Caffeine Nights Publishing

THE CREW

Dougie Brimson

Fiction aimed at the hea... the head…

Published by Caffeine Nights Publishing 2013

Published in Great Britain by Caffeine Nights Publishing

www.caffeine-nights.com

British Library Cataloguing in Publication Data.
A CIP catalogue record for this book is available from the British Library

ISBN: 978-1-907565-44-1

Cover design by

Mark (Wills) Williams
Image of Leo Gregory by Julia Underwood

Everything else by
Default, Luck and Accident

This book is dedicated to all those who have stabbed me in the back or tried to shaft me over the years.

Fuck you.

PRELUDE
Saturday, 16 November 1996
18.25

Paul Jarvis lay on the floor of Euston underground station, clenched into a ball, in a vain attempt to protect himself while he waited for rescue or unconsciousness. Whichever came sooner. As he waited, he tried to remember everything that others had told him in the past; never expose your face – and protect your head at all costs. Everything else will heal in the end, but not that. The blows were coming less frequently now. Sporadic but no less violent. But the noise was still ferocious. Screams and shouts, mixed with fear and aggression.

Opening one eye, he turned his head to try to see what was happening around him. Feet were rushing past and, every so often, someone would either stop and aim a kick in his direction or simply run over him, stamping on him as they passed. He shut his eye again and relaxed. The noise was receding. Was that because the trouble had moved on, or was it because his brain was switching itself off? Putting him to sleep for a while to escape the nightmare.

Suddenly, he felt a hand grab his hair and pull his head away from the safety of his arms. He tried to resist but had no strength for any kind of fight, and so he opened one eye to see who it was. He could just about make out a snarling face, but couldn't focus properly. It seemed to be twisted with hate and was shouting something at him. What was it? Something about West Ham. West Ham cunt. Yeah, that was it. He almost laughed at the irony of it all. 'He thinks I'm West Ham, but I'm not. What kind of tosser makes that sort of mistake?' he thought. The blurred face pulled away and he waited for the blow – but it never came. Just a sudden shove back to the floor and a crack as his head hit the hard concrete. If anything else came, he didn't feel it. Unconsciousness had arrived at last.

Suddenly, he was awake. Something was touching his face, and he winced. But this was different. No aggression this time, just compassion. He opened his eyes and turned his head. A young woman in a police uniform was kneeling down beside him. She was crying. Jesus, was he hurt that bad? He tried to speak, but no words came out. Just a groan of agony. 'It's OK,' she said. 'They've gone and an ambulance is on the way.' He tried to move, in an effort to sit up, but she held him down.

'Stay where you are, you may have broken something. Best wait for the ambulance.'

She reached behind his head and gently lifted it, sliding her coat underneath for him to rest on. He relaxed into it and looked at her. Her eyes were red, full of tears and so he looked away. Across the concourse, something caught his eye and he tried to focus on what it was. A group of men in black uniforms were standing around something on the floor. They were just looking down, heads bowed. What was it? A pile of clothes, or was it a man? Christ, it was. 'He looks in a right state,' he thought. 'Why aren't they helping him?' One of the men began taking off his coat, but the hand touched the side of his head again and gently turned it away.

'You mustn't look,' the policewoman said, tears still streaming down her face. 'Just you relax. The ambulance will be here in a second.'

He closed his eyes again and tried to relax, but the pain was beginning to take hold now. A dull ache eating its way up through his body. He opened his eyes again as two men in green overalls knelt down beside him. The policewoman was speaking to them, telling them who he was and what had happened to him. He tried to speak, but nothing came out. Just a gasp as the medics put a mask over his face and lifted him onto a stretcher. And then they were moving, past the coat and up into the fresh air. Away from the battle ground and the dead policeman.

* * *

Billy Evans sat in his car and stared out of the windscreen at the front of his house. It was late, but he knew that once he left the confines of his Mercedes and went indoors, the most satisfying day of his life so far would end. He wasn't ready for that. Not just yet. Reaching across to the passenger seat, he pulled a cigarette from a half empty packet and lit it with his Zippo lighter. The first lungful relaxed him a little and he allowed a smile to spread across his face as he thought about the older lads in the firm. He couldn't begin to imagine how they must be feeling tonight. Gutted was probably an understatement, but that's what happens when you fuck up. And boy, had they fucked up. Just six short months ago, they had called the firm together and announced that the Cockney Suicide Squad, one of the most notorious fighting firms in football, were not taking part in any organised trouble during Euro 96.

He had stood up and asked if this was a joke. The greatest tournament in England for over thirty years, with the Jocks walking into their backyard, and they weren't going to do anything about it? It had to be a joke. But they had shouted him down. The top boys from all the London firms had met and decided that while it was OK to fight together abroad, it wasn't on at home – and especially not in London. Those particular rivalries were just too deep to be put aside, and so it was best to keep the firms out of it. Then he had stood up again and told them that they were wrong. This was the chance to show everyone what they could really do – and if they didn't take it, they were making a major mistake. But still they had shied away. The decision had been taken, and that was that. And so he had stormed out. Furious at the lost opportunity. For a while, he had toyed with the idea of putting together a new firm and taking them. He certainly had enough support among the other lads but, in the end, he had decided against it. He was a part of the CSS and he had to obey the rules. It was tradition.

But then he had been proved right – and in the worst possible way. Not only had the northern firms come down to the capital and taken the battle to the Scots in Trafalgar

7

Square, but Chelsea, Spurs and Arsenal had shown. Not at the front, where the provincial firms from clubs like Sunderland, Stoke, Plymouth and Leicester had done the business, but lurking in the back streets of the West End. Picking off little mobs and doing just enough to let everyone know they were there. And then the rumours had started. The CSS had let the side down, they had lost their bottle and they were living on past glories.

At first, they had ignored it, but then, just three weeks ago, they had travelled to Sheffield and listened to the Wednesday fans singing about how they had done their fighting for them and stood as mobs of northern bastards taunted them with cries of 'Are you Orient in disguise?'. That had been it. No firm worth its salt could put up with stuff like that, and so he had gone to the top boys and put forward the plan to hit Millwall at Euston. At first, even after what had happened in the summer, they had taken the piss, but he'd forced it through. Convinced them that if they were ever to repair the damage done to their reputation and re-establish themselves, they had to stage a big hit. Who better than the Scum from across the river? Their biggest rivals and one of only three or four other firms in the country who could hold a candle to them in terms of status.

In the end, they had gone for it – and what a success it had been. His plan had worked to perfection. Seventy lads, split down the middle. Half sent to Warren Street station and then on foot to Euston. The others, spread around the various walkways of Euston underground. Hiding among the shoppers until his spotters told him a mob of Millwall lads had arrived. As soon as the Scum were below ground, he had formed his lads up and that was it. By the time Millwall had realised what was happening, it was too late. Fair play, they had stood for a time, but then the second group had come pouring down the escalators and hit them from the rear. The classic pincer movement.

Thankfully, casualties among the CSS had been light, but the Millwall firm had taken a real hammering. He had seen one lad at the top of some escalators who looked like he'd been stabbed, but that was too bad. If you run with a firm, you take a risk every time you turn a corner. He took a final drag on his cigarette, dumped the stub in the ashtray and shut his eyes. He could have happily fallen asleep, but his head was buzzing. Reminding him of small details and conversations that had taken place that day. So he opened his eyes and lit another cigarette.

A light went on in his house and he smiled again. Wondering if it was Samantha or one of his boys. What would she say if she knew what he had achieved that very afternoon? Would she be proud, shocked, maybe even disgusted? Maybe she knew already but didn't care. He drew on his cigarette and let out a sigh. All he knew was that today had changed everything. Today, in just five short minutes, he had not only started a war with Millwall, he had put the CSS firmly back on the map. As if that wasn't enough, by the time they had made it back to the East End, his lifelong ambition had been realised. The old guard had stepped aside and he had been installed as top boy. Years of fighting, planning and hoping had finally paid off. He had thanked them all, bought them a pint – and that was it. No arguments, no violence, just a grudging acceptance that a new era was about to begin and a new regime was in place.

And now the real work could start. There were scores to be settled and reputations to rebuild, but beside that, he had other plans for the CSS. Big plans, and not all of them involved football, either. Having an active firm at your beck and call was a valuable commodity and he hadn't built up his business from scratch without seeing an opportunity when it presented itself. This was another one. Perhaps the biggest he had ever seen.

His mobile rang and he looked at it for a second before answering.

'Hi Billy, where are you?'

He smiled to himself. The spell was broken, his day was over. 'Hello sweetheart. I've just pulled up outside. Put the kettle on, I'll just be a second.'

Part One

Chapter 1
Saturday, 4 September 1999
11.15

Gary Fitchett closed his eyes and slowly exhaled. Letting the cigarette smoke drift out through his nostrils. 'Fuck me! That's better.' He opened his eyes and glanced around before stepping out into the Saturday morning mayhem of Camden High Street. The relief at escaping the confines of the underground was almost tangible. He hated it down there. It was the one thing that genuinely scared him. A legacy of a school trip to Wales when he'd been messing about in some potholes and become separated from his mates. Not for long – a matter of minutes – but it had been enough. A quick look at his watch told him it was almost eleven thirty. Time to look for a pub where he could get a decent pint. A fairly tall order, given that in his opinion every landlord in London was a thieving bastard and what they laughingly sold as bitter was invariably watered down and tasted like piss.

A woman bumped into him and, without thinking, he apologised and then increased his pace to fit in with the speed of the shoppers. 'What the fuck am I apologising for?' he murmured, and slowed down again, forcing the other pedestrians to slow down to his pace or move around him. He hated London, it was a shit hole. The place was filthy and the people were worse. Rude ignorant bastards. He'd only been here half an hour and he already felt dirty. No, not dirty, contaminated. He'd be glad to get back to Birmingham tonight. At least the sun was shining. He didn't even want to think about how bad this place would look in November.

'Whose fucking idea was it to come here?' he said out loud.

'Yours actually,' came the instant reply. 'You said, and I quote, everyone will expect us to go to the West End, so if we go to Camden, we'll be out of the way for a while and can have a few beers before the game, end of quote.'

He stopped and turned round.

'And I must say Fitch,' the voice continued, 'it was a fucking top idea. I mean, instead of eyeing up all the tourists, we get to see all these fucking weirdos and faggots instead.'

Fitchett smiled. 'You're such a twat Baz. If I'd known you were going on the pull, I'd have taken you down to Soho where all the real ponces hang out.'

They both laughed and Fitchett turned and began walking again. He liked Baz; he was one of those blokes who always had something funny to say. You need lads like that sometimes.

They had a decent turn-out today, forty-three lads. The usual twenty-two hard-core of course, lads who he knew well and trusted, and another twenty-one besides. The cling-ons. Good scrappers, but not yet accepted into the fold. Maybe today would be the day for some of them. The day they'd make the grade. That was the thing about football, you just never knew when and where it would happen. To be honest, that was why he had decided to bring them to Camden today. There were no Premiership games on because England were playing on Wednesday – and usually, if you were in London, that meant trouble. If their clubs weren't playing, then their lads certainly wouldn't be on a day off or out shopping. They'd be looking elsewhere, and with the Blues in town, that meant they'd be prime targets for a hit. After all, Fitch might not support a Premiership club, but he led a Premiership mob and they had certainly had their run-ins with the big clubs over the years. Only last season, they'd been involved in a pitched battle with some Arsenal fans outside a pub in the West End and had really turned them over. Well, if Arsenal wanted another go, Fitch and his lads were ready, but the Gooners would have to find them first. They were the rules of the game, and he wasn't about to make their job any easier.

'Something's not right here; it's not fucking right at all.' Fitchett stopped and turned round.

'What is it, Al?' he asked.

'See that kid over there, I've seen him about four or five times since we left Euston. He was on the tube with us. He's fucking scouting, I'm sure of it.'

Fitchett looked across the road and just caught sight of a young lad dressed in a beige Adidas sports top as he vanished into a McDonald's opposite. If Alex said something was wrong, then it always paid to listen. He'd saved them from walking into trouble so many times it was ridiculous.

'Anyone else?'

He looked around at the others, but everyone within hearing distance just shrugged their shoulders. He already knew that none of them had seen anyone. After all, he hadn't – and he'd been looking for it. That's why Alex was so handy, and that's why Fitchett always kept him at his side. He had a sixth sense about trouble and that was as valuable as another twenty lads. Fitchett quickly looked up and down the road, but all he could see were cars and shoppers. No mob, not even any obvious football fans. Shit, that was one of the reasons they'd come into Camden rather than the usual West End. All they wanted was a few beers away from any other mobs and the watchful eyes of the Old Bill. Then a short trip down to Loftus Road to give Rangers a spanking.

He glanced across the road at the front of the McDonald's. If the kid was scouting, then that meant someone was looking for them and he would be on the phone right now, calling up the troops. More likely, if he had a mobile, then they would already be on the way. But who? It could be anyone. Chelsea, Arsenal or Spurs. The one thing he was sure of though, it wouldn't be West Ham or the South London vermin. Not this far up North. And it certainly wouldn't be Rangers. Even the thought of them having a pop made Fitchett laugh.

'Right, if we're walking into anything, then we'd better find out who or what the fuck it is.' He looked at Pillow, a tall gangly black man who'd gained his nickname years ago when he'd brought a blow-up doll with him on a trip to Everton. His excuse, that he needed something to rest his head on if he fell asleep, had settled into legend when he was seen on *Match of the Day* that night with this plastic woman sitting on his shoulders. He might look a bit daft, but Fitchett knew that it was all a front. Underneath, he was a clever bastard and was one of the most trusted men in the mob. Fitchett nodded to him and, without question, Pillow leapt over the steel barrier segregating them from the traffic and ran out into the road. The screaming of tyres, punctuated with the blasting of horns and shouts from irate cabbies, had everyone within a hundred yards turning round to see what was happening. 'Fuck me, talk about letting everyone know where you are.'

As soon as his man had vanished through the plate glass doors and into the burger bar, Fitchett instinctively moved back and leant against the shop front. A brief glance back up the road simply confirmed what he already knew, that everyone else had done the same. It's what they did, kept out of sight, blended in. That's why there were no colours. Replica shirts were for other football fans, not them. Another world watching the same game in a completely different way. He dumped his cigarette, lit another and smiled as the Saturday-morning shoppers walked past without even seeing. Forty-three lads right in their midst, and all of them ready to go at a moment's notice. So much potential violence simmering in the middle of a sea of blandness. His eyes remained fixed on the front door of McDonald's.

'They haven't a fucking clue,' he thought, 'all these Cockney bastards so wrapped up in their own little world and not giving a shit about anyone else. Arrogant cunts who think they're better than we are. They're just scum.' He smiled to himself; he was beginning to look forward to hurting someone later on.

'Fitch.' The noise made him start a bit, and he looked round to see Alex discreetly nodding up the road. Leisurely turning round, he spotted a small group heading in their direction, but on the other side of the road. About fifteen lads, aged between sixteen and twenty-five, their clothing smart but anonymous. The uniform of hooligans everywhere.

'Who are they?' he asked.

'Fuck knows,' replied Alex, 'but they haven't seen us yet. My guess is that they're about to walk into Pillow.'

Fitchett slowly returned his gaze to the front of McDonald's. The last thing he wanted was to be spotted and rapid movements were a dead giveaway. Keep the element of surprise, the greatest weapon any hooligan firm ever had. 'Baz, take your lads back up the road and get over there. Dave, get up to that crossing and get in behind them. I'll cross here with Al and Nick.' He barked out his orders like a military commander, and as he did so his troops obeyed without question. His troops.

'They still haven't seen us,' Alex whispered, his words coming like a running commentary, keeping his leader informed, 'and Pillow is still inside.'

Fitchett surveyed the battleground and then looked back across at the front of McDonald's. 'If he comes out now, we'll be all right. Otherwise ...'

'We can't do this in there Fitch, there's too many kids.'

Fitchett looked up to see Nick looking at him. In other people, he would have thought that their bottle had gone, but not Nick. He was a mate and he was sound. He'd been an accepted member of the hard-core for around two years now and Fitchett trusted him totally. After all, Nick had been the one who'd saved him when he'd been battered unconscious by the 657 Crew at Portsmouth. You don't forget things like that. 'We might not have any choice mate. We can't let Pillow take a spanking.'

Nick smiled and turned back to face McDonald's. 'I don't know, he's an ugly cunt. It might be a giggle.'

The three men laughed quietly, but they all knew Fitchett was right. If they went inside and sussed Pillow, then they'd have no choice but to go in and get him out. And that would mean only one thing.

'Here we go.' The small group of lads stopped outside McDonald's for a moment and then began walking up the road again. Past the red and yellow neon, the plate glass and the laughing kids. And Pillow.

'Shit,' said Alex. 'I was sure they'd go in.'

Fitchett spun around and looked up the road, frantically searching for Baz and his fifteen lads. 'Where the fuck are they?' he said out loud, spotting them even as he spoke. They were all but invisible among the shoppers as they made their way towards their foe.

'This could be fun,' said Alex. The three of them watched as the drama continued to unfold. Two groups of lads, on a collision course in the middle of a North London street. Violence a split-second away.

Suddenly, there was a shrill whistle and they turned to see Pillow standing outside McDonald's. He had a mobile phone in one hand and was holding the young kid by the collar in the other. 'Got the fucker!' he screamed, his thick Brummie accent cutting through the traffic noise like a Stanley knife. 'He was hiding in the bog!'

Fitchett looked round at the group of lads, half hoping that they hadn't heard him shouting, but knowing that they had.

'Fucking idiot,' said Alex. 'D'you think they've seen the others?'

'No. Not yet. But they've seen us.' The small group, the enemy, had stopped and were now talking excitedly among themselves, their discreet glances merely confirming the fact that the four of them had been sussed. Fitchett looked across at Pillow in an attempt to catch his eye, but he was preoccupied with the kid who was struggling in vain to get away.

'Here they come,' said Nick, his voice calm and steady without a hint of fear. 'They're going for it!'

Fitchett looked back up the road to see that the enemy were now moving quickly back down the street towards them. He was about to shout out to Pillow when the enemy broke and ran out into the traffic, forcing drivers to slam on their brakes. The squealing of rubber was punctuated with a loud crunch as a taxi ran into the back of a small yellow van. No abuse from the drivers though, not this time. That could wait.

Fitchett smiled to himself. He loved this bit, when it was about to kick off. Half terror, half ecstasy. The adrenalin surging through him like an electric current. His breathing coming in short gasps and his stomach trying to push its way up through his throat. 'The Buzz', they called it. And they were right. Fitchett was buzzing, this was what it was all about for him. This blast of magic. He glanced at the other two, knew they were feeling exactly the same and then looked up and down the road to check on his troops. Baz and his lads had worked out what was going on and were now closing in behind the enemy, still unseen. Dave and his group were fifty yards down the road but had stopped to watch what was happening. Not fear, but common sense. They knew the score and, if they were needed, they'd be there like a shot. Fitchett looked back at the enemy. 'OK then, we're set,' he thought. 'Come and get it.' The enemy, his enemy, were walking into the classic football ambush and they didn't have a fucking clue. Fitchett moved forward until he was in front of all the shoppers and against the steel barrier. That way, he could get a few digs in as they tried to get over it. The best way.

Then the shouting started. 'Come on then! Come on you northern wankers!' Ugly Cockney accents and swearing, just noise designed to gee themselves up and disguise their fear. 'They think they're something. Fifteen onto four, but they're shitting themselves and they're about to get spanked.'

Still Fitchett kept quiet. 'Let them come,' he thought, 'and then we'll do them properly.' He looked across at Pillow, who had let go of the kid and was now running across the road towards the enemy, catching them by surprise as they had half-expected him to do a runner. Without even slowing, he steamed in, his first punch a vicious right hander which sent one of them sprawling across the bonnet of a black cab. Within seconds, he had vanished under a pile of bodies. Fists and boots flying out like an old Andy Capp cartoon.

Now they were at the barrier. No, wrong, some of them were over the barrier. Shit, Fitchett hadn't seen that. They were working their way through the shoppers, who were suddenly waking up to the fact that they were in trouble: Saturday morning and standing slap bang in the middle of a riot. That'd give them something to talk about in the pub later on. Something different. Fitchett reached into his pocket, the black canister in his hand like an old friend. Grabbing one of the enemy, he pulled him forward and lashed him across the face with the red spray before stepping to one side and throwing him past. The lad screamed in pain as the pepper spray burned into his eyes. Fitchett moved forward, away from the spray, to avoid breathing it in himself. And then the shouts went up,

'Selector, Selector.' Baz and his lads. And the fear in the faces of the enemy as they realised that they had been ambushed. The realisation that they were being hit by the Selector, one of the most infamous and dangerous hooligan groups in England. And they were fucked.

Fitchett leapt over the barrier and stood there, like some working-class Napoleon. The whole thing going on around him like it had been captured on video and he was watching it at home with the sound turned down. The background of the North London high street blurred out of focus, the shoppers, running for cover from the battlefield, just grey formless shapes. And the lads, vividly graphic as they battered and bullied their opponents. Miller, normally a quiet bloke bordering on shy, but when it kicked off, he became a fucking madman, grabbing some piece of scum round the neck and running him full pelt into the side of a courier's van. Stevie, the new boy desperate to be accepted into the hard-core, straight-arming some little Cockney shit across the Adam's apple. Johnny the boy, dragging someone off Pillow and throwing him face down onto the road before dropping on him. The motion punching his knee into the small of the scum's back with a force that would leave him in agony for days. Good lad, he's learning. Bodies everywhere and his lads were dishing out a real lesson. His lads, and he'd led them as they battled their way up to the top. Chelsea, Sunderland, Leicester, Millwall, Forest: they'd been to all of them over the years and done them all.

And suddenly, there's their top boy. His arrogance almost tangible and marking him out better than any colours could ever do. Standing there in the middle of it all and screaming, trying to rally his troops. 'Stand, you cunts, stand. They're fuck all!' And Fitchett's across the bonnet of a black cab and at him like a wild animal. The first head butt exploding the bastard's nose across the front of his face, leaving Fitchett covered in blood and someone else's snot. And then his trademark, the elbow. Delivered with a sickening crunch into the right cheek. Their top boy is down and they're all over the place.

'Go-go-go!' comes the desperate cry, and they're off. Dragging their casualties with them. Up the road and into the waiting arms of Dave and his lads. Running into another kicking, and on their own ground. The ultimate humiliation. Two minutes. That was all it had taken. Two minutes.

And now they were moving. Instinctively. Away from the scene of their triumph. Away from the stunned shoppers and the furious cabbies and away from recognition. The troops falling in behind Fitchett as he walked.

'Fuck me lads, that was fun.'

Fitchett turned to see the cause of all the problems walking right beside him. A trickle of blood coming from his nose. 'Pillow, you tosser,' he laughed. The tension gone, the adrenalin flowing back into its reservoir for later on.

'Where the fuck did they come from?' Pillow asked.

'Never mind that, who the fuck were they?'

'Well the kid was scouting for Arsenal,' said Pillow. 'But Christ knows who they were.'

'Best we find out then,' said Nick. 'You still got that mobile?'

Pillow took it from his pocket and hit the redial button before handing it over.

'Who's that? ... Who's this? ... Oh we're just a few tourists from Birmingham way and I've got news for you me old cock sparra'; I think we've just met some of your lads in Camden High Street. Well, I think they were your lads; they were wankers and they were covered in red. Or at least they are now.' He listened intently for a moment and then took the phone away from his ear, looked at it with a mocking expression of shock on his face and then threw it into the road. 'Well really! Have you ever heard such language!'

'Were they Arsenal?' Fitchett asked.

'He said not. Nothing to do with them. The Gooners were waiting for us in the West End, but the coppers are all over them now. Seems someone tipped them off and we wrong-footed 'em. They won't be seeing us today after all.'

'Well whoever that lot were, they won't forget that in a hurry,' Baz added, 'but we'd better get the fuck out of here.'

Fitchett looked at Alex as the noise of approaching sirens punctured the air, the still static traffic giving them precious time to escape from the scene of their victory.

'Back onto the tube,' said Alex. 'Go right at this next junction and there should be a station about twenty yards up the road. Mornington Crescent.' Fitchett looked at him, always cool and always collected. 'And you'd better lose the shirt, Fitch.'

Fitchett looked down; their top boy's blood was all over his new Ralph Lauren shirt. 'Bollocks,' he said.

And they were off. The leader, his general and his troops. Another victory for the battle flag.

Chapter 2
Monday, 6 September 1999
07.05

Paul Jarvis parked his BMW and climbed out. Grabbing his briefcase from the passenger seat, he slammed the door and pressed the alarm button on his key ring. The car gave a satisfying bleep and a flash of its indicators as he walked through the almost empty underground car park towards the lift. Usually, he loved Monday mornings, but today, well he wasn't expecting to get home much before the end of *EastEnders*. Not that he watched it anyway, but that wasn't the point.

He pressed the lift button and waited for a few moments before angrily pressing it again three or four times. 'This poxy bloody lift,' he said out loud to himself, glancing across at the door to the stairs before quickly deciding against it. His office was six floors up and he hadn't even had a cuppa yet, never mind any breakfast. 'Bastard cleaners have probably propped the door open,' he thought, giving the button yet another prod.

The sound of a car entering the car park made him start and he watched as a blue Ford Escort slid immaculately into the space next to his BMW. 'Smart arse,' he thought. 'I bet he couldn't do that again. I must have left loads of room.' He turned as the lift doors opened behind him and, with a brief and barely audible 'thank fuck for that', walked in and hit number 6 on the panel. The doors stayed stubbornly open and he hit the button again. 'Come on you bastard,' he hissed, desperate for the doors to close. He didn't want to have to wait for the driver of the car because he wanted, no needed, that last moment of peace before the chaos of the day began. Of course, there was another reason he wanted to get moving. After all, he'd been made to wait, so why shouldn't they? Let their day start off on the wrong foot as well. It was petty, he was the first to admit that, but it was one of those little things that made life all the better. Like climbing out of an empty lift and pressing all the buttons. Get one over on everyone else. He knew it was sad and childish, but he loved doing that.

The doors began to slide shut – and as they did so, a woman's voice rang out, 'Wait for me!'

'Shit,' he thought, and stuck out his foot to keep the doors from closing. He looked across the car park and watched as a woman walked briskly towards him. Quite slim, about thirty, very pretty and very blonde. Her long hair tied tightly behind her head with a black ribbon and dressed from head to foot in black. It was a look he loved. The smell of her perfume entered the lift before she did and he made a mental note that she pressed the button for the fourth floor. Jarvis took a deep but discreet breath. Sucking in as much of the perfume as was humanly possible without drawing attention to himself. 'Jesus Christ,' he thought.

'Hi,' she said with a beaming white smile and a voice that held a faint southern accent. 'Thanks for waiting for me. This lift is awful, isn't it? You would have thought that someone would have done something about it by now.'

Jarvis smiled and quietly thanked God for sending this vision to him just in time to kick-start his day. 'Excuse me asking,' he said, 'but how the bloody hell can you look so good this early on a Monday morning?'

She looked at him, blushed and laughed. 'Lots of love from a good husband and a ton of make-up.'

Jarvis laughed out loud and clicked his fingers. 'Damn,' he said. 'Well, when you get home, make sure you tell him how lucky he is.'

The lift stopped and she smiled at him as the doors opened. 'I'll do that,' she said, 'but I'm sure he knows already. See you later.'

The doors closed behind her and the lift began its journey upwards. 'He better,' he said to himself, 'or he's a fucking idiot.'

The doors of the lift opened and he surveyed the familiar scene in front of him. He hated open-plan offices. There was no privacy. Just a sea of desks, a hundred computers and total chaos all illuminated by a thousand strip lights. He didn't want to get out. He knew that the second he did, the spell would be broken and the week would start. The lingering smell of perfume infinitely preferable to a day spent rummaging around in a sea of paper.

'What are you doing?' a male voice asked.

'Dreaming,' he said. 'Just dreaming.'

'Well sod off and dream somewhere else.' Jarvis stepped out of the lift and smiled. A well-built man in his early forties stood in front of him, his white shirt straining to keep the beer-fuelled contents of his stomach under control.

'And a good morning to you too, Al,' he said. 'Nice weekend?'

'Not bad. Made a nice change, no football. You heard about the Camden thing?'

Jarvis shook his head. 'Haven't seen anything yet. I need tea first.'

The man stepped into the lift and the doors began to shut. Jarvis turned round and put his hand in between them. Forcing them back open. 'Smell that,' he said. The man standing in the lift took a deep breath and smiled. 'That is the smell of a vision and I had it all to myself for about forty-five seconds just now.'

He took another breath. 'That's Chanel that is. Right classy. Who was she?'

'Don't know,' said Jarvis. 'Never seen her before. Blonde hair, very pretty. Works on the fourth floor.'

The man looked at him with a quizzical look on his face. 'About thirty? Hair tied back? Nice figure?'

'That's the one. Who is she?'

'Don't know, never seen her before!'

They both started laughing. 'You wanker,' said Jarvis. He couldn't believe he'd fallen for that. He leant in and ran his fingers down the lift panel. Pressing every button so that it would stop on every floor. 'Revenge is swift and it is mine!' Jarvis shouted triumphantly. The lift doors shut and this time he let it go, the round man's cursing muffled by the metal sheeting. Turning on his heels, he took a deep breath and walked into the office.

For once, his desk was reasonably tidy. On the left-hand side, in a tray marked 'Bullshit' were a small pile of green files which he no longer needed but couldn't be arsed to put away. Next to them were two coffee cups, one of which was just about empty, while the second was half full and coated with a strange green substance. Each one had a small post-it notice stuck to the handle with the legend 'wash me up, you bastard' written on it in red ink. In the centre of his desk sat his laptop, humming away to itself, while on the right, in the tray marked 'Urgent' sat three files and two videotapes. He sat down with a sigh. There had only been one file in there when he'd left on Friday. That meant work. He picked up the two cups, poured the contents into his neighbour's plant pot and dumped them in the bin. 'Job jobbed,' he thought.

Reaching over, he lifted out the two new files and the two tapes. Usually, the tray would have been bulging on a Monday morning. But with no Premiership games and only QPR and Orient at home, the weekend had probably remained reasonably quiet compared to a usual mid-season Saturday in the capital. He took the thinner of the two files and lifted out the contents. It was a simple report on the policing for the Orient game. Very low-key and very quiet. 'Typical Orient, in fact,' he sighed. 'A bit like the club.' He put the report back in the folder, signed the front and threw it into the 'Bullshit' tray. Picking up the second folder, he immediately noticed it was much heavier than the first and bore the legend 'Report into Crowd Control at Queens Park Rangers vs Birmingham City fixture. Loftus Road 04-09-99'. He looked at the cover and then set it down. 'Can't start this on an empty stomach,' he said out loud to the still-empty office. 'I need something to get me going.' He stood up and walked out of the office in the direction of the canteen.

He was halfway through his breakfast when the tannoy system burst into life. 'Detective Inspector Jarvis, please report to your office immediately.' He looked at his watch. 'Bloody hell, I don't believe this!' It was only seven forty-five, he wasn't due on duty until eight. He shovelled what remained on his plate onto a slice of bread and, after gulping down his tea, headed for the lift.

He was still chewing his makeshift sandwich as he walked out of the lift to see the very unwelcome sight of two men standing next to his desk. One was his boss, Detective Chief Inspector Peter Allen, but he didn't know the other. He had a feeling he was about to, though, because they were looking through the file he had left unopened and were in deep conversation about something. This didn't look good. He gulped down what was left in his mouth and quickened his step.

'Morning, Guv.'

'Ah, Paul. This is Chief Inspector Morgan from Kensington.' Jarvis looked into the face of the second man. He didn't exactly look pleased. 'Have you read the report into the incident in Camden High Street on Saturday?'

Jarvis shook his head. Camden again, what was that all about? It must have been serious to warrant all this attention. 'No Guv, not yet, I've only just got in.' Jarvis noticed a very faint shake of the head and an exhale that was rather too powerful for his liking. 'What happened?' he asked.

Another shake, and then the uniform spoke. 'I'll tell you what happened, Detective Inspector. My son was attacked and nearly blinded in broad daylight by a group of Brummie bastards – and I want to see the one who did it in court.'

Jarvis looked at him and then at Allen.

'Have a look through the report and the tapes, Paul, and let me have a report by lunchtime.'

'Of course, Guv.'

The man in uniform gave Jarvis a glare and the two men walked off, leaving him staring at the file in front of him. So that was what it was about; some high-up's little lad got a spanking and he wants somebody to pay.

'Cheeky fucker,' he thought. 'Who the fuck does he think he is, coming down here dictating what I do and don't do? As if I haven't got enough on.' He took out the paperwork and flicked through it. According to the report, nothing much had happened during the game. Just the usual drunks and abuse.

Seven ejections and one arrest for threatening behaviour. Jarvis shrugged his shoulders. That was quite good for a club with the number of travelling fans Birmingham usually had. Especially with their mob, the Selector. He certainly hadn't been warned about anything beforehand, or he'd have put a few of his lads on it. He carried on reading and came to appendix a: a report into an incident in Camden High Street. It was, to say the least, brief. Very few witnesses and only two statements. One from a passer-by who had remained on the scene and another from an eighteen-year-old man named Barry Morgan, 'Detained in hospital with damage to his eyesight as a result of an attack with a substance believed to be pepper spray'.

He read through them: the two accounts were so different they could have been of two separate incidents. The witness described how fighting had started in the middle of the road outside McDonald's and had spread down Camden High Street towards the tube station. It had lasted a couple of minutes and there were a few vague descriptions. Barry Morgan's version basically revolved around the fact that he'd been shopping on his own and had been mugged by a group of men with accents that weren't local.

Jarvis smiled. He'd seen enough of these reports over the years to know straight away that young Barry Morgan was obviously a bit of a lad who had got caught. 'I'm surprised he didn't add he was shopping for his mum's birthday present,' he thought, and reached over for the two tapes. They were both marked with the serial numbers of the cameras and 'Camden High Street 04-09-99 11.00 to 13.00 hours'. He stood up and walked to the machine in the corner. The office was beginning to fill up and, as he started the first tape running, the level of noise began to rise to its normal manic level. The quality of the tape was rubbish and, using the remote control, he flicked through it until the fighting started. He watched, totally detached from what he was seeing. This was just one in a thousand such tapes he had watched in the past four years since he had joined the NFIU, the National Football Intelligence Unit. He had to admit, though, that this was a good one. The way the larger group, the Brummies he assumed, had worked out the ambush so quickly was a bit clever. Once it had finished, he stopped the tape and put in the second one. The angle was different and he was pleased to see a much clearer shot of a small group of young men seemingly taunting four other men before coming under attack themselves. 'Christ,' he thought. 'They'll do well to live that down if word gets out.'

He continued to watch the tape and smiled to himself as one of the youths was sprayed across the face with something. 'Barry Morgan, I presume,' he said out loud. He rewound the tape, ejected it and put it back in its box. Looking around, he caught sight of a young-looking copper busily hammering away at a keyboard. The new DC, Phil Williams. He'd come to the unit with good credentials, and by all accounts was learning fast. Jarvis had high hopes for him. He walked over and put the two tapes down on the desk in front of him.

'Phil, take these two and have a flick through them, will you? Anyone doing anything stupid, blow up their faces, print them off and run them through the computer. See if we get lucky and can give at least one of them a name.' He tapped the second cassette. 'And on this one is a very good shot of someone giving a lad a face full of pepper spray. I want prints of both their faces. All right?'

The man at the desk looked up and gave a sigh. 'Yes Guv,' he said.

Jarvis smiled as he walked back to his desk. He loved being a DI; a bit of power never hurt anyone and, after all, he'd spent long enough being ordered about and shat on. He sat down, switched on his laptop and began typing his report, based on what he knew of the Camden High Street incident. He was about halfway through when he decided to have a quick chat with Allen, his DCI. If this was the son of a Chief Inspector, it could be embarrassing and he might just want it buried. It certainly wouldn't be the first time.

Allen's office door was open and he was sitting at his desk reading the paper. Jarvis tapped on the door and stuck his head in. 'Guv, could I have a quick word?' Allen put down his paper and motioned him in. 'This guy Morgan, I think he may be in for a shock. If his lad was the lad I saw on the tape, then he's in the shit. Looks like it was him who started it.'

Allen looked at him and smiled. 'That could be interesting.'

'Sir ...' They both looked round as the young Detective Constable walked in holding a small pile of paper. 'The faces you asked for.'

Jarvis flicked through them, handing each one on to Allen. The tape had been bad enough, but these enlargements were awful. Not one of them showed a likeness that was good enough to have stood up in court. However, Williams had printed off a sequence of the lad getting sprayed across the face and Jarvis held one of them up.

'Barry Morgan I presume.' He dropped the picture in front of the DCI and turned back to Williams. 'Any names, Phil?'

'Only three, sir.' He leant in and took the photographs from the desk, leafed through them and pulled three out. He looked at one and handed it to Jarvis. 'This guy is called Fitchett, and this other one is Alex Bailey. Neither has any previous at home, but they're both well known. It's thought that they're the two top men of the Selector, the ...'

Jarvis looked up from the photos and interrupted him. 'We know who the Selector are thank you, Detective Constable.'

'Sorry Guv,' said Williams, his face almost scarlet with embarrassment. 'They've both been seen abroad with England a lot and Fitchett was thought to be involved with the planning of the riot in Dublin, although nothing could be proved. They were also both deported from Norway in 1996. Nothing serious though, just drunk and disorderly.'

Jarvis held out the photographs for Allen, but he waved them away and looked at Williams. 'You said there were three names ...'

'Oh, yes Guv.' The young DC fumbled for a picture and pulled it out. 'When I tried to identify this face, all I got from the computer was a message referring me to the DI.' He looked at Jarvis with a puzzled expression on his face, but Jarvis didn't respond. Instead, Allen reached up, took the picture and placed it face down on the desk without even looking at it.

Jarvis gave Williams back the two pictures he had in his hand. 'Get the computer boys to clean these two up and then send them up to Brum. See if the local lads can fill us in a bit more.'

Williams waited for a second, before realising that nothing else was required of him and left the office. Jarvis reached over and pushed the door shut.

'Is it Terry Porter?' he asked. Allen handed him the photo. 'Yes. Get hold of him and let him know he's been spotted. See if he can give you anything else on the other two.'

Jarvis nodded. 'To be honest Guv, I think we're wasting our time here. He's been undercover with them on and off for almost two years now and he's not even close to getting anything worthwhile yet. And from what I know of the Selector, this is as far in as he's going to get.'

Allen looked at him and smiled. If anyone knew about undercover operations of this nature it was Jarvis, and he trusted his judgement on such matters. After all, it had been Jarvis's idea to keep all details of any undercover operations totally secret apart from the two of them. Although at first the others on the Unit had been aggrieved, they hadn't had a single leak of information since the policy had been implemented, and it was now accepted practice. 'Fair enough, if the local lads come up with anything then we'll see about pulling in the top boys. Other than that, give him a week or so and pull him out.'

Jarvis got up and went to leave. He stopped at the door and turned back. 'What about Morgan?'

The DCI laughed and said, 'I'll send the picture to Mr Morgan, see if he wants us to proceed.'

Jarvis smiled and opened the door. 'Somehow I doubt that,' he laughed, 'but I'll get that report for you Guv. Just in case.'

He was about to walk out when Allen called him back. 'How's the briefing for Wednesday coming?' Jarvis looked at him and slowly nodded his head. 'Fine Guv, it'll be ready by the morning.'

Allen smiled. 'Might as well stick this lot in with it. Keep it right up to date. I'll let you know what Mr Morgan says.'

Jarvis nodded and walked out. 'That's all I need,' he thought. 'More bloody work.'

After two hours, Jarvis got up and stretched his back to relieve the stiffness. His briefing for the England game on Wednesday night was almost complete, but he needed one last file. As a DI, he could have got one of the others to get it for him but he needed the exercise and, besides, a visit to the fourth floor might well result in another look at the blonde from earlier on. He was about to head for the lift when the phone rang. It was the DCI requesting his presence. He gave a sigh and walked over to the desk of the young DC. Grabbing a pen and a stick-it note, he scribbled down a name and handed it to the young copper. 'Phil, go down to the fourth floor and bring me up the file on this gentleman. Sign it out under my name and make sure it's right up to date. When you've got it, keep hold of it until you can hand it to me personally.' Before Williams could answer, Jarvis was out of earshot and walking towards the DCI's office.

He knocked on the door and was in before the answer came. 'Yes Guv,' said Jarvis. 'What's up?'

DCI Allen looked up and grinned. 'I've just spoken to Mr Morgan. You'll be amazed to know that he wants us to stop proceedings. He's slightly embarrassed, to say the least.'

Jarvis smiled. 'Thought he would,' he said. 'It's amazing what a bit of parental embarrassment can do, in my experience.'

'Anyway,' went on Allen, 'finish the report on the incident and stick it on file. You never know when it'll come in handy.'

DC Williams was waiting by Jarvis's desk when he got back, a large green folder tucked under his arm. 'The file you wanted, Guv,' he said.

Jarvis took it from him and weighed it in his hand before dropping it on his desk. It was heavy. 'Pull up a chair, Phil,' he said. 'If you're going to do the job, you need to know everything there is to know about this face.'

As Williams scuttled off to grab his chair, Jarvis sat down and opened the folder. It was packed full of statements and photographs. He pulled a picture out and stared at it. A round face with short dark hair stared up at him, the expression completely indifferent, yet with a strange kind of menace.

'He looks a nasty bastard.' Jarvis looked up as Williams put the chair down and sat on it, dragging it the last few inches so he was tight up against the desk like an excited schoolboy.

'He is,' said Jarvis, returning his gaze to the photograph, 'he most certainly is. Phil, this is one Billy Evans. Thirty-two years old, a car dealer from Romford. On the face of it, he's a respectable man with a nice house, nice family and a successful business. However, just after Euro 96, he became the king-pin of the West Ham mob, the Cockney Suicide Squad. It's also believed that he has a record of involvement with the planning of trouble involving England fans abroad, including the riots in Dublin, Oslo and Rome.'

Williams took a photograph and looked at it. 'Nice bloke. Anything else?'

Jarvis dropped his photograph and picked up a sheet from the file. 'Aside from his involvement in football, there's been a lot of rumour over the years suggesting that he's also been involved in the distribution of drugs to clubs all over the southeast and that he's also done some protection work in the East End.'

Williams looked up. 'Rumour?'

'Yes, that's all we've ever had, rumour. We've never been able to get anything concrete on him, despite undercover operations and surveillance. I've been through his house twice myself – and nothing. We did get him in court once, for affray.

'He was arrested during a ruck at a game in Coventry but the charge was dropped when the local plods dropped a bollock with the evidence.'

Williams let out a slow whistle, but Jarvis went on. 'Six months ago, he vanished from the football scene and we thought he'd given it up to concentrate on his other "activities". We even handed his file over to the organised crime lads, but a few weeks ago, when West Ham were playing at Elland Road, he was spotted in Leeds with some of the serious lads from the Service Crew. Since then, he's been spotted at all of West Ham's away games and always in with the local firm. The odd thing is, he hasn't been seen at Upton Park all season.'

Williams looked at his DI but he was miles away. This was clearly a talk he had given many times before.

'The DCI thinks he's just keeping up with old mates,' Jarvis continued. 'Me, I think it's something more than that. I think he's up to something and I want to know what it is. That's why he's in every briefing I have to give and I want you to go through this file so that you know everything about him. If you ever turn up anything, I want to know – and I want it written down and put in here.'

Williams had been staring at Jarvis, but his DI was clearly unaware of it. 'Guv.'

Jarvis turned to face him. 'What?'

Williams was a little unsure of how to do it, but there was a question he had to ask. 'Guv, judging by the stuff here, this guy has been at it a while. If nothing's ever turned up on him despite all this work, why are you ... I mean, why are we still after him?'

Jarvis's expression changed instantly. He glared at Williams and lowered his voice. 'Because I say so. And if I'm sure of one thing, it's that one day I'm going to put this bastard inside.'

Chapter 3
Wednesday, 8 September
16.20

Fitchett and Alex stepped out into the late-afternoon sunshine. Both were relieved to escape the frantic din of Baker Street tube station, but for different reasons. Alex because it got on his tits and Fitch because of the oppressive atmosphere. Two trips to London in four days would normally have been their idea of hell on Earth, but this one was different. This one was more social than sporting, and the first blast of the England fans in full cry brought an instant smile to both their lips.

'I love this place,' said Alex. 'Every time I come here, it's like a reunion.'

Fitchett laughed out loud. 'You fucking idiot. Half the lads here would kick your arse, given half a chance.'

'Wouldn't get near me, mate. I'm like Linford Christie on acid when I do a runner.'

'Yeah I know, I've seen it enough times.'

Alex stopped and raised his eyebrows. 'You've got a bloody nerve, you cheeky bastard. You're like the fucking roadrunner when you do the off. And I've seen that enough times!'

Fitchett looked at him and laughed again. 'You bloody tart.'

And there it was, the Globe. The unofficial meeting place of England's finest. The front of the building almost hidden behind a huge mob of men and a sea of red crosses, each flag covered in black writing, marking out who they were and which club they were from. Like a sea of battle flags. The two of them stopped for a moment to take it in, and then set out across the busy West London road to take their place among their peers.

Like many of the people there, neither Fitchett nor Alex felt any kind of affinity with the national side when they played at home. They cared, of course, but England and Wembley in the caring, sharing nineties was all about kids and corporate money, the atmosphere under the twin towers more akin to a

Spice Girls concert than a football match. Not for the likes of them, the true fans who made all the noise and carried all the pride and passion with them in their hearts. They were only ever seen on the away trips these days. But when England played, they still came down. It was a social thing, when they could meet up with friends and acquaintances from former trips, exchange information about various mobs, or just catch up on the gossip. And the Globe was where they met. It was neutral ground. Everyone knew that.

At the traffic island in the middle of Baker Street, they both felt a tap on the shoulder and spun round to see the face of someone they had first met in Rimini during Italia 90. Graham Hawkins, known universally as Hawkeye. As ever, his clothes were immaculate and Fitchett noted them in an instant: brown Camel boots, beige Diesel jeans, blue checked Teddy Smith shirt and a beige Burberry jacket that must have cost over £200. Flash bastard. Yet despite his expensive clothes, his bony features and cropped hair always gave him the appearance of being ill. Alex had once said he reminded him of an AIDS victim and it had become something of a running joke.

' 'Ello lads, long time no see. What brings you down to the land of class and style then?'

'Fuck me, Hawkeye. You're still alive then? I didn't know they'd found a cure for the old arse fever.'

''Course boy. It'd take a fuckin' double dose to put me away.'

They all laughed as the lights changed and they made the final short trip across the road into the welcoming environment that can only ever be created by groups of football fans. Without a word, the three of them forced their way through the melee outside and made their way inside. Only once they were in did they visibly relax, and Alex pushed through the crowd and headed for the bar. It never did to hang around outside the Globe. It wasn't the uniformed police who were the problem – although there were always plenty of them hovering around – but the plainclothes lot from the NFIU. Hiding in the windows opposite with their video cameras, recording every face and hoping to get lucky. Best not to give them the chance if you could avoid it.

Fitchett and Hawkeye moved over to the side of the pub and settled against the wall to wait for Alex. 'Back in a sec,' said Hawkeye, and walked over to another group, leaving Fitchett standing there soaking in the atmosphere. He genuinely liked Hawkeye. He wasn't bad for a Cockney, and a West Ham one at that. Fitchett was, however, slightly puzzled. Despite his sickly appearance, Hawkeye was a nasty piece of work – Fitchett had seen him in action enough times to know that. But he wasn't the top man at West Ham: that was Billy Evans. And, like Alex and him, they were rarely seen apart at games. But Evans was nowhere to be seen.

He shrugged and looked around. The Globe was a typical pub. Wood panels on the walls, beer stains on the carpet and the ceiling stained yellow by a million cigarettes. But there was something about it. It had a mood, an ambience. Fitchett had never been able to put his finger on what it was, but Alex was right, this was a great place to be. There were lads from all over in here, you only had to listen to the accents to realise that. Hereford, Exeter, Stoke, Newcastle – almost every top boy in England standing within fifty feet of each other, and not a hint of trouble. Fucking amazing, he thought, as yet another chorus of the obligatory 'No Surrender to the IRA' broke out outside.

As he stood there, a few people looked over at him and nodded. Fitchett returned the compliment, but that was all. No conversation. Not yet. He was the top man of one of the biggest mobs in the country and he was under no misapprehensions that everyone who counted knew who he was and where he was from. You didn't play the game as long as he had without people knowing. That's what it was all about. Reputation. If they wanted to talk, they would come to him. Another round of singing broke out among the crowd outside, but inside the pub, the atmosphere remained loud, but almost dignified. His eyes settled on a table in the corner and he made a mental note of the people sitting there. They were talking among themselves but Fitchett knew from numerous trips abroad who and what they were. He had never been into all that and neither had any of his lads. He wouldn't allow it and, in any case, they had a few black lads in the Selector, Nick for one and Pillow for another. They were good lads and, what's more, good scrappers. He'd gone to Dublin, of course, and played the right-wing game, but that had been an exception. And for once, Alex had refused to go with him. 'Waste of fucking time,' he'd said. 'That's not what football's all about, not for me anyway. That's all bollocks.' And he was right.

'How've you been then, you old wanker?' Hawkeye was back, charming as ever.

'Yeah, we're all right mate.'

'So I hear. In fact I heard you had a bit of a result Saturday.'

Fitchett looked at him and raised an eyebrow. 'What d'you hear then?'

'Just that you stumbled across some Chelsea lads and gave them a lesson. They're none too pleased, I can tell you. They were on their way to a meet with some Spurs.'

Fitchett was still laughing as Alex appeared back with a handful of plastic glasses. 'You're not gonna believe this. That lot in Camden were only fucking Chelsea!'

Alex put his hand to his mouth. 'Oops!' he said sarcastically. 'Well if they were Chelsea, then that club has gone right downhill, I can tell you. Either that, or it proves how top we really are – because we gave them a right spanking!'

Hawkeye laughed, 'No I'm telling ya, they were from Slough way. A right tasty little firm by all accounts.' He paused, took a long drink from his pint, and then added, 'Mind you, we did them a few weeks ago. I mean, they ain't that good. We put the Under Fives on 'em, just for a bit of training.' More laughter.

'Yeah, right-oh! The fuckin' Cockney Suicide Squad? You'll be getting your pensions soon. You're a right bunch of old cunts.'

Hawkeye rubbed his eyes and said, 'That hurts, that does.'

Alex gave him a broad wink. 'Truth always does mate. Face it, your lot are finished. History.'

Hawkeye reached into his pocket and pulled out his cigarettes as a chorus of 'Come on England, Come on England' broke out by the door.

'Where's that twat Evans?' asked Fitchett over the noise, 'I'd have bet money that he'd be here.'

Hawkeye looked around and said quietly, 'He's out the race mate. He hardly even goes to games any more. Just had enough, he says. Fuckin' tragic.'

'Bollocks,' said Alex. 'They'll bury that cunt in Upton Park.'

Hawkeye shook his head. 'I'm telling you straight, lads, he's given it all up.'

Fitchett looked at Hawkeye. He couldn't believe it. Billy was the nearest thing to a mate he had ever had at another football club. They'd even met up a few times, when he had been in Birmingham on business. 'He is going to Italy though? I mean, it's the Euro 2000 qualifier for fuck's sake!'

Hawkeye shook his head. 'Tell you what mate, I don't know. Haven't spoken to him for a while now. His business takes up all his time, these days.'

Alex shook his head. 'Well fuck me, I'd never have thought it.'

'He won't miss Italy,' said Fitchett. 'Not in a million fucking years. I'll give him a bell this week.'

They were still discussing Billy Evans twenty minutes later when Fitchett suddenly became aware that they were surrounded by a group of men. Instantly, he recognised one of them from the Saturday, although it wasn't that hard. His face was still badly bruised and he was clearly none too pleased.

'You're one of the cunts we met on Saturday,' one of them said.

Fitchett looked him up and down, West London, mid-twenties, smartly dressed and full of himself. Everything he hated. The enemy. 'Hello mate,' he said, 'I knew I'd seen you before, but I just couldn't place it. How's your top boy? Last time I saw him he was rolling around in the road trying to hide under a taxi.'

By now, Alex was standing next to Fitchett and was about to speak, when Hawkeye jumped in. 'And you are ...?'

The enemy glared at Hawkeye. 'This has got fuck all to do with you, wanker.'

Fitchett moved forward and discreetly touched his friend on the back. Just enough to let him know that he wanted him to move out the way. He had been in situations like this enough times to know that the best way to deal with scum like this was to front them up. Show a bit of bottle and they always backed down. Besides, he wasn't bothered about this runt. 'Listen shit head, you got a seeing-to on Saturday; don't make me give you another one. Not here. You know the rules. If you want another go, then let's sort it out and we'll be there. Any fucking time you want it. But bring some better lads this time. The ones you had with you Saturday were fuck all.'

The enemy looked Fitchett up and down. 'You northern cunt. Who the fuck d'you think you're talking to? I should kick your arse back up the M1.'

Fitchett moved forward as he spoke. His voice lowered almost to a hiss. He was getting angry now and he wasn't going to put up with this bollocks from anyone. 'You could try, boy. But this time I won't let you run away. This time I'll do you myself – and I'll make sure you never walk properly again.'

They were now almost standing nose to nose, and he was just about to lash out when Alex moved forward and got between them. 'Pigs,' he hissed. Fitchett continued to glare at his adversary as Alex pushed him backwards. His eyes were narrowed and his lips were clenched tight shut. Each second that passed, he could feel the tension rising inside him. This wanker would back down before he would. He was looking for a flicker, a blink. Something, anything that showed a weakness, but so far there was nothing.

'Fitch, the coppers.' Alex's voice was becoming concerned, but Fitchett held the stare.

'What's going on?'

'Nothing, officer, just an argument about a spilt pint, that's all.'

Fitchett heard it all; he even felt the jostling as the police moved in, but it was all happening somewhere else. He wasn't going to back down. Not from some little shit who should be showing him respect. 'OK son.' The hand on his shoulder tugged him round, breaking the spell.

'I'm not your bloody son,' he said. 'I'm fuck all to do with you.'

The policeman looked at him. 'Oh, is that right?' he said.

'Well you are now sunshine. Come with me.'

Fitchett was led out of the pub, round the corner and pushed against the wall. He lost sight of Alex and the enemy, but could see that Hawkeye had followed and was within earshot.

'Listen, you fuckwit, I don't know what's going on there, but it stops right now, is that clear?'

Fitchett looked at the policeman in front of him. They were probably the same ages, around thirty, thirty-one. In a different time and a different place, they might have been mates. Now all Fitchett saw was a wanker in a uniform. PC 3876. But the line had been reached – and if Gary Fitchett knew one thing, it was when to back down from the law. That was what had kept him out of the courts all these years. 'Sorry officer,' he said apologetically, 'I don't know what came over me. But you know what it's like in there. It takes ages to get served and then some prick knocks your pint over. I just lost it for a bit. Sorry.'

PC 3876 looked at Fitchett and noted his accent. 'Brummie are you? What club d'you follow?'

'England of course.'

'Don't get funny, sunshine. What club side do you support?'

'I'm Villa,' said Fitchett. 'Always have been.'

PC 3876 stared at Fitchett for a few seconds. 'Empty your pockets, will you please.' He knew Fitchett was lying and he half thought he had seen him somewhere before. Maybe on one of the bulletins issued by the NFIU. If he remembered, he'd look into it later on.

Fitchett held out the contents of his pockets. Fags, lighter; train ticket, money, keys. 'No wallet?' asked PC 3876. 'And no match ticket?'

'Never bring a wallet to London,' said Fitchett. 'I had it stolen once. Cost me a bloody fortune and I'm meeting someone up at Wembley who's got a ticket for me.'

PC 3876 handed Fitchett back his things. He knew that there was only one reason why people who came to the Globe carried no identification, and that was to make sure that if they were nicked they'd be difficult to trace. 'What's your name then?'

'Gary Fitchett.'

'Lying fucker,' thought PC 3876. He half thought about giving him a tug but decided against it. After all, he was set to leave for the stadium in half an hour and was due a break when he got there. Dealing with this yob would take hours, and what would be the point? He hadn't really done anything. 'All right, off you go. But no more bother, all right?'

'Thanks officer,' said Fitchett, the relief in his voice almost believable. 'It won't happen again.'

Five minutes later, Fitchett had worked his way back into the welcoming environment of the Globe and had found Alex and Hawkeye. Alex handed him back his pint and, after a long drink, he asked, 'What happened to Chelsea then?'

'He said he'll be seeing you again,' said Alex. 'I told him we'd look forward to it. Next time they were up our way.'

'That's a date then,' said Fitchett. 'We'll do them and Villa at the same time.'

Hawkeye looked at Fitchett and shook his head. 'Did you give that copper your real name?'

'Course, we always do,' smiled Fitchett. 'What's the point in lying? I had no ID on me and the chances of him knowing me are zero. Best tell the truth. After all – one of the others could have asked you or Al who I was, and what would you have said? Tell them my real name, then whatever I say will match. Makes the rest of it more believable.'

Hawkeye looked at him and shook his head. 'You're fucking mad. But why d'you tell him you were Villa then?'

Alex stood bolt upright. 'You fucking traitor.'

Fitchett pulled out a cigarette and then offered the packet to the other two. 'Had to, didn't I? Better one of them cunts get in trouble than one of ours.'

The three of them were still laughing when a familiar voice spoke out. 'I see they've relaxed the quarantine laws then.'

'Well fuck me!' said Hawkeye. 'Look what the cat dragged in. Mr Evans. How the devil are you?'

Fitchett turned and looked at Billy Evans with a mixture of happiness and relief. Like Hawkeye, he was immaculately dressed. A mixture of Ralph Lauren and Pepe topped off with a very nice Burberry jacket. Obviously, a label back in favour among the Eastenders this year. He looked fatter though – well, not fat, more round. Probably a lack of action. One thing Fitchett was sure of, though, he was a vicious bastard when he wanted to be. He hadn't been top boy at West Ham for nothing. Fitchett reached out his hand and Evans took it.

'Hello my son, I see you've come down for some culture.'

They all smiled. 'What's this bollocks Hawkeye's been spouting about you turning into a scarfer then?'

Evans looked at his friend and laughed. 'It's all true, I'm afraid. It's all right for you lower-league lads, but us kingpins running with the big boys, well it's a strain. Gets to you. Know what I mean?'

He pulled out a packet of cigarettes and offered them around before realising that all three were already smoking.

'You're a fuckwit Billy,' said Fitchett as he held out his lighter. 'You are going to Italy, though?'

'Course I am. Matter of fact, I was gonna give you a bell this week, Fitch. I've got something on that might be right up your street.' He moved forward and pulled Fitchett over to one side.

As he did so, Hawkeye and Alex instinctively moved out of earshot and began talking. They knew their places in the pecking order of their respective mobs – and if their top boys wanted to talk, then their job was to make sure no one else listened. They didn't need to know what they were saying, and in truth they didn't want to know. That was the key, keep it quiet and exclusive. That way, if anyone got arrested then they had nothing to say.

Evans took a quick look around and leant forward so that he wouldn't have to speak too loudly. 'Listen Fitch, how d'you and Al fancy a trip to Rome with me and a few others? It'll be a giggle and there may be an earner in it? What d'you reckon?'

Fitchett looked and grinned. He knew all about Billy and his trips with England. Christ, he'd been on enough of them. 'Count us in. You know us, anything for a crack.'

Evans looked at him and gave a broad wink. 'Top man,' he said, 'I'll be in touch.'

They stood there and looked at each other for a second before the two of them burst out laughing and walked back across the pub to join their friends.

As kick-off time approached, PC 3876 watched the crowd make their way across Baker Street and vanish into the tube station. The British Transport Police were stopping everyone and taking any alcohol off them, which was annoying a few people but that was their problem now. He'd done his bit. This had been his first time at the Globe and he had quite enjoyed himself. Truth to tell, he'd actually been a bit apprehensive when they dropped him off. After all, at the briefing they'd told him that the place was a haven for football hooligans and he hadn't been that keen. I mean, judging by the photographs he had looked at, who in their right mind would want to walk into the middle of that lot? But apart from the Brummie bloke getting a bit stroppy, it had been all right. He looked across at the others. They were getting a bit worried that the van taking them up to Wembley would be late and they might not make kick-off, but he wasn't concerned. He'd never been that much of a football fan anyway. Motorsport was his thing.

Rather than listen to the others moaning, he decided to have a final look inside the pub, and after telling them where he was going, walked round the corner and through the front door. It was only two-thirds full now and, in any case, was under orders to shut at 7.00 p.m., which was only ten minutes away.

It looked a right toilet. The kind of place he wouldn't normally be seen dead in. Glancing round, he caught sight of the guy he had pulled earlier, the Brummie. He was laughing and joking with three other men, and PC 3876 smiled when he realised he hadn't left for the match. 'I knew he was lying,' he thought, congratulating himself on his powers of deduction. 'Probably gave me a false name as well, the twat.' He was just about to leave when something about one of the men he was standing with clicked. The stocky one: he was one of the faces he'd been shown earlier at the briefing. No doubt about it. PC 3876 turned and walked out. The van was waiting for him and his colleagues were all inside. It didn't take any of his considerable powers of detection to work out that they were, to say the least, agitated.

'For Christ's sake Dave, get a hurry on. We'll be late.'

He walked over and climbed inside, the vehicle moving even as the door shut with an almighty bang.

PC 3876 settled into his seat and pulled out his pocket book. He wanted to write down a quick description of the two men in the pub before he forgot it. He could do with a few brownie points.

Across the street, Paul Jarvis leant back away from the net curtains and shouted out, 'Get the number of that van and make sure that crew reports to me tonight before they go off shift.'

'Yes Guv,' came the instantaneous reply, the voice speaking on the phone almost before Jarvis acknowledged it. He wanted to speak to the copper who'd gone into the Globe to try to find out if he'd seen Evans inside and who he had been talking to. If that meant pissing the others off for a while, then too bad.

He let out a sigh and looked around. He hated this room, it was a right shit hole. Full of rubbish and smelling of stale fags and sweaty coppers. Every time England played at Wembley, he was guaranteed to spend at least four hours in here. Watching the front of the Globe and taking pictures of low-lifes getting drunk across the road. Tonight, rather than sit there on his own, he'd had three other members of the Unit for company and they had watched while the targets had gathered.

Pointing out the faces of the known hooligans and trying to identify new faces. It had been no different from any other night and then, in the space of ten minutes, it had all changed. First, he'd spotted the Brummie lads from the Camden High Street ruck. It had been a good move by the boss to stick their pictures in the briefing, although he would never acknowledge that. Then he identified the lad from West Ham, Hawkins, and had been very surprised to see him speak so openly to the Brummies. He had been very careful to get lots of pictures of the three of them for future reference. But what had really made his night was the appearance of Billy Evans. Jarvis hadn't expected that and had been almost apoplectic with delight. He'd been alone, but had headed straight into the pub without speaking to anyone outside. It was too purposeful, Jarvis had thought. If it was a social visit, then he'd have talked to some of the lads outside. Jarvis knew from experience that he was familiar with at least fifteen of the lads drinking outside the pub.

'Guv, it's Evans!' Jarvis span around and caught sight of Billy Evans as he stepped out of the Globe. The sound of clicking cameras and winding motors filled the room but Jarvis continued to glare at his adversary, his head straining forward until it was almost touching the glass. As the three men walked out behind him, Jarvis raised his eyebrows in feigned surprise, and even though he knew it was already being filmed, called out, 'Get that, someone.' As if making sure to himself. Only once the four men had crossed the road and vanished into the tube station underneath them, did the men in the room relax. Jarvis stood up straight and rubbed his hands together in delight. 'Well lads, that was a fucking turn-up. Our old mate Evans is out and about then, is he? I wonder what that little shit's up to?' He looked across at the other people in the room. They were busily packing up their gear but glanced across at Jarvis and smiled as he spoke. 'If he's back in the game, then this time I want him. The twat's got it coming.'

Chapter 4
Thursday, 30 September
05.24

Jarvis pulled his collar up around his neck for what seemed like the hundredth time and took a long look at the clock on the dashboard of the Ford Mondeo. Five twenty-four. Six minutes to go. He leant forward, picked up the radio and mentioned this fact to the other members of the team before settling back into his seat. He'd be glad to get going, just to get some warmth through him.

To get his mind off the cold and on to the job in hand, Jarvis began running over the events of the past three weeks: the fight in Camden High Street; the sighting of Billy Evans at the Globe; the debrief of PC 3876; it all led to here. A small two-bedroomed house on a mid-eighties housing estate on the outskirts of Birmingham. Jarvis had taken the decision to raid the homes of both Fitchett and Bailey the day after the England game. He knew he was sticking his neck out, but the photographs from the fight in Camden High Street had been cleaned up and even the DCI thought that they were now good enough to stand up in court. In fact, they were so good that when Jarvis had met Terry Porter to tell him he was being pulled out, Porter had been able to put names to most of them. With any luck, they would all be picked out on CCTV and arrested at the next Birmingham City home game. Jarvis, however, was convinced that Fitchett and Bailey could give him information on Billy Evans, and that was why he wanted to get them in custody fast and then search their homes. If he could get that link, then he might be able to use it as a lever, and then, who knew where it would lead? That's why he was here personally – and why he had another team waiting outside Bailey's house in Bordesley Green, who would go in at the same time as he did. He hadn't left it to the West Midlands coppers because he couldn't afford to miss anything.

His thoughts returned to Terry Porter. That had been a bit strange. Usually when he told undercover coppers they were being pulled off an operation, they were pissed off. After all, it was a good earner for most of them and Jarvis knew better than most that the majority of them enjoyed it. Usually for the wrong reasons. But Porter had been obviously relieved. He'd actually said he'd be glad to get back to doing proper police work. Jarvis would speak to him when he got back off the three weeks' leave he had been given. If there was a problem, it needed sorting.

'Guv.' The voice jolted him back to life and he looked across at his young DC, Phil Williams. It had been Jarvis's idea to bring Williams along. He wanted to see how he performed under pressure and, besides, if he was going to stay on the squad he needed to learn some of the tricks of the trade. 'The light's come on.'

Jarvis looked across at the front of the house as, one after another, the downstairs lights went on. 'Shit,' he said out loud, before grabbing the radio and saying, 'Target is mobile, repeat, target is mobile. Go-go-go.' He dropped the microphone and leapt out of the car. Within seconds, the street was alive with uniformed coppers and the noise of stomping Dr Martens. To Jarvis, as he strode purposefully towards the front door, it seemed deafening. He wanted to be one of the first there, but wasn't going to run. This was his operation and he wanted to show he was calm and collected. He couldn't do that if he was running, and anyway, he had the warrant in his pocket. Nothing would happen until he was there.

At the top of the short path, he stopped and glanced around. The others had slowed and were now falling in behind him. 'OK,' he said. 'Let's do this.' He stepped aside as two uniformed officers leapt forward with a bright red battering ram in their hands. One crash and the door went in. A flood of policemen poured through, some running upstairs and others down the short downstairs corridor, vanishing into the rooms on each side. Jarvis was last in, and he waited to see what response came from the others as they searched through the house. A shout drew him towards the end of the downstairs corridor and he walked along and into the kitchen. Sitting at the breakfast bar was a man in a very smart and obviously expensive pale yellow shirt with a blue tie. In front of him was a bowl of cornflakes and a glass of orange juice. He looked at Jarvis and smiled.

'Come in, why don't you? If you'd have just given a ring on the bell, I'd have let you in.'

Jarvis looked down at him and grinned back. 'Hello Gary,' he said, 'you're up early aren't you?'

Fitchett turned back to his breakfast and drained the glass of orange juice. 'I was expecting guests. You know how it is.'

Jarvis grinned and looked around the kitchen. It was immaculate. All white wood and glass. 'So, expecting us were you?'

Fitchett smiled and returned to his cornflakes.

Jarvis pulled the warrant out of his pocket and dropped it on the table. 'Gary Fitchett, I am Detective Inspector Paul Jarvis from the National Football Intelligence Unit. I've a warrant here for your arrest – and you, my son, are nicked.'

Fitchett looked up at him, his face almost expressionless. Jarvis made a mental note of the fact that he hadn't shown the slightest sign of fear, anger or anything else since they had come through his front door. It wasn't just as if he knew they were coming: it was something else. A kind of arrogant acceptance. He'd seen it before but he couldn't work out where. Yes he could, the last time he raided Billy Evans's house.

Fitchett stood up and looked Jarvis straight in the eye. 'What about my rights?'

Jarvis stared straight back at him and laughed. 'Gary, what makes you think you've got any fucking rights?'

Jarvis walked through the house trying to work out where to start. Fitchett had been taken to the local nick, where he would charge him later on. They had him bang to rights for the Camden High Street assault and the local plods had enough other stuff on him to make sure he was facing a stretch of some sort or another. But that wasn't what Jarvis wanted. He wanted a link with Billy Evans and he was certain that there was one somewhere. He carried on his stroll through the house. There were no shrines to Birmingham City, no shelves full of National Front propaganda or anything of the kind most people would expect from a hooligan of Fitchett's obvious status. In fact, every room was immaculate. When he opened a cupboard on the landing to find it full of neatly stacked towels, Jarvis almost laughed out loud. 'He'd make someone a lovely wife,' he thought.

He moved back to the kitchen and noticed a laptop computer sitting on the breakfast bar. Sitting down, he switched it on and searched through the software directory to see what it contained. Nothing unusual, just tons of documents relating to work. Not even any games or hidden stuff that he could spot. He moved through the programme to the address book and searched through for any names he recognised. Nothing. 'Bollocks,' he said out loud and slammed the lid down. Someone would need to have a look through it later on, in case anything was on there he hadn't spotted. He stood up again and walked through to the lounge. The phone was on a table by the door and he picked it up and looked at the list of stored numbers. Mum, work, takeaway, ticket office, and a list of names. Both male and female. He put it back down and walked over to a shelf stacked out with tapes and numerous books. Nearly all the videos were about football and most of those were Birmingham City. Greatest goals, season reviews, etc. The books were the predictable ones you'd find in any male household: Nick Hornby, Andy McNab, some joke books and loads about football. No different from most fans and, in truth, much the same as Jarvis had on his shelf. 'No hooligan books though,' he mused. With a sigh, he stood up and called out.

Within a few seconds, the young face of DC Williams appeared. 'Yes Guv?'

'Phil, make sure the laptop comes with us back to London. I also want someone to check out all the numbers on this phone. Anything turned up yet?'

'Not yet Guv,' said the young copper; 'but the Brummie lads are still looking.'

'Get someone up in the loft as well and make sure that we get all his phone bills including any mobile ones. And where the fuck is his mobile? He's a rep for God's sake. And when we get back to the local nick, make sure someone gets onto his work and gets any phone bills from them too.'

'Yes Guv.'

The young face vanished and Jarvis walked back into the kitchen. He sat down and ran through everything he had to do: phones, phone bills, address books, computer; that was it. He stood up and walked out to the garage adjacent to the house. A red BMW 3 series not unlike Jarvis's own sat there, a black helmet sitting on the roof. 'Anything?' called Jarvis.

'Nothing yet,' said a voice from the back of the car. 'Just the usual stuff you'd expect. You sure this is the guy you're after? I mean, nice house, flash car. He's not your usual yobbo, is he?'

Jarvis thought for a moment and watched as the uniform climbed up from the boot. 'He's our man all right. No doubt about that.'

The uniform shrugged his shoulders. 'Well, there's nothing in here sir.'

Jarvis sighed and walked back into the house. This was odd but not unusual. When he'd first turned over Billy Evans about three years ago, it had been the same. Nothing to suggest he was anything other than a regular football fan.

'Guv!' The shout made him start and he walked back into the corridor.

'Who's calling?' he shouted.

'Up here!'

He almost sprinted up the stairs and ran into the bedroom. Unlike all the other rooms, this one was a mess, but Jarvis had no doubt that what he was looking at had been caused by the two men in there. He looked at the man in uniform, who was idly flicking through a wardrobe packed with freshly ironed white shirts and smart dark suits, and then at the young copper from his own nick, who gave a broad grin, handed Jarvis a photo album and simply said 'bingo'.

Jarvis took the book and turned it round so the pictures were the right way up.

'It was under the mattress.'

Jarvis nodded and stared down at the faces on the pictures in front of him. A series of photographs showed Gary Fitchett and Billy Evans standing in front of a fountain, wearing the regulation clothing of football fans abroad. Shorts and England shirts. Draped on the floor in front of them was a flag, the cross of St George, and, in the background, a group of Dutch policemen in full riot gear. Underneath in neat black ink read the legend 'Rotterdam 1993'. Jarvis looked up at the young copper and smiled. 'Well done Phil. This'll do nicely.'

Chapter 5
Friday, 1 October
14.30

'Here's your coffee, Guv. Watch out, it's bloody scalding.' Jarvis looked up from the stack of papers and took the polystyrene cup. 'Cheers Phil,' he said. 'I'm ready for this.'

The two men sat silently drinking as the train thundered its way towards Euston. 'I'll be glad to get back to London,' said the young DC. 'I hate going up north.'

Jarvis laughed. 'Bloody hell Phil, if you think Birmingham's north, then you need to get about a bit more. I'll have to sort you out a transfer to Newcastle.'

Williams laughed out loud. 'Bollocks to that Guv, they're all mad up there. I went out with a Geordie bird once: she drank more than I did and I couldn't understand a bloody word she said.'

Jarvis put down his cup and smiled at the young DC. He'd done all right. The photo album was a godsend and he'd done well when they'd charged Fitchett. In truth, the atmosphere in the charge room had been a bit strained. Jarvis had insisted all along that details of the raids remained a secret and he had been very wary of the local coppers. This had pissed them off a bit and although he understood that – after all, no one likes being told what to do in their own nick – he hadn't been too concerned about who he had upset. It had been left to Williams to smooth things over with a charm offensive that had been frighteningly convincing.

Jarvis took another sip of coffee and turned his thoughts to the two men arrested. All he knew about Bailey was that the raid had gone to plan and he, like Fitchett, was on his way to London for questioning. Fitchett, though, was another matter. As Jarvis had expected, he was an arrogant bastard. Even in the charge room, Fitchett had maintained an air of defiance. As if at any moment he expected to be released and given an apology. He'd glared at Jarvis a couple of times, probably for effect, but had just received a smile and a wink for his trouble. Jarvis never spoke to people he'd nicked until he had them in an interview room – and he was saving that pleasure for when they were back in London. It was a trick he'd learned from his first DI. He had said that the best way to get results from an interview was to have the prisoner questioned by someone he hadn't met. For some reason, it threw them completely. Jarvis had worked out that it was all to do with being familiar with voices, and so now he didn't speak to prisoners until he had to. A few of his colleagues over the years had thought he was mad, but the fact was it worked for him and he'd certainly got enough results.

The look on Fitchett's face when they'd come through the door still worried Jarvis a little. He didn't like working in other people's nicks: too many strange faces, and he was very aware of the possibility that their arrival had not been unexpected. That was one of the reasons for taking the two prisoners back to London. Besides, he felt tired and dirty. He needed to go home, have a bath and get some decent sleep before having a crack at an interview. Especially these two.

'You found anything in there?' asked Williams, nodding towards the pile of papers on the table.

'Nothing yet,' said Jarvis. He picked up a photocopy of a telephone bill and passed it across the table. 'It's all just normal stuff. We'll have to get all these numbers checked out, but to be honest I doubt we'll find anything. I reckon he's got another mobile stashed somewhere for Saturdays. People like him usually do: that way, unless we find it, we can't trace any of the numbers he rings when he's planning an off.'

Williams looked through the bills on the table in front of him. 'Well, if you're looking for an Essex number, there's none here,' said Williams. 'And I should know, being an Essex lad.'

Jarvis looked at him with feigned surprise. 'Don't tell me you know every telephone code in Essex,' he said.

'No Guv,' laughed Williams, 'but I know the code for Romford, and that's where Evans lives, isn't it.'

It wasn't a question, it was a statement, and it threw Jarvis a bit. Williams saw that and quickly began working through the papers on the table leaving the two men in an embarrassed silence. Jarvis took a mouthful of coffee and broached the subject that had been on both their minds for days but for different reasons. 'When are you going to ask me then?'

'Ask you what, Guv?'

'About Billy Evans.'

Williams shrugged his shoulders. 'I know what you told me, of course, and there's the stuff I got out of the file. The other lads on the unit have filled me in on a lot.'

Jarvis looked down at the table and then back at Williams. 'Did they mention Euston at all?'

Williams looked uneasy. This was before his time and he knew it still rankled with a few of the older hands. 'Some of it,' he said, 'but ... well, you know Guv.'

Jarvis nodded. He did know. The death of a fellow officer always left a scar and it was something you didn't talk about if you didn't have to. After all, it could happen to any of them at any time. They all knew that. Jarvis sighed. If Williams was going to hear about it, he'd best hear about it from him. He took a deep breath and began.

'About a year after I joined the unit, we had a tip-off that a mob of Millwall were going to be ambushed by West Ham at New Cross station. Word was that this was revenge for an attack on a Hammers pub the previous season, but we were certain it was to give a boost to the CSS after their no-show during Euro 96. Anyway, we did know that the West Ham boys weren't going to mess about. They were going tooled-up and they wanted to settle things once and for all. I was a DS at that time, and our advice to the Met lads was to flood the place with uniforms and simply keep the two groups apart. We went along to observe and see if we could identify any of the main players.'

He took a sip of coffee and glanced out of the window. 'Millwall were at West Brom that day while the Hammers were at home, and so we thought we'd have plenty of time to get everything in place for them coming back. What we didn't expect was for the West Ham lads to throw us a curve and head off on the tubes to kick it off at Euston.'

Jarvis stopped talking and watched as a young woman walked past the two of them. He leant forward and continued, his voice lower than before. 'I was one of three spotters at Euston. Me, and two DCs. We were supposed to follow the Millwall lads when they got off the train, to let the Met know where they were. But when they got to the bottom of the second lot of escalators, the West Ham appeared from somewhere and it all kicked off. There were probably a hundred lads rucking down there – and this was on a Saturday night in a tube station. It was bloody chaos.'

'Shitty death,' said Williams.

Jarvis took another mouthful of coffee and continued. 'Anyway, what could we do? We just had to keep out of the way until the cavalry arrived, but after a couple of minutes, more West Ham must have turned up because the Millwall lads came steaming back up the escalators and past us, trying to get away. That's when we got attacked. They must have thought we were West Ham.'

'And that's when DC Peterson was stabbed,' interrupted Williams.

Jarvis leant back and raised an eyebrow. 'So you did know,' he said.

Williams shrugged his shoulders. 'I'd heard,' he said, 'but what else could you have done?'

Jarvis looked at him. 'Nothing,' he said. 'Except get the bastard who set it all up.'

'Billy Evans,' said Williams.

'Exactly. From what we found out later, he made it to top boy just after that, so this would all have been down to him. But even though we bust our nuts, we could never prove anything. Not about that, nor about anything else. I've turned over his house, his business – everything, but nothing. I know that he's responsible for the death of a police officer, but I'd begun to think we'd never get the bastard. Maybe now we've got another chance, because I just know he's up to something. Let's just hope the DCI has got the balls to let us run with it.'

Gary Fitchett sat in the back of the police van as it sped down the M1 towards London. He was desperate for a cigarette, but when he'd asked for one the two coppers in the front had just laughed at him. 'Pair of wankers,' he'd thought. He let out a loud sigh, shut his eyes and leant his head back against the metal panel. For the thousandth time, his thoughts returned to the raid on his house. He'd always known, deep down, that one day the police would come through his front door. It was an occupational hazard and, to be honest, he was surprised that he'd got away with it for so long. After all, he'd been at it since he was thirteen. When they'd told him he was being charged in connection with affray and an assault in Camden High Street, he'd almost laughed out loud at the irony of it. After all the rucks he'd been in with his lads, not to mention the stuff with England, he ends up getting tugged for a nothing off with a few Chelsea faggots. 'Fucking cameras,' he'd thought. 'That was careless; we didn't check for cameras.'

He opened his eyes and stared at the roof of the van. The idea of the police going through his house annoyed him a bit. He knew they wouldn't find anything, because there was nothing to find. If you live your life expecting to be raided, you're not going to give them any help when they do come, are you? But that didn't make it any easier to take. And who was to say they weren't nicking anything they could get their hands on? Bastards. And the copper who'd nicked him was an odd one. Fitchett smiled at the thought of him being all silent and moody in the charge room, trying to wind him up. 'What a tosser,' he thought. 'He must think I give a shit.' He had a sneaky feeling they would meet again, and in a perverse kind of way he was looking forward to it. The next part of the game. See what they throw at me and see how I deal with it.

He'd been lucky over the years, in so much as he'd never been arrested or charged with anything. He'd spent a few nights in the cells, but had always been kicked out in the morning. He was careful like that. Tow the line and grovel for all you're worth, then get back out there and do the business. But it would be interesting to see what it was like being interviewed. 'I wonder if it really is like *The Bill*?' he thought. He could handle it, no problem. One thing he was sure of though, they had more on him than the fight in Camden. They had to have, otherwise they wouldn't have got authority to mount a raid on his house. But what was it? That was the only thing that worried him.

The thought that someone could have grassed him up for something entered his head but he dismissed it immediately. He knew his lads and trusted them all without question. None of them was capable of anything like that. He wondered if they'd raided anyone else. No one had said anything to him and he hadn't seen anyone he knew in the police station. God only knew what Al's missus would have said if they'd gone through his front door at five thirty in the morning. Fitchett wasn't afraid of much, but she scared the shit out of him.

Sitting up straight, he turned his mind to work, but that was even more depressing. Even though he was sure he'd walk in the end, he knew that his boss would give him the elbow. Not even being the top salesman last year could save him from the sack if there were the remotest hint of a scandal. You just couldn't afford it in his line of work. Still, he knew what he was risking every time he walked out the door to go to a game. To be honest, that was part of the attraction. Seeing how far he could push his luck. Maybe he'd pushed it just a bit too far this time.

He shifted around on the hard seat. 'Do you lot make these fucking things uncomfortable on purpose?' he called out to the two policemen.

The passenger looked round. 'Give it a rest. You'll be back in a cell soon, then you can moan all you want.'

He shut his eyes again. He hadn't enjoyed last night, sleeping in a cell. The smell had been disgusting. Stale piss and vomit. For a time, his old fears about being closed in had resurfaced, but he had learnt long ago that simply looking out of a window had helped. Even if it was frosted, like the one in the cell. It was a link with the outside world and that was all he needed to calm himself down. He certainly wasn't looking forward to doing any time. He'd heard enough stories over the years to know what went on in prisons – and none of it appealed. He let out another long sigh. 'What a fucking waste,' he thought.

He needed cheering up and began to hum some of his favourite songs to himself, but one of the coppers in the front turned round and told him to be quiet. He thought about starting again to wind them up, but decided against it. 'Why rock the boat?' He looked at the two men in the front, separated from him by the mesh screen. He hated coppers. They were the scum of the earth. Everyone goes on about hooligans, but what about the coppers? They're just as bad, but because they wear a uniform, they get away with it. Like the time they had been arrested in Liverpool and the coppers there had beaten the shit out of him and Al, and then dumped them down the docks with no shoes on. Or at New Street station, where that copper had whacked him across the kidneys with his truncheon. The bastards abroad were even worse. Rome, Katowice, Marseille, Stockholm, fucking savages. They'd had their moments, though. Like at Derby, when they'd got the copper off his horse and kicked the fuck out of him. Or the time in Norwich, where Baz had stolen a bottle of oil from a garage and thrown it on the road in front of a police biker. He'd gone down with an almighty crash and had then slid along the road on his arse. Funniest thing he'd ever seen.

He was smiling now. Looking back at happier times. The great away trips and the rucks. Wolves, when they'd ambushed the Bridge Boys at New Street and kicked the shit out of them. Boro away, when their pub had been attacked by the Frontline, but they'd fought back and run them. The time at Sheffield United where the Blades Business Crew had tried to trap them in a cul-de-sac, but Al had taken half the lads through an alleyway and attacked them from the back. What a ruck that had been. Or the time they'd been on a coach stuck in traffic and someone realised that just behind them was a bus full of West Brom's Section Five. 'Mayhem on the M6', the headlines had read. Swansea in the cup a few years ago. Cheeky Jack bastards, thinking they could do us at home. His lads had taught them a lesson they'd never forget. Portsmouth away, where he'd earned the title of top boy by throwing the leader of the 657 through the front window of Tesco's and then diving straight in after him.

Barnsley away, when Al and him had walked into a pub full of Five-O by mistake and had to sneak out the toilet window.

What else? Oh yeah, Luton, when they'd gone through the Arndale Centre like a whirlwind and run their crew around all afternoon. Bradford, when they'd met up with the Ointment at Corley services on the M6. The Selector had given them such a hammering, they'd ended up running across the motorway to get away. Leicester, when they'd set fire to a hot-dog wagon to keep the police busy while they went off to ambush the Baby Squad's main pub. Stoke: they'd had some major offs with the Naughty 40 over the years, but the attack on their buses when they'd come to Brum had to be the best. Pillow's idea to throw paint bombs at the windscreens had been inspired. And Millwall, fucking Millwall. He hated going there; it was the only ground that really scared him. The locals were mental.

He took a deep breath and shifted around on his chair. He ached all over. He turned his thoughts to England and the trips he'd had with them. Christ he'd been in some right scrapes over the years. Poland, Holland, Sweden, Italy, Norway, France. Turkey was the worst. He shuddered at the memory of it. When he'd been pissed and dropped his trousers at the train station. Fucking stupid. The police had grabbed him and dragged him off before the others could protect him. They'd beaten the shit out of him, stolen everything he had and then kicked him out. It'd taken ages to find his way back to the others. Dublin. What a crack that was! Someone else picking up the tab for two days on the piss and the biggest result of all time. Best of all, when they'd battered the Scots in Trafalgar Square and almost had the coppers on the run in London. They'd been so close, but the Cockneys had fucked up by not organising things better and the police had got themselves together just in time.

The memories of Euro 96 were still passing through his head when Fitchett became aware that someone was pushing him in the side. 'Wake up fuckwit, we're here.'

He opened his eyes to find the van had stopped and the back doors were open. One of the policemen was reaching inside and motioning him out.

'Shit, must have dozed off,' Fitchett said as he climbed out and stretched himself. He was stiff as a board. Looking around, he could see he was in a yard surrounded by a tall brick wall and which was half full of cars. To his left was a tall, grey, nondescript building with windows which betrayed nothing. He assumed it was a police station and he knew he was in London. But apart from that, he could have been anywhere.

Jarvis grabbed his briefcase and his overnight bag and climbed out of the taxi. He was halfway up the stairs to the station before Williams had paid the driver, and by the time the young DC arrived at the front desk, Jarvis was already in the lift. He hadn't wanted to come back to the office at all, but he wanted to speak to the DCI before he went home.

Although it was almost seven, the office was still half full of people when he walked in. 'Is the DCI in?' he asked.

'No Guv, he's gone home for the weekend. There's a note on your desk and DS Harris is in the briefing room.'

Jarvis dropped his bags, sat down and grabbed the envelope. He read the contents eagerly and, as he did so, a broad smile spread across his face. He'd been given exactly what he'd asked for. Three men and DS Al Harris as the office manager to co-ordinate things. On the bottom of the letter, Allen had scrawled 'You've got seven days to convince me'.

He heard the lift doors open and looked up as Williams came in. 'Phil,' he called as Williams approached. 'We're on.'

The young DC's face broke out in a broad grin. 'That's great, Guv.'

Jarvis stood up. 'It's not just great, it's fucking tremendous.'

He picked up the phone and dialled the number of the custody sergeant, but put it down before it could ring. He told Williams to go home and then headed for the briefing room.

He bumped into Harris on the way. 'Sorry Guv, I didn't know you were back, I was on my way home.'

Jarvis looked at him and smiled. He really rated Harris as a copper and liked him as a bloke. He certainly hadn't asked for him by accident. 'It's OK, Al,' he said. 'Just fill me in on the details and then you can get off. I know this has all been a bit of a rush job.'

Harris looked at him and nodded. 'That's the truth; I didn't know anything about it until two hours ago. Anyway, you've got me, of course, DS Steve Parry and DC Neal White, who arrested Bailey, and Phil Williams who was with you in Brum. I've briefed Steve and Neal already and they're back in at nine tomorrow. I haven't spoken to Williams yet, but I'll give him a ring at home.'

Jarvis nodded thoughtfully. 'Is everything in place in there?'

'Yes Guv, the board's been done and all the files are in there and locked up.'

Jarvis rubbed his hands together and grinned. 'Nice one Al. You get off – and say sorry to Sue for me. I know she already hates my guts.'

Harris laughed out loud and began walking towards the lift. 'See you in the morning, Guv,' he called over his shoulder.

Jarvis walked towards the briefing room and tried to open the door. It was locked. 'Shit.' He suddenly felt very grubby again and was incredibly hungry. After all, he hadn't eaten since breakfast. He walked back to his desk and picked up his bags. Before he went home, there was one last thing he wanted to do.

Gary Fitchett lay on the hard mattress and stared at the ceiling. He was bored out of his mind. To relieve the monotony, he began singing some of his favourite football songs. At first quietly and then at the top of his voice. *'My old man said be a Villa fan, I said fuck off bollocks you're a cunt.*

'When I was a little boy, my granddad brought me a brand new toy, a Villa fan on a piece of string, he told me to kick his fuckin' head in. Fuckin' head in, fuckin' head in, he told me to kick his fuckin' head in ...'

The hatch on the door flew open and an angry face pushed itself forward, filling the small metal frame with rage. 'Shut the fuck up!' it screamed, but Fitchett could only laugh.

Someone had scratched the shape of a backside around the opening and the face looked like a talking ring-piece. 'Any more noise like that and I'll sort you out.'

The hatch slammed shut and Fitchett laughed out loud. 'Twat,' he shouted. As he lay there, something caught his attention and he sat up. He could have sworn he could hear someone else singing. Moving over to the door, he pressed his ear against the closed hatch and strained for all he was worth. The unmistakable sound of a Brummie voice could be heard and at once he knew who it was.

'Alex!' he shouted out and, again, an angry voice shouted down the corridor at them to shut up. After a final burst of the Birmingham City anthem 'Keep right on to the end of the road', the cells went quiet.

Fitchett sat down. So Alex had been raided as well. And he was down here. 'Bollocks,' he said to himself.

The sound of approaching footsteps made him turn towards the door, and once again the hatch flew open. This time, however, he was surprised to see the face of the copper who had raided his house. Fitchett stood up and stared at the face in the hatch for a few seconds before he spoke. 'Well, well, well,' he said, 'we meet again. I see you got my mate as well.'

Fitchett swore he saw a look of shock pass across the face of the copper, before the hatch slammed shut. He ran over to the door and shouted, 'You ignorant bastard, you could have said hello at least!' Sitting down on his bed, a smile spread across his face. 'One nil to me, I think.'

Jarvis was furious. He stormed back up the corridor and slammed the door shut before letting both barrels go at the custody sergeant. 'I gave express orders that these two were to be kept well apart and were not to know the other had been arrested. The Brummies managed it, I even sent them down in different vehicles – and then, when I get them in my own nick, what happens? You might as well have put them in the same fucking cell!' Before the sergeant could answer, Jarvis had turned and stormed out of the room.

By the time he'd got to his car, he'd calmed down a bit. To be honest, it wasn't the end of the world, but it might make things difficult later on. He'd have to deal with that if it arose, but at the moment he needed a shower and something to eat. Fitchett and Bailey could wait until the morning.

Part Two

Chapter 6
Saturday, 2 October
08.30

Jarvis stood at the door to the lift and pressed the button repeatedly. After some food, a shower and a decent sleep, he was raring to go – and the wait for the lift was making him impatient. He gave it a final thump and was about to give up and head for the stairs when the metallic chime of the lift bell told him there was no need. He gave a curse to all things mechanical and walked in, hitting the number 6 as he did so. No Chanel-breathing blonde this morning, but he wasn't worried about that. Indeed, he was so keen to get to work, he threaded his way through the lift doors as they opened and, strolling out into the office, was relieved to see a light already on in the briefing room. 'Morning Al.' Jarvis could hardly contain his anticipation.

'Guv,' replied Harris without even glancing up from the computer he was busily typing away at. Jarvis waited for a further response but, when none came, he took a look around the room. It was large and windowless with a second door at the left-hand end leading to a small office. It was also quite sparse: three desks, three telephones, two computers, a television and video, four filing cabinets and a large white board containing relevant names, photographs and dates. He walked over to the board and took a close look at the pictures. Two stills from the video of the Camden High Street fight showed Fitchett and Bailey. From each of them, a thick blue line pointed towards a single picture, the likeness on it so familiar to him: Billy Evans.

With a snort, he turned away from the board and walked towards the small office. It was empty, save for a desk, chair and a further filing cabinet. At least it had a window, but the view of various air-conditioning units stuck to the side of the office block next door was hardly inspiring. After abandoning his briefcase on the empty desk, he walked back out to the briefing room and looked at Harris. On the floor next to him sat a steaming cup of tea and a half-eaten bacon sandwich. 'I see you've got your priorities right, Al,' he laughed.

Harris looked up and smiled. 'Well, someone's got to. My old lady ain't speaking to me any more. Not since I told her I was back working with you.' They both laughed and Harris bent down and picked up the sandwich. He stuffed it in his mouth and carried on typing with it hanging from his lips.

Jarvis shook his head and turned away; he suddenly felt hungry again. He was about to head for the canteen when the other three members of the team strode in. They were all laughing at something or other and Jarvis immediately took that as a good sign. He'd never really worked with Steve Parry before and hardly knew Neal White, who looked even younger than Phil Williams. But first impressions were vital, and this one was positive. The last thing he wanted was any grief among his own team.

'Right,' he said, instantly gaining everyone's attention. 'Has everybody eaten?' The question seemed to faze the others, who replied with a mixture of ers and ums. 'Well, I'm off for some breakfast, so if anyone wants to join me, feel free. Back here in twenty minutes for a briefing.'

Jarvis strode out and, within seconds, the heavy sound of footsteps followed. At the lift, he turned round and was amused to find, not just the three men, but Harris as well. He had a cup of tea in one hand and the final remnants of his sandwich in the other. Jarvis looked at him and then let his eyes fall down towards his bulging waistline.

'Well, I don't know when I'll get to eat again, do I Guv?'

Twenty minutes later, the five men were back in the briefing room. They were all in good spirits, which was exactly what Jarvis had wanted. He had learnt long ago that the police canteen had far more value than just the provision of food and drink. It was where ice was broken and teams were formed. Twenty minutes of telling jokes and talking about football, telly or women was worth a thousand hours of lectures or interviews.

'All right, gentlemen, listen up.' Jarvis walked over to the board and the other four men turned to face him. The silence was instant. He looked at the board and then turned round to face his team. 'As you all know, we have two bodies downstairs for an assault on a Mr Barry Morgan in Camden High Street on Saturday, 4 September. They are Gary Fitchett and Alex Bailey. Both these men are known to be the kingpins of the Birmingham City hooligan group the Selector. Fitchett is top boy, Bailey his number two. Neither of them has been questioned yet; we'll do that later when we've collated all the stuff found in their homes. However, there are two things that you do not know. The first is that Barry Morgan is the son of Chief Inspector Morgan from Kensington.' He watched as ironic smiles broke out on the faces of the team. 'It is therefore fairly certain that charges will not be pressed and so we will only get the two men on affray. That information is not to go outside this room, is that clear?' He looked around and the four men nodded and grunted in agreement. 'The second thing you do not know, and the real reason for this operation ...'

'Legion, Guv.'

Jarvis turned to look at Harris. 'What?'

'It's Operation Legion.'

Jarvis nodded. 'Right, the reason Operation Legion has been set up is to target this man ...' He turned and tapped the photo. 'Billy Evans. You should all have heard of him by now, but if you have any doubts, DS Harris will fill you in.'

He sat down and listened as Harris stood up and began going through a detailed briefing on the history of Billy Evans. When he had finished, Jarvis stood up.

'As Al has just said, it looks like our man is back in the game again. He's obviously planning something – and judging by the fact that he's been seen all over England in recent months, it's something big. We need to know what it is, and fast. Hopefully, the two men we have downstairs will be able to throw a little light on it, but at the moment we're in the dark.' He stopped talking and looked around. 'So, what could it be gents? Anything spring to mind?'

The room was quiet for a moment and then Williams stood up. 'Well if Evans really is a major player, could he be setting up some kind of supercrew?' He looked around for a response but none was forthcoming. He went on. 'Well, everyone's always talking about the so-called England national crew, maybe he's trying to put it together.' He shrugged his shoulders and sat down.

Jarvis rubbed his chin. 'I can see the sense in that. But why now?'

Steve Parry piped up: 'It has to be Italy, Guv.'

Jarvis looked at him. 'Go on ...'

Parry stood up and faced the other men. 'England are playing out there later this month aren't they? Maybe he's planning something for then. After all, there's a lot of lads who are very bitter about what happened in Rome last time. He wouldn't have much trouble getting two or three hundred together.'

The others all nodded. 'Makes sense,' said Neal White. 'Especially if he's got a history of this type of thing ... You know, Dublin and all that.'

'Yeah.' Harris was on his feet. 'But he's been out of it for months now. He hasn't even been at West Ham much this season and there's nothing to suggest he's back to cause trouble. It could be he's just going round meeting up with people he's known over the years.' He stopped and looked at Steve Parry. 'You never know, he might even be watching football.'

The sarcastic tone in Harris's voice didn't fool Jarvis a bit. He was playing devil's advocate to get the others thinking. 'He wouldn't be the first person to get out of it in this way. I've seen hundreds in my time. It could be that we'll go digging around and there's nothing to find. We may have just missed our chance.'

'Or it could be that he's planning to go out with a bang,' said White. 'And put himself in the history books along with names like Harry the Dog and Ned the Shed.'

Jarvis looked around the four faces. 'OK,' he said, and wrote down the words 'Italy' and 'supercrew' on the board in large blue letters. Then, as an afterthought, he wrote a large question mark beside each one.

'Of course there is the chance that this is nothing to do with football at all ...' Jarvis and the others turned to face Steve Parry. 'Well, let's face it. Most of these people aren't exactly law-abiding are they? What if this is something to do with something else? Drugs, for example?' Harris reached down into Evans's file and pulled out a sheet of paper and read it while Parry went on. 'It's long been suspected that Evans is involved with drugs, right? Well maybe he's using these other lads to farm them out around the country. I mean, he's only ever been photographed inside grounds with these lads hasn't he? But how did he get there? It could have been in a car full of "E"s, coke or crack for all we know.'

Jarvis turned back to the board and, with a smile, wrote 'drugs' on the board. Again, a question mark was added. He was impressed. Five minutes and they had come up with two ideas, both of which were reasonably sound. He put the pen down, turned back to the four men and rubbed his hands together.

'Right gents,' he began, 'we've got something to think about. So let's try and find out if any of it's right, shall we? Steve, I want you and Neal to check out every phone number we found in the two houses. That's the ones stored on the phones and the ones listed on the itemised bills. See if anything comes up.' The two men nodded. 'And I take it you found nothing of any use in Bailey's house?'

'No Guv, it was clean as a whistle. There wasn't even a mobile. It looks like one of the Selector holds them all at another address.'

Jarvis nodded. 'OK, Al, get on to all the networks and see if they have a customer listed under either name. I doubt they will, but it's worth a try.' He turned to Williams. 'Phil, I think we'll have a crack at our two lads. Bailey first. Get on to the custody sergeant and set him up in the interview room, will you?'

The four men began busying themselves, but Jarvis had one more thing in store for them. 'Oh yes, gents,' he called, patiently waiting until they were all focused on what he had to say. 'The DCI wants something concrete on this within seven days or he'll fold this operation and settle for the affray charge on the two downstairs. What that means in real terms is that this could be the last chance to put away the man who killed DC Graham Peterson. I don't need to tell you that I do not want to lose that chance.'

A policewoman walked into the interview room and slid a tray of plastic cups full of canteen tea onto the table between the four men. Jarvis reached forward, picked one up and took a mouthful. He took another cup, handed it to Williams and then slid the third across the table to Alex Bailey. The fourth sat untouched and, after a brief pause, Bailey's solicitor reached forward and took it himself.

Jarvis watched as Bailey took a slow and deliberate drink from his cup. 'That's a fuckin' top notch cuppa that. Give my compliments to the chef.'

Jarvis smiled. 'I'll make sure he knows that. He'll be so thrilled you're pleased.'

He took another mouthful from his own tea and busied himself with his notes. The interview so far had not gone smoothly and he was actually glad of the break. Bailey was clearly no mug and knew exactly what to say to counter everything Jarvis had thrown at him so far. He had gone straight on the attack and told Bailey that the charges relating to the fight in Camden High Street were just a start. That he was also under investigation with regard to incidents at a number of other games as well as the planning and organisation of football hooliganism dating back a number of years.

However, Bailey had laughed out loud at this and after a brief chat with his brief, had denied any knowledge of or involvement with organised hooliganism. He had, however, admitted being involved in the fight in Camden but had said that he was with a group of friends who were looking for a quiet pub when they'd been attacked. They were simply defending themselves. He then shook Jarvis by adding that if they had CCTV footage of this, then it would back up everything he said. It wasn't even a bluff, it was more than that. Jarvis could see in his eyes that he knew they had tape of it and that it backed up his story. Undeterred, he had continued, asking Bailey to give his account of what had happened. But his version of events had tallied almost perfectly with what was on the film. Jarvis had balked a bit at this; he had not expected the interview to go this way. He was losing control and had decided to take Bailey in another direction.

'Tell me about Gary Fitchett,' he had said. But Bailey hadn't even flinched. 'He's my best mate,' he'd begun, and then gone on to explain how they went to football together every week. But that was all. When Jarvis had suggested that Fitchett was actually the leader of the Selector and that he was his number two, Bailey had roared with laughter.

'The Selector aren't a firm,' he'd said. 'They're just a group of lads who go to games together. Yeah, we're a bit loud sometimes, but we never go looking for trouble. That's fucking stupid.' Jarvis had then gone over some of the intelligence reports that the locals had provided on the Selector but again, Bailey had laughed them off as pure speculation and certainly nothing to do with him.

'If you have any proof that my client has been involved with anything other than the incident relating to the charge of affray, then please produce it,' Bailey's brief had said.

Jarvis had merely replied, 'All in good time,' and then told them that they were taking a short break.

The four men were drinking their tea when Jarvis broke the silence. 'Tell me about Norway.'

Bailey looked at him over the rim of his cup. 'It's in Scandinavia.'

Jarvis smiled. 'Very good. Now tell me about the events surrounding the England game in 1995.'

Bailey put down his cup and furrowed his brow. 'Like a load of others, I got pissed and got mouthy with the local police and so they threw me out. Nothing else to it. If we'd been anything other than English they'd have left us alone.'

'You were deported?' asked Williams.

'Yes, that's right.'

'And who was with you?'

Bailey picked up his cup but it was empty. He crushed it and dropped it on the tray. Jarvis could see he was stalling for time. 'You know Fitchett was there. So what? I've told you, we always go to games together. He's my best mate.'

'And he was deported as well?'

'You know he was, otherwise you wouldn't ask. Anyway, you've got him downstairs so ask him yourself.'

Jarvis looked down at his notes and sent a silent curse to custody sergeants everywhere. 'Right, let's move on then shall we? What about Dublin?'

'It's the capital of Ireland.'

Jarvis looked up at him and scowled. His patience was wearing very thin, primarily because he wasn't getting anywhere. 'Tell me your version of the events surrounding the England game in 1995.'

'Why? Don't you know what happened? It was in all the papers. I thought you lot were supposed to be on top of things?'

Jarvis glared across the table and Williams again broke into the conversation. 'Tell us why you didn't go to Dublin.'

Bailey settled back in his chair He knew exactly where this was leading. 'Who said I didn't?'

'We do, Alex.'

After a pause, Bailey gave a barely perceptible nod and leant forward. 'I couldn't get a ticket.'

Jarvis almost laughed. 'So you're telling us that you didn't go to Dublin, for what was almost certainly going to be the most controversial England game in recent memory, because you didn't think you'd be able to get in?'

'That's right.'

'Even though you knew that tickets would be openly on sale?'

'That's right.'

'And that given the sensitivity of the political situation at that time, there would almost certainly be violence?' Jarvis waited for the right response, but it never came.

'Which was another reason why I didn't go. I've told you, I'm not involved in football violence. Never have been.'

'Except for Camden ...'

'As I said earlier, we were looking for a pub and got attacked.'

Jarvis almost bit through his lip in frustration. Williams took up the assault. 'But Gary Fitchett went...'

'And so did a few thousand others, and I didn't go with them either.'

Jarvis took a deep breath. They were getting nowhere and he was about to end the humiliation when he decided to try one last tack. 'How do you know Billy Evans?'

Jarvis almost smiled when he saw a flash of surprise cross Bailey's face. 'Gotcha,' he thought.

'Who?'

Jarvis pulled out a photograph and pushed it across the table. 'This man, Billy Evans. How do you know him?'

Bailey was on his guard now; the arrogant smile had gone from his lips and had been replaced by a slightly puzzled expression. He clearly hadn't expected this at all. 'Who said I did?'

Jarvis pulled out another photograph, this time one of the ones taken at the Globe. It clearly showed him with Fitchett and Evans. 'I do.'

Bailey picked up the photograph and looked at it before dropping it down on the desk. 'So, I met a bloke in a pub, big deal. Christ, is that a crime as well now?'

'But you said you didn't know his name?'

'I didn't. I knew his first name was Bill but I didn't know his second name. Why should I? And what's all this got to do with me anyway?'

Jarvis looked at him across the table. He could tell by the look in his eyes that he'd finally got him rattled. He left the silence hanging for a second and Bailey took the bait. Jumping in again unprompted and slightly agitated. 'We met a bloke in a pub and went for a beer together to watch the England game. That's all there was to it. Anyway, why were you taking pictures of me? I've done fuck-all and you know it.'

Jarvis began flicking through his notes and left another long pause. He had Bailey on the defensive now and he wanted to leave him hanging there for a bit. He had one last thing to throw at him and he wanted to time it just right, for maximum effect. He closed his eyes and took a deep breath. Now or never, he thought. Opening his eyes, he fixed them on Bailey. 'We have evidence to suggest that Billy Evans is involved in the supply of illegal substances and that he uses known hooligan groups to distribute those drugs around the country. That's you and your mates, Alex.'

He could have sworn he heard Williams draw a deep breath but Bailey's reaction was instant and explosive. 'Drugs!' He exclaimed, slamming his hands on the desk and standing up. 'No fucking way!'

Williams was on his feet like a shot. 'Sit down!'

'You're not getting me on anything like that. That's total bollocks.'

'Sit down now!' shouted Williams.

Bailey fell into his seat and crossed his arms. His brief leant forward to speak to him but he pushed him backwards and sprang forward again. Jarvis noted with some relief that this was the first sign of aggression he had shown throughout the entire interview. 'You cunts, so that's what this is about, is it? You want to fit me and Fitch up. What for? To boost up your arrest figures? Yeah, well fuck you. If you think I'm selling dope then fucking well prove it. I ain't saying nothing else.' He leant back in his chair and crossed his arms again.

Jarvis raised his eyebrows in mock surprise and smiled. 'Hit a chord there did I, Alex? A bit too close to home maybe?' The glare from Bailey was so vicious it almost hurt, but Jarvis knew he'd got him rattled. 'So come on Alex, you tell me. Why did you meet Billy Evans?'

'Fuck off. I told you, I ain't saying nothing else.' Jarvis looked at Bailey and knew he'd got as far as he would for now. It was time to leave him to stew for a while and let him do some serious worrying. He gave Williams a nudge on the leg and the young DC stood up. 'This interview is terminated at 11.48 a.m.' He reached over, switched off the tapes and handed one to Bailey's brief, adding, 'We may well want to speak to your client again.'

Jarvis didn't relax until he was back in the briefing room. It had been a battle of wits but in the end he'd left Bailey seriously concerned about his fate – and that was exactly what he had wanted. Maybe he would be a bit more forthcoming when they spoke to him again. But now he turned his mind to Fitchett. In truth, he'd used the interview with Bailey to sound out a few ideas and get himself into the swing of things. He had always believed that, of the two men, Fitchett was the key to getting at Evans. The photographs found in his home had been a good indication of that. But they also had more on Fitchett than they had on Bailey. The wounding of Barry Morgan for one thing and the stuff from Dublin for another. The West Midlands Police had also given them a few more odds and sods to throw in, but everything depended on how he would react under questioning. If he was half as cocky as Bailey had been, then they would be in for a hard time. Somehow, they would have to get him rattled. And they might only get one good crack at doing that.

Chapter 7
Saturday, 2 October
13.45

Jarvis and Williams sat impassively as Fitchett talked through the events of the fight in Camden High Street, his Brummie accent interrupted only by frequent whispers to the smartly dressed, middle-aged woman sitting on his left. It came as no surprise to the two policemen that his version of events matched that of Bailey almost perfectly, although there was one notable exception.

When he had finished, Jarvis leant forward and picked up a sheet of paper. 'That's all very good Gary,' he said, 'but aren't you missing something out?'

'Like what?' asked Fitchett.

'Well, why don't you tell us? But before you go on, I have to tell you that we have CCTV film of this incident and everything that took place.'

Williams gave Fitchett a grin and a broad wink and Fitchett, seeing this, cursed under his breath. His brief leant forward and they began a whispered conversation. After a minute or so, they sat up and the woman spoke: 'My client has told you everything he can remember, Detective Inspector. Perhaps we could see the film to refresh his memory.'

Jarvis reached into the folder and pulled out some photographs. 'All in good time,' he said, 'but at the moment, I don't think there's any need. For the benefit of the tape, I am handing Mr Fitchett a set of photographs taken from the CCTV film. Can you describe what is on those photographs please Gary.'

Fitchett looked at the photographs and swallowed. Jarvis waited for a response and then, when none came, he continued. 'You have already admitted to taking part in this affray, Gary, but these photographs clearly show you attacking someone with an offensive weapon. The hospital who treated the victim of that attack confirms that the weapon was some kind of pepper spray, which is illegal in this country. That's at least two more charges you will be facing.'

Fitchett shrugged his shoulders again, settled back in his chair and stared up at the small window above the door. There was nothing else he could do.

'So you have nothing else to say?' asked Williams.

'He attacked me first; I was defending myself, that's all. I know I shouldn't have had the spray but I'd found it in the street and didn't want to throw it away.'

Jarvis took back the photographs and put them in the folder. 'It may interest you to know that the gentleman you assaulted was the son of a senior police officer and he was almost blinded by that spray.'

Fitchett reached for a cigarette and lit it. 'Well I'm sorry and all that, but to be honest, it's tough luck,' he said arrogantly, through a cloud of smoke. 'He shouldn't have come for me, should he? He won't press charges though.'

Williams looked up from his notes, a puzzled expression on his face. 'What makes you so sure of that?'

Fitchett drew on his cigarette. 'Two reasons: first, he's the son of a copper and you lot will want to bury it just in case the press make a big thing of it. Secondly, I've been going to football for long enough to know that people who go looking for trouble don't use the law to fight their battles. That's all.'

'So you go looking for trouble then?'

'That's not what I said, is it? I said I know people who do, but I'm not one of them.'

'People like Alex Bailey for example?' Jarvis stared hard at Fitchett as he said it, to see what reaction there would be, but he merely laughed out loud. Not what Jarvis had hoped for.

'Al! He's my best mate. I've told you that already. He doesn't go looking for trouble and neither do I. Still, I'm sure you've spoken to him so he'll have told you that himself.' He took a long drag on his cigarette and blew the smoke across the table towards the two policemen. Despite the fact that he was in serious and deepening trouble, his air of arrogance was still quite annoying. He was obviously enjoying this. Jarvis rustled through his papers for a moment and then looked up again.

'Tell me about the Selector'

A look of puzzlement passed briefly across Fitchett's face. 'What about them?'

'Well, tell me what you know.'

'They're a group of lads who follow the Blues. That's all.'

'So you're not a member, then?'

'You don't become a member, you either are one or you're not.'

'Well, what does that mean?' Jarvis's voice was calm but his mind was racing. He was circling, looking for a way to attack and wipe that arrogant look off the face of his prey.

Fitchett rocked back on his chair and looked at the ceiling. 'Well, it's hard to explain really. It's sort of, an unofficial supporters' club. Yeah, that's a good way to describe it.'

'So it's not an organised group, as such?'

'No.'

'And are you a part of this group?' Williams cut in.

Fitchett rocked his chair back onto its feet, exhaled and stubbed out his cigarette. 'I suppose I am.'

Jarvis reached into his pocket and pulled out a packet of polos. He unwrapped one and took it before passing the packet over to Williams. He sat there, sucking and slurping on the small round mint for a moment and then crushed it. He noticed with some satisfaction that the noise registered a momentary flicker on the tape machine's sound meters. 'So the Selector isn't an organised and very well-known group of football hooligans then?'

'Not to my knowledge.'

'And you are not the leader?'

Fitchett laughed. 'No ... no way.'

Jarvis sniffed and then scratched the side of his nose. 'Well that gives me a problem, Gary,' he said. 'Because when I asked Alex Bailey those questions this morning, he answered them completely differently to you.'

Fitchett's face remained unmoved, but his eyes registered a brief moment of shock. Williams saw it and smiled to himself.

'Why, what did he say?'

Jarvis noted the change in the tone of his voice. The arrogance was still there but this time it contained a very slight tremble. 'I'm afraid I can't tell you that, but suffice to say his answers were not the same as yours.'

Fitchett ran his hand over his forehead and then leant over to talk to his solicitor. After a brief few seconds, she spoke up: 'My client cannot answer questions relating to something someone else has told you if you will not even tell him what that is. Surely, Inspector, even you can see that.'

Jarvis smiled. 'Of course. Then let's move on shall we?'

The solicitor, however, hadn't finished. 'My client would like to use the toilet first, and so would I if that is acceptable.'

Williams reached forward. 'Interview suspended for toilet break and refreshments at 14.15.' He turned off the tapes and stood up, adding, 'Wait there a moment will you, and I'll get everything sorted out,' as he left the room. Jarvis remained seated, his eyes fixed on Fitchett and a broad smile on his face. He'd ruffled him a little. At last he was winning.

Gary Fitchett stood at the urinal and stared at the white tiles in front of his face. He'd always wondered what it was like being interviewed, but he'd never imagined it would be like this. All this twisting and turning, jumping from one thing to another, it was getting too confusing and he was finding it hard to keep track of what he had said. One thing he did know though, if he made a single mistake then that bastard copper would jump on it. The other thing that was getting to him was the room. It was too small and badly lit. The window above the door was a lifeline but it was getting harder to bear. The stupid thing was that every time he lit a cigarette, he made it worse, but what could he do? He had to avoid letting the coppers know he had a weakness. Do that, and he was fucked. He shook his head and turned his thoughts to Alex and the things the coppers had said. It was all bollocks, the copper was bluffing, he had to be. He would trust his mate with his life. But surely the copper couldn't try stuff like that while his solicitor was sitting there, could he? He didn't know and couldn't even guess. He tried to remember what people had told him in the past and even what he'd seen on *The Bill,* but his head was spinning and so he gave up. What if Alex had grassed him up to save himself? Or had made a mistake and dropped them both in it? No, no way. His best friend wouldn't have grassed him up, not in a million years. He was certain of that – or at least he thought he was.

He shook his head and moved across to the wash basin. He had to calm down, get his head together. 'Jesus!' he muttered as he caught sight of his face in the mirror. He looked totally drained and suddenly realised he was shattered. Spinning the cold tap, he began filling the sink with cold water but kept his eyes firmly fixed on his reflection. 'What if they've got more stuff to throw at me?' he thought. 'Christ almighty! What else do they know?' There was so much more. Stuff he'd probably forgotten about. If it all came out he could go away for ever. He turned off the tap and lowered his face into the water. It felt fantastic and he felt the tension draining out of him, but when he could hold his breath no longer and lifted his head up, the reflection in the mirror looked even worse than before. This was all too much, too confusing. He took a few long deep breaths before shaking his head and moving across to the hand dryer in the corner; stealing a wary glance at the uniformed policeman by the door. He didn't like this, not one bit. This was one part of the game that he clearly wasn't any good at.

'Shall we begin again?' Williams reached forward and restarted the tape. After the formalities, Jarvis again went on the offensive. He'd been surprised how easy it had been to unsettle Fitchett, but now he had him on the run he wasn't going to let up. 'Time to throw him another curve,' he thought.

'Let's leave the subject of Camden High Street and this group of so-called supporters, the Selector, shall we, and move on to other things.'

The look on Fitchett's face was one of bewilderment. This wasn't what he had expected at all. 'Like what?'

'Tell me what happened in Norway, Gary. In 1995.'

Fitchett's eyes widened. 'Norway!' he exclaimed. 'That was fucking years ago! What do you want to know about that for?'

'Just tell us what happened, will you?' Jarvis gave a discreet grin as Fitchett appeared to shrink before his eyes.

'I got drunk and was arrested. Then they deported me and a load of others. That was all there was to it.'

'So you think getting deported is no big deal, do you, Gary?'

'They were throwing people out for nothing. My mate had a piss in an alley and he was lobbed out as well.'

'Was that Bailey?'

'No. Someone else.'

'Who?'

'I can't remember'

'But you said he was your mate ...'

Fitchett looked across the table at Jarvis, the look of bewilderment replaced with an expression of hatred. 'When you go abroad with England, you're all mates. That's what I meant. You fucking coppers all think that every England fan who goes abroad wants to cause trouble, but you're wrong. We go to have a laugh. That's all.'

Jarvis leant across the table and went for the jugular. 'Is that what happened in Dublin then, Gary?'

The look of shock on Fitchett's face almost made Jarvis laugh out loud, and when he answered, the hesitation in his voice was clear. 'What do you mean?'

'Did you go to Dublin to have a laugh and it got out of hand? Or was it something more sinister than that?'

Fitchett sank even further into his seat and stared at the small window. 'I didn't do anything in Dublin. Nothing at all. Anyone who says I did is a fucking liar.'

Jarvis took a sheet of paper from the desk and made a great play of reading it before handing it to Williams.

'Well, the Garda think you did, Gary. In fact, there are a few things here which suggest to me that they think you were one of the men who organised it.'

The gravity of what Jarvis had said took a while to sink in and then Fitchett began laughing. 'You what! Me? Set up the riot in Dublin? You must be fucking joking, I don't have those sort of connections.'

Both Jarvis and Williams sat up with a start. 'What do you mean ... connections?' Fitchett almost turned white with shock at what he had said, and Jarvis certainly wasn't about to let it pass. 'You said "I haven't got those kind of connections", Gary. What did you mean by that?' Jarvis asked, his normally relaxed manner replaced by a tone which was intimidating, bordering on aggressive. 'Come on,' he repeated. 'What did you mean?'

Fitchett stared up at the window. His breath was coming in short, sharp gasps and beads of sweat were bursting out on his brow and slowly dribbling down the side of his head. He couldn't take much more. The old fear was back. He closed his eyes and leant forward, his head in his hands. He was all over the place and had to get out of there. Into the fresh air and sunlight.

Williams glanced at Jarvis. Something was wrong. He thought Fitchett was about to faint. 'Are you all right, Gary?' he asked. His voice was calm and relaxed, in total contrast to the oppressive atmosphere in the small room. Before he answered, Jarvis interrupted. He could see something was wrong with Fitchett but wasn't sure if he was faking or not. And he wasn't going to take the risk that he was. 'Gary,' he said aggressively, 'are you saying you know the names of the people who organised the riot in Dublin?'

Fitchett continued to stare at the window – and when he did eventually answer, what he said was barely audible. Williams quietly asked him to sit up and repeat what he had said, and when he did so, his voice was flat and monotone. Typical of someone who has simply had enough. 'I don't know anything about Dublin. I was there, that's all I can tell you.'

Jarvis stared at him. He'd known all along about Fitchett's suspected involvement in the Dublin riot, but hadn't for one moment considered that they might get the names of the people who set it all up. Clearly, given the state of Fitchett, that information was there for the taking. For once, he wasn't sure what to do next, but help, when it came, was from an unlikely ally.

'I think I need to speak with my client, Inspector.'

Jarvis looked at the woman in the corner and nodded. 'Yes, I think that would be a good idea. You've got five minutes. I'll get some tea or something sent in.'

'I need some air,' said Fitchett urgently.

Jarvis shook his head. 'I can't do that Gary, you have to stay in the interview room.'

Fitchett looked at him; his eyes were blazing and his skin looked pale and clammy. 'You don't understand, I gotta get some air.'

The desperation in his voice was almost scary and Jarvis stole a quick glance at his brief. She was starting to look concerned, and he knew that if he resisted any longer, she would start screaming for him to see a doctor. 'OK, I'll get you taken outside for a short while.'

He nodded to Williams, who began dealing with the tapes, and then walked through the door and leant against the wall outside. He stood there for a moment, eyes closed. Then, after a deep breath, he pushed himself off the wall. He was about to start walking when the door opened behind him and Williams came out.

'Guv,' he began excitedly, 'you know what's wrong with him, don't you?'

Jarvis shook his head. 'I know he doesn't look too hot.'

Williams shook his head. 'He's claustrophobic. I've seen it before. A kid at my school suffered from it. Sweating, pale skin and short, sharp breaths. They're classic symptoms. But the big giveaway is that he keeps looking at the window above the door. He's using it as his link with the outside.'

Jarvis furrowed his brow. 'You what?'

'It's a subconscious thing. He believes that if he can see glass, the barrier between him and the outside world is breakable. In other words, he isn't totally closed in.'

Jarvis nodded thoughtfully. 'So that's why he's so desperate to get some fresh air?'

Williams nodded. 'But why not tell his brief? She'd get him out like a shot.'

'It's my guess that he's probably suffered with it for years and has learnt to work around it. But it's his weakness and he'll never admit to it. Certainly not to a woman.' Jarvis gave a wry smile. 'Makes sense I suppose. Let's see if we can play on it, shall we?' He glanced at his watch. 'Look, you'd better get them sorted. I need to speak to the boss.' He turned and headed along the corridor in the direction of the DCI's office.

'This is Special Branch territory Paul, and you know that. The Dublin investigation was taken out of our hands over two years ago.' DCI Allen sat behind his desk and watched as Jarvis strode up and down the tiny confines of his office. 'We have no choice in the matter.'

Jarvis stopped and turned to face his boss. 'Listen Guv, he's all over the place in there and I haven't even mentioned anything about Evans yet. That was the whole point of this thing – and if we lose that, then it's been a complete waste of time.'

Allen raised an eyebrow. 'A waste of time ... the names of the organisers of the biggest riot in the history of British football. I don't think so.'

Jarvis shrugged his shoulders. 'Yeah, yeah, you know what I mean Guv.' He ran his fingers through his hair and walked over to the desk. 'Look, we may finally have the chance to nail Evans and we'd be mad to give that up. Let me have one more go at him, and if nothing turns up, then we'll hand him over to the spooks. Just give me an hour to see what I can come up with.'

Allen looked up at his DI and then stood up. 'You have an hour, Paul. If anything comes of it, I want to be the first to know, understand?'

Jarvis grinned. 'No problem, Guv. No problem at all.'

By the time Jarvis returned to the interview room, the other three people were already waiting for him. Williams switched on the tape and recorded the resumption of the interview as he sat down and looked at Fitchett. He was smoking again but every time he took a drag, his hand was shaking badly. His eyes were fixed on the window above the door and he refused to make any kind of eye contact. He was clearly in a terrible state and Jarvis was suddenly certain that Williams was right.

Fitchett was indeed suffering from being closed in. 'So let's go for the jugular,' he thought. He looked at Fitchett and smiled.

'OK, Gary. I want to leave the subject of Dublin for now.' He opened his file, pulled out a photograph, and pushed it across the table towards Fitchett. 'Do you know the man in this photo, Gary?'

Jarvis noted an almost imperceptible glance downwards. 'Never seen him before.'

'I think you'd better take a long, hard look before you answer that question again Gary. Do you know the man in the photograph?'

He quickly looked down and nodded before returning his gaze to the window. The answer this time came in a quiet and guarded voice. 'Yes.'

Jarvis took the photograph and put it back in the folder. 'Do you know his name?'

'Yes.'

'Well, what is it?'

'Billy ... Billy Evans.'

'Where do you know him from?'

'We've met a few times. I can't remember when.'

'Do you know if he is involved with a group called the CSS or the Cockney Suicide Squad?'

'No.'

'No you don't know, or no he isn't?'

'No, I don't know.'

Jarvis nodded and then flicked through a few sheets of paper. He allowed the silence to drag on for a while, every so often lifting his eyes up to look at Fitchett. It was an old trick and it always worked, winding him up just that little bit more. When he spoke again, it was almost a relief. 'Have you ever met him abroad?'

'I can't remember. Why are you asking me questions about a bloke I hardly know?'

Jarvis pulled out one of the photographs taken from the album found in Fitchett's house and pushed it across the table. 'Gary, why are you wasting my bloody time? That's you and

Evans in Rotterdam in 1993. We found that photo and an album full of others just like it in your house.'

Fitchett stubbed out his cigarette, took another one and lit it, his hand shaking even more violently than before. 'If you know so much, why do you need me to keep answering your poxy questions?'

Jarvis looked across and tried to catch his eye, but Fitchett's gaze remained fixed on the window. 'Gary, let me tell you a few of the things I know, shall I, just to save us all some time? You have already been charged with affray and I will be adding assault with an offensive weapon and possession of an offensive weapon to that. Given the current thoughts on football hooligans, that almost certainly means that you are going to prison. That's inside, Gary,' Jarvis added for effect. 'Locked up.' He looked for a response, but there was none. At least none that he could see, and so he went on.

'Furthermore, I know you were in Dublin at the time of the riot involving England fans and that, for reasons that will be investigated further, you were in the company of one of the persons believed to have been instrumental in the planning of that riot, one William or Billy Evans. I also believe that you know the identities of others who were involved in that incident. Furthermore, I know that you and Alex Bailey met Evans in the Globe on the eighth of September this year.'

Fitchett finally turned his eyes and glared at Jarvis. 'So fucking what?' The voice was trembling but full of fear and hatred.

Jarvis looked at him across the table and continued. 'I also know that you were seen in deep conversation with Evans inside the Globe and that you left the pub with him.'

'Big deal! Is that a crime as well now?'

Jarvis hesitated for a moment and then slammed his hand down on the table. The sharp crack made the other three people in the room jump. He leant across the table, and when he spoke, his voice was low and intimidating. 'Listen Fitchett, right now I have two choices. I can hand you over to Special Branch, who will want to speak to you about your involvement in the Dublin riot – and believe me, their questioning will make me look like Dale Winton. Or, you can stop being a wanker and help me out. I don't want you, I want Evans, but if you won't help me out, then I'll just have to settle for what I've got. And that means you.' He glanced at his watch and nodded to Williams. 'We'll take a five-minute break, and when I come back I want a decision. It's up to you, Gary.' Without waiting for a response, he turned and stormed out.

Five minutes later, he walked back into the room and looked at Fitchett. The expression on his face was astonishing. The arrogance had gone completely and at the table sat a defeated and ashen-faced man. Williams restarted the tapes as Jarvis sat down.

'My client wishes to be as co-operative as possible.'

The female voice seemed strangely out of place in the smoke-laden atmosphere, but Jarvis had no hesitation in interrupting it. 'I can't promise anything, but if what is said proves to be of use, then I will of course do what I can.'

He looked at Fitchett; he was nearly in tears. Jarvis almost felt sorry for him.

'He will not, however, admit to anything other than the assault in Camden High Street. He refutes any allegations of involvement in the planning and organisation of violence at any time or in any form.'

Jarvis nodded. 'Understood,' he replied. He looked at Fitchett and smiled. 'OK Gary, let's get down to what I really want and then we can get you out of here. Tell me what you know about Billy Evans.'

DCI Allen stood up and walked over to the window of his office. Strangely, the chaos of the London streets below always helped him relax a little. He stared out for a few seconds and then turned round. 'Run through it again.'

Jarvis nodded and picked up his notes. 'Fitchett said that Evans told him he is putting something together for the Italian game on the twenty-seventh and he wants him to go along. He doesn't know what it is yet, but he thinks it's more than just a jolly for your average mob. In any case, Evans will contact him and give him all the details some time next week.'

Allen turned back to the window and nodded. Jarvis knew from previous experience that this was a good sign. Allen always stared out the window when he was thinking.

'Do you believe him?'

Jarvis nodded. 'Guv, he was all over the place in there. Listen to the tapes, you'll hear it. He'd have shopped his own mum if he'd thought it would have helped.'

Allen turned back to the window. 'And he has no idea what is being planned?'

'No Guv, not yet. But he will – and then he will pass that information on to us,' Jarvis added, pre-empting the next and obvious question.

Allen turned round and faced Jarvis. The look on his face was one which suggested he wasn't best pleased at being placed in the situation his DI had just put him in. 'You know what you're asking, don't you Paul? The risk we're running? He could tell Evans we're on his case or he could even vanish altogether, and then what would we have?'

Jarvis reached round and scratched his neck. 'Look Guv, we'll be all over him like a rash. We'll be on his phone, everything. When Evans rings him, we'll know, and then we'll pull him in again.'

Allen sat down at his desk and nodded. 'OK, Let's do it. But first I'll have to speak to Special Branch and see if they're OK with it.'

Jarvis was taken aback. 'But Guv ...'

Allen lifted a hand and stopped him. 'I have to Paul, you know that as well as I do. If he has information relating to the Dublin riot, then they will want to talk to him at some point. Hopefully, they'll give us time to complete this investigation, but if they don't...'

He left the sentence hanging. The meaning was obvious. Jarvis stood up and began pacing around. He knew the DCI was right, of course – they had no choice in such matters. He stopped pacing and turned to face Allen. 'We're close Guv, I can feel it. We have to make this work.'

Allen looked up at him. 'I know what this means to you, Paul. I'll do my best, all right?' Jarvis nodded, turned and started to leave.

'Paul ...' He turned and looked back at Allen. 'I'll only ever say this to you once. If we get the nod for this, don't fuck it up.'

Jarvis smiled, turned and walked out. He could hear Allen dialling the phone even before the door was closed.

Gary Fitchett lay on the bed in his cell, his face buried in the mattress and a pillow covering the back of his head. The events of the day had left him feeling physically sick and dirty. He half imagined that this was how a woman must feel when she'd been raped. Empty, violated, disgusted with yourself, that was how he felt, and worse. He'd given up everything he'd ever believed in: loyalty, pride, respect, the lot. And for what? To get that bastard copper off his back and escape from that hell-hole of a room. He turned over and stared at the frosted glass windows above him. He didn't know how he would ever live with himself when this was all over – but he just hoped it would be, and soon. Suddenly, he realised it was Saturday and his thoughts turned to his beloved Blues. They were at home to Bury today and he began to wonder how they might have got on. But then, in an instant, he realised that he didn't care any more. That part of the game was over.

Chapter 8
Monday, 4 October
12.00

Neal White pulled the red Ford Mondeo into the car park of Euston station and turned off the ignition. He climbed out and, after telling the other two men in the car that he'd only be a minute, headed for the ticket office. Jarvis wound down the window and then looked across at Fitchett. 'You all right Gary?'

'I'm fine,' he said bluntly.

'You sound knackered.'

'Well wouldn't you be if you'd had all the shit I've had over the last few days?'

Jarvis nodded. 'Fair point.'

Fitchett ran his hands over his face and then entwined the fingers, stretching them out so that they gave a resounding crack. 'Do you have to do that?' asked Jarvis. 'It's gross.'

Fitchett gave him a grin and lit a cigarette.

'Right,' began Jarvis, 'as soon as DC White gets back with your ticket, that'll be you on your way back to Brum. Now, are you clear on everything?'

Fitchett exhaled deeply. 'We've been over it a hundred bloody times,' he replied, the irritation in his voice clear for Jarvis to hear.

'Well one more time won't hurt, will it?'

Fitchett sighed, took another drag on his cigarette and sank back into the seat as Jarvis began running through the details. 'You and Alex Bailey were arrested for the assault in Camden High Street and have both been released on bail. That's all anyone needs to know. Just carry on as normal and, as soon as Evans gets in touch, let us know immediately.'

'I thought you were tapping my phone?' said Fitchett.

'We are,' Jarvis replied, 'but who said he's going to ring?'

Fitchett shrugged and then flicked his cigarette stub out the window. 'Well I'd best lay off the 0898 porno lines then. I'm not giving you bastards a free thrill.'

Jarvis ignored the attempt at humour and continued: 'You've got my card; I can be contacted on that number at any time, day or night. And remember no one must find out about this, Gary, no one. If it leaks out, then we'll have you back inside so fast you won't know what happened.'

Fitchett raised an eyebrow. 'Do you think I'm going to tell anyone that I'm grassing them up? What kind of fucking idiot do you have me down for? They'd slaughter me if they knew.'

'Don't worry about them; they can't send you down like I can.'

'No,' said Fitchett, 'but they sure as shit can put me somewhere else. I tell you, this'd better be worth it. You have no idea what I'm doing for you.'

The car door flew open and Neal White climbed back into the front seat. Reaching over, he handed Fitchett an envelope. 'Here's your ticket Gary. The train's in thirty minutes, platform 11.'

'First class, I hope?' he said, stuffing the envelope in his pocket.

The DC clicked his fingers. 'Sorry, I knew there was something I'd got wrong.'

'Can I go now?' Jarvis nodded and Fitchett got out. Before he closed the door he leant in. 'I'd like to say it's been a pleasure, but I'd be lying through my arse.'

'You too,' said Jarvis and then leant over, grabbing Fitchett's jacket. 'Don't even think about fucking us over Gary, it would be a massive mistake.'

Fitchett shook him off. 'Fuck you,' he said. And was gone.

'Can we trust him?' asked Neal.

'We have to,' sighed Jarvis. 'He's the only chance we've got. Come on, let's get back to the nick.'

Jarvis stared out the window and reflected on recent events as White steered his way through the London traffic. It had been a hectic couple of days and he felt shattered, most of it through worry that they would have to settle for what they had

– which, certainly as far as Bailey was concerned, was very little. Indeed, he'd been released on bail the day before. Luckily, the DCI had come through in the end and had approved his plan to use Fitchett as an informer, at least for a while. Mind you, word was that, initially, the Special Branch lads had been far from accommodating. That was until he had mentioned Billy Evans, then they'd been all ears. In the end, they had been happy to let the Football Unit run with it for a while, on condition that they were given Fitchett when the operation was over. To Jarvis, this had meant only one thing, that Evans was known to them, probably for Dublin, he had guessed, and as soon as Jarvis nicked him, they would come in and steal the glory. He was happy with that though – after all, they were all on the same side. He just wanted the bastard sent down. There was, however, one nagging doubt which kept returning. When Evans made contact with Fitchett, just what could they get out of it? He might say nothing of value over the phone, or Fitchett could tip him off in some way and then they'd have nothing. After all, what did Fitchett have to lose? Even he must have had no doubt that he was going inside at some point. Maybe he was just clinging on to the hope that, by helping them, he'd spend less time in the nick.

He was still pondering this when the phone in the car gave out a shrill ring. He picked it up, spoke his name and then listened intently. 'Well bugger me,' he said, 'thanks for that

We'll be back in about ten minutes.' He put the phone down and gave out a yell which made White jump and give out a curse. 'You're not gonna believe this,' Jarvis said out loud, as much to himself as to his DC. 'The BT boys have just connected up the tap on Fitchett's phone and it looks like there's only a message from Evans on his fucking answer machine! Can you believe that!'

White looked across at Jarvis and grinned. 'Do they know what it says?'

'Not yet,' said Jarvis, shaking his head. 'They just know he's had a recent call from Romford and that a message was left. It must be Evans. It must be!'

Gary Fitchett climbed out of the taxi and took the short walk down the drive to his house. He looked at the front door, made sure that the damage to it had been repaired and then went in. Once inside, he stood in the hall and took a deep breath. It had been tidied but felt odd, as if he'd been burgled, which of course he had. At least in all but name. He caught sight of himself in the hall mirror and suddenly felt filthy dirty and very tired. He needed a shower, and until he'd had that, everything else, including the pile of mail by the front door, could wait. There'd be time enough for all that later on.

An hour later, clean and refreshed, he strolled down the stairs and picked up his mail. It was the usual mixture of bills and junk and he threw it all onto the table by the hall mirror. He couldn't be arsed to deal with that just now. Walking into the front room, the beeping of the answerphone caught his attention and he strolled over to it. 'Fourteen messages,' he said out loud. 'I am popular.' He pressed the button and the machine began to replay. The first was from work, asking where he was; the second, also from work, was more insistent. His appointments had all been cancelled and they clearly weren't happy. After that came a few from various mates asking about football on Saturday and there was one from his mum. She'd heard about the raid and sounded seriously worried. He let out a sigh and shook his head. The next message was from work – he was to contact his boss immediately – and then there were more from his mates. Word was out and they were all worried. Not just for him and Alex but, from the tone of their voices, for themselves. Two messages to go. The voice of his best friend rang out, Alex. 'Ring me when you get home,' was all he said before hanging up. Then the last message began and it sent a shiver down his spine. 'Hello you northern twat. It's Billy, Billy Evans. Give me a call as soon as you can.' He left the number and then he was gone, the three beeps from the machine announcing that there were no more messages.

Fitchett looked at the machine. He hadn't expected this at all and was at a loss as to what he should do next. He replayed the message and wrote down the number before picking up the phone and then putting it down again. 'I need a beer,' he said to himself, and walked through to the kitchen, grabbed a can from the fridge and took a long drink from it before returning to the phone. He took another long drink, and then rang his mother. She was furious with him, not just for what he had done but for what he had put her through. After promising to go round later on, he rang work. It came as no surprise to learn that they had also found out about the raid and wanted to discuss it with him at nine in the morning. It didn't look good.

He lifted the phone again to ring Alex, but then the thought struck him that everything he said was being heard by someone else and he put it down again. Suddenly, even the phone was his enemy. He walked out to the hall and reached into his jacket pocket to find the card the copper had given him. He took it out and studied it for the first time. Such a small piece of card and so much trouble. He walked back into the living room, dialled the number on the card and was surprised when the phone was answered on only the second ring.

'DC White.'

'Hello, it's me, Gary Fitchett.'

'Hang on, I'll get DI Jarvis.'

He waited and then Jarvis came on the line. 'Hello Gary, what have you got for me?'

Fitchett felt a lump rising in his stomach, as if he had indigestion. 'He's called. He wants me to call him.'

'Then call him, you idiot. We'll talk afterwards.'

The line went dead and Fitchett took the phone from his ear and stared at it. 'What a cunt,' he said. And put it down. He took another drink from his can and then drained the remainder with a single gulp. He walked back to the kitchen and got another. He needed something to calm his nerves so that he could work out what to say when he rang Billy. How could he act as if nothing was wrong, when all the time he was setting him up? But what choice did he have? If he didn't ring, then that bastard Jarvis would be on his case again – and he didn't want that. Not for a while.

He moved back into the living room, lifted the phone and dialled the number on the pad. After ten rings, the phone was picked up and a metallic voice answered. 'Hello, this is Billy, I can't ...' Fitchett slammed the phone down. 'I don't fucking believe it,' he thought. He was actually shaking, he was that nervous. He took another mouthful of beer and sat down to calm his nerves. After a few minutes, he picked up the phone and dialled again. 'Hello, this is Billy, I can't take your call at the moment but leave a number and I'll get back to you.' There was a pause, seven short beeps and then one long one. 'Er ... Billy, it's me, Fitch. Just returning your call, give me a ring when you can.' He put the phone down and sighed. That was it, there was no going back. The process of grassing up had begun. He felt sick.

The insistent ringing of the phone woke him up with a start, and for a moment Fitchett struggled to work out where he was. The room was in half darkness and the news was on the television. He blinked and then realised he was at home. 'Shit,' he shouted, and dived for the phone. 'Hello!'

'Hi, Fitch, it's Billy. Where the fuck have you been?'

Suddenly, he was wide awake. 'Billy, er ... hi mate. Shit, sorry, I must have dozed off. What time is it?'

'It's nearly six o'clock, you sound all over the place mate, d'you want me to call you later on?'

'No!' he exclaimed, a little too urgently. 'No, it's fine, just give me a minute will you. I need to wake up a bit.'

'Listen, don't worry. I'm in a bit of a rush myself. Are you still up for a trip to Italy?'

Fitchett rubbed his head and stifled a yawn. 'Yeah, of course.'

'Well can you get down to London on Wednesday?'

'Yeah, I guess so.'

'Then be at the Victoria Hotel in Great Portland Street for two o'clock. Ask for the conference suite and I'll meet you there.'

Fitchett's mind was racing; should he ask Billy for more information or just leave it? 'Erm ... yeah, that'll be great. I'll see you there then, all right?'

'Top, see you mate.' With a click, the phone went dead.

Fitchett stood there for a few seconds and then put the phone down. He looked at it for a while and then picked it up, dialled and waited while he was transferred.

'Jarvis.'

'Hello, it's me, Gary,' he said nervously. 'He's called again.'

'And?'

'He wants me to come to London on Wednesday and meet him.'

'Where?'

'In a hotel in Great Portland Street, the Victoria, at two o'clock.'

'What for?'

'I don't know, he didn't say and I didn't ask.'

There was silence for a moment and then Jarvis came back on the line. 'Let me know what train you're on and I'll meet you at Euston.'

'Fuck off!' Fitchett barked, the worry in his voice clear. 'You don't really think I'm going, do you?'

'You are, Gary. If you're not there, then we'll want to know why. And don't think about doing anything stupid. It wouldn't take long to track you down.'

Fitchett paused for a few moments and then sighed. He had no choice. 'All right, I'll be there. But don't meet me at Euston, someone could see me. I'll get off the train at Hemel Hempstead, there's a cafe in the car park outside. That's where we'll meet.' He put the phone back on its hook, sat down and put his head in his hands. This was all getting too much. He needed to clear his head and then work out what the bloody hell he was going to do.

At that exact moment in time, Jarvis knew exactly what he was going to do. In fact he was already doing it. Sprinting down the stairs, he ran to his car and headed for Great Portland Street as fast as he could.

Chapter 9
Tuesday, 5 October
10.00

'Right, so that's the story so far. Any questions?' Jarvis stopped pacing around the Incident Room and looked around at the four faces of his team. They had been listening intently, but were all well aware that the DCI had come into the room and was standing behind them.

'You have to admire his cheek,' said Steve Parry. 'I mean, booking the conference room for the Two Waters Athletic Team – the TWATs.'

Jarvis laughed along with the others. 'I know, when I spoke to the manager last night he still hadn't twigged. Probably still hasn't.'

'Can't we just go in and nick the lot of them for conspiracy?'

Jarvis looked at Williams and shook his head. 'No evidence of anything. They could be having a reunion, for all we know.'

'Is there any chance we can put a listening device in the room, Guv?' asked White.

Jarvis shook his head again. 'Too risky. One thing I've learnt over the years is that these lads are no mugs. You can get a sweeping device for fifty quid these days. No, we have to rely on Fitchett.'

'What about a wire?'

This time it was Parry who shook his head and spoke up. 'They'll search everyone going in.'

'Will Fitchett come through?'

Jarvis looked across at Al Harris. 'He has to. Or he's history.'

Jarvis walked over to the large board on the wall and looked at it for a moment. It was now covered in various lines and pictures. He turned round to face his team. 'OK, let's sort ourselves out for tomorrow. DC Williams and I will meet

Fitchett at Hemel Hempstead train station and then brief him on what we want him to do after the so-called meeting. We will then make our way down to the empty office block opposite the hotel and join DS Parry and DC White, who will have been keeping it under observation from mid-morning. DS Harris will be sorting out the details of that this afternoon and will also stay in the Incident Room tomorrow and keep everything together.'

'Have we any idea of anyone else who will be there?' asked Parry.

'No. None at all. The usual thing with these kind of meetings is that only one person from each firm is invited. Anyone could turn up at this one. Literally anyone. We don't know who he's invited, but the conference suite they've booked holds up to forty people.'

The room fell into silence and the men all turned to face the DCI as he spoke up. 'Have we any idea what they're up to?'

'Not yet Guv, at the moment it's all just guesswork. But whatever it is, it's big. It has to be. That room costs not far short of £200 to rent for the afternoon. You don't spend money like that for a get-together with your mates, do you?'

The DCI nodded. 'But you must have some ideas?'

Jarvis scratched his head. He hadn't expected the third degree from his boss, and it was making him uncomfortable.

'Well, if Evans set up the riot in Dublin, as many people seem to believe, then this could be something like that. Other than that, it could be drugs. We're almost certain he's a supplier.' Allen nodded, let out a deep breath and, after motioning Jarvis to follow, left the room. As he walked towards the door, Jarvis rubbed his hands together and a broad smile spread across his face. 'Ain't this fun.'

Harris watched him leave and gave an almost imperceptible shake of his head. 'He's too involved with this one,' he thought. 'Way too involved.'

'What's the plan afterwards, Paul?'

'Guv?'

Allen looked up and raised his customary eyebrow. 'Come on Paul, what do you plan to do once Fitchett tells you what took place? You can't pull them for conspiracy: as you said yourself, you'll have no evidence.' Jarvis looked out the window and shrugged his shoulders. 'To tell you the truth, Guv, I'm not sure yet. Everything depends on what Fitchett comes up with.'

Allen stood up and walked round to the front of his desk. 'If he comes up with nothing worthwhile, pull him in and hand everything over to Special Branch.' He turned and looked at Jarvis. 'But whatever happens, I want to be the first to know, is that clear?' Jarvis nodded. 'Of course Guv. It goes without saying.'

Gary Fitchett walked into his front room and slumped down on the chair. He rubbed his eyes and then remained staring at the ceiling for a while. 'That's that then,' he thought. 'Out of work.' He felt gutted. His life was falling apart and there was nothing he could do about it. It was all out of his control. He thought about the events of the past few days, but that made him feel even worse. And he had tomorrow to deal with as well. Jesus, walking into a room full of lads and knowing that he was about to drop them all in it. The very thought of it scared the shit out of him. He stood up and noticed the answerphone blinking furiously away to itself. Two messages. He pressed the button and they began to play. Both were from Alex, the first asking him to ring urgently, and the second telling him he'd be round after work. 'After work,' he thought. 'That's a fucking laugh.' He looked at his watch; four thirty. He'd be here soon. Fitchett sat there for a while and then got up and went out. He had enough on his plate without coming face to face with Alex Bailey. On top of everything else, that would have been just too much to handle.

Chapter 10
Wednesday, 6 October
11.15

Gary Fitchett stepped off the train at Hemel Hempstead and made his way out of the station. It came as no surprise to see the red Ford Mondeo parked opposite the entrance, and he walked straight over to it and climbed in the back seat.

'Morning Gary,' Jarvis said. 'Pleasant trip?'

'Let's get out of here, I feel like a fucking criminal.'

Jarvis laughed out loud. 'But that's what you are Gary, don't forget that.'

Phil Williams started the car and drove out of the car park.

'This won't take long,' began Jarvis. 'We'll drive around for a bit and then drop you back here. There's a train into London every fifteen minutes. In the meantime, we just need to make sure you know what's what.'

Fitchett stared out of the window as the car sped along the A41. 'I know,' he said without looking round.

'Gary, it's in your interest to take notice of what I have to say. After all, you're the one going in.'

Fitchett turned his head round. The expression on his face was a bizarre mixture of hatred, fear and loathing. Jarvis wondered if that was for himself or for the police in general.

'Thank you. Now all you have to do is behave normally. After all, I'm sure you've been to these sort of things before.' He waited for a response, but nothing came other than a single grunt, so he continued. 'I want to know everything that happens and everything that's said. If you can tell me who was there as well, then that'll be great.'

Fitchett let out an ironic laugh. 'Stick a broom up my arse and I'll sweep the corridors on the way if you want.'

Jarvis carried on, almost without drawing breath. 'Afterwards, I want you to go to Neal Street in Covent Garden. Find the Italian cafe and wait there. I'll meet you.'

Fitchett turned back to the window and ran his hand over his face. 'All right. I get it.'

Jarvis took out a packet of cigarettes and offered them across. Fitchett took one and lit it without offering to light anyone else's. 'Gary, I know how hard this is for you, but remember, the more you co-operate, the more I can help you later on.'

The look on Fitchett's face showed he wasn't that convinced. 'Yeah, that's a good point. What is gonna happen when I've done your dirty work then? You haven't told me that yet, have you?'

'You'll be fine,' said Jarvis. 'Let's get this afternoon out of the way before we sort out how we can help you.' The car settled into silence and the two men in the back smoked their cigarettes, each totally absorbed in their own concerns, as Williams headed back to the station.

Ten minutes later, Fitchett had left the car and was back on the platform. He was clearly visible from the car park and the two policemen watched him until he climbed on a train and was heading in the direction of Euston.

'D'you know, I almost feel sorry for him,' said Williams as he started the car and pulled back out of the station on to the main road. 'He's probably quite a decent bloke.'

Jarvis, now sitting in the front seat, looked across at his DC. 'Well don't. You saw the film of him in Camden, he's an animal – and as soon as I have what I want from him, he'll be exactly where he belongs, and that's inside.' He looked at the queue of traffic and, in a voice that contained a little too much irritation for Williams's liking, added: 'Come on Phil, get a bloody move on. We need to be somewhere.'

Gary Fitchett took a final breath and ground what was left of his cigarette into the pavement. He'd arrived at the Victoria Hotel twenty minutes earlier, but hadn't been able to summon up the courage to go straight in. Instead, he had stood across the street and watched while a succession of faces from his past had walked up the stairs and into reception. But now, he'd begun to worry that someone would see him standing there and get a bit twitchy. And so, after a glance at his watch had shown the time to be almost five to two, he had decided that he couldn't put it off any longer. He exhaled sharply and walked over to the crossing. It was full of media types and women in short skirts, but he hardly noticed them as he crossed. His eyes were focused on the front of the hotel.

After a brief pause at the bottom of the steps, he climbed up and strolled through the swing doors into a dimly lit reception that was dominated by burgundy upholstery, oak panels and stale cigarette smoke. At the desk, he was directed to the third floor and, after a visit to the toilet, and a sprint up the stairs to avoid the lift, found himself standing outside the Conference Suite. He cocked an ear to the door. It was rowdy inside, plenty of laughter and loud conversation of the type you only get in a room full of males. He closed his eyes and, after another deep breath, opened the door and walked in. The noise exploded in his face. It was chaos, full of cigarette smoke and a group of men dressed in what must have been thousands of pounds' worth of clothing. He stood there for a while, returning the wary glances that the men in the room were throwing in his direction.

'Fitch!' He looked up as Billy Evans strode over towards him and shook his hand. 'About fucking time! I was wondering where you'd got to, you old cunt.'

Fitchett looked at him. He felt desperately sorry for himself, and for what he was about to do. 'Sorry mate, poxy trains. You know what they're like.'

'Yeah, course. Listen, I'm really glad you're up for this. It'll be just like old times.' He laughed, and Fitchett gave a smile and a nod.

'Yeah, well whatever it is, it'll be a crack.' Evans gave him a broad wink. 'This is a good 'un mate. Trust me. But Fitch, first, well I don't want to be a pain but ... well you know the score.' Evans gave a nod over Fitchett's shoulder towards the door where two men stood looking at him.

'Oh yeah ... course.' He walked over to them and lifted his arms as they searched him thoroughly and then thanked him. 'No worries,' he said before turning round.

Evans had vanished into the crowd and so he walked over to a table in the corner that was almost hidden by beer bottles, cans of soft drinks and plates of food. Picking up a Coke and a handful of crisps, he surveyed the room. It was clear Evans had been busy as it contained about twenty men, many of whom he recognised – and not just from trips abroad with England either. There were some serious faces from clubs up and down the country.

'Hi Fitch.'

He turned to face the familiar figure of a tall gangly man with thick brown hair. 'Fucking hell! Danny! I haven't seen you since Toulouse. How you doin'?'

The tall man took a drink from a bottle and smiled. 'Yeah, all right. You?'

Fitchett nodded and smiled. 'Yeah, good. What d'you make of all this then?'

The tall man looked around. 'Don't know, but I reckon we're about to find out.'

They both turned as Evans suddenly appeared at the far end of the room and called for quiet. He motioned to the two men by the door and they walked out, closing the door behind them. 'Can you all grab a seat and we'll get on.' He waited while everyone in the room sat down and it fell silent.

Three hours later, Gary Fitchett walked into the Italian cafe in Neal Street. He was slightly relieved to find Jarvis already sitting there and walked up to the table. He was visibly nervous.

'Well?' Jarvis asked.

'No, not here, no way.' Fitchett looked around anxiously.

'Well where then, d'you want to come back to the nick?' He was shocked when Fitchett nodded. 'OK, you know where it is. I'll wait for you in the car round the back and we'll go in that way, all right?'

Fitchett nodded, got up and walked out.

'Fuck me,' thought Jarvis. 'This must be serious.'

'Look, I'm telling you, that's what happened. If you don't believe me, then screw you.' Fitchett settled back in his chair and lit another cigarette.

Jarvis stood up and rubbed the top of his head. He was finding this difficult to comprehend. 'Right, let's go over it again. Evans told everyone in the room that he has been contacted by an Italian right-wing group and asked to stage a riot when England play in Rome.' Fitchett nodded. 'But he didn't say who?'

'No.'

'And that everyone who goes with him will be given transport, a match ticket and some cash.'

'Yes, I told you all this already,' added Fitchett.

Jarvis went on: 'And no one backed out?'

'No, everyone in that room said they were up for it.'

'And he hinted that there were others?'

'Yes. I told you. He said some were going by coach, others by train. We're the ones going by car. That's why we have to take someone with us. To share the driving.'

Williams looked up from his notes. 'So there could be sixty or seventy lads going?'

Fitchett nodded. 'And they're no mugs either. There were some serious lads in that room, I can tell you.'

'What, besides yourself you mean?' asked Williams.

Fitchett gave him a glare as Jarvis continued. 'So now all you have to do is carry on as normal and wait for him to contact you to give you details of the meet?'

'That's right,' said Fitchett irritably.

'And he didn't say anything about anything else?' Jarvis was fishing, just in case Fitchett knew more than he was letting on.

'Like what?' he asked.

Jarvis looked at Williams. 'Forget it, it doesn't matter.'

He sat down again and stared at Fitchett. 'Gary, if we can swing it, would you go and take an undercover officer with you?'

Fitchett almost jumped out of his skin with shock at the suggestion. 'What!' he shouted. 'You're off your fucking head you are. No way. No fucking way.'

Jarvis looked at him and replied to the onslaught in a calm, almost pleading voice. 'Come on Gary, why not?'

Fitchett looked across the table at the two policemen as if they were raving mad. 'Because it'll be fucking dangerous, that's why. You don't get it do you? These lads'll spot a copper a million miles away – and then what? I'll be fucking dog meat, that's what. And besides, why should I? I've done exactly what you wanted me to do. I'm fucked if I'm doing any more.' He returned Jarvis's stare and took a final drag from his cigarette, lighting another from the stub.

Jarvis looked at him, a faint smile on his face. 'Why should they spot a copper Gary? You didn't – and you're exactly the same as they are.'

Fitchett's face went white. 'What d'you mean?' he barked.

Jarvis gave a wry smile and went on. 'Listen Gary, we need you to go and in the end you will. Because if you don't, I'll have you inside like a shot. This way, at least you get to go home for a while longer.' He took a look at his watch, it was late. Nearly eight o'clock. 'Think about that when you're eating your tea in a cell tonight.' Jarvis stood up, collected his notes together and went to walk out.

'You cunt!' shouted Fitchett, the fury in his voice almost tangible. 'Is that it, is it? You're locking me up again! I fuckin' knew you'd screw me, you wanker! And what do you mean ... I didn't?'

Without looking round, Jarvis said, 'All in good time Gary. All in good time.'

Chapter 11
Thursday, 7 October
09.15

DCI Peter Allen sat at his desk and read through the report of the previous day. As he read, he clicked the top of his retractable Biro with such ferocity that Jarvis began to wonder if the poor thing would last for much longer. When he had finished, he put down the report and his pen and looked across at Jarvis who, Biro fixation aside, had remained impassive while he read. 'Are you sure of this Paul? One hundred per cent sure?'

Jarvis nodded. 'From what he said and from what we know, we're looking at a repeat of the Dublin riot.'

Allen stood up and turned to the window, his hands behind his back. 'And Evans didn't discuss drugs or anything else?'

Jarvis shook his head. 'No Guv, as far as Fitchett is concerned, they're going out there to kick things off. That's all.'

'But you think there's more?'

Jarvis nodded his head again. 'I'm sure of it. In fact, I'd put my career on it.'

Allen turned and gave him a look that suggested he might have to do just that. 'So you want to let Fitchett go and send someone undercover with him. Any ideas?'

Jarvis walked over to the window and stood next to his DCI. 'Yes Guv, Terry Porter. It's perfect, he's just come out of the Selector. Fitchett doesn't even know that yet.'

Allen stared at the London traffic for a while and then turned. 'OK Paul, I'll speak to the chief and we'll also need to discuss it with Special Branch. If they give it the nod, then we'll see what the Italians have to say. We've already had a few meetings with them about security for the game, so finding the right person to talk to shouldn't be difficult.' He sat back down at his desk and picked up his pen again. 'In the meantime, you speak to Terry Porter and see if he's up for it.'

'Yes Guv. And thanks.'

He went to leave but the DCI called him back. 'Paul, no risks here. You know the problems with working abroad. We can't afford to mess up.' Jarvis nodded and left.

The incident room was full of smoke and noise when Jarvis walked back in. The four members of his team were talking excitedly, but they stopped and watched their DI as he walked across the office and stood in front of the incident board. He told Harris to get hold of Terry Porter and then began talking.

'OK, this is the score as we see it. Evans has been asked by an Italian political group to recruit a firm to stage a repeat of the Dublin riot when England play in Rome. That's on ...' he looked at Harris who grabbed a diary, flicked through the pages and said, 'October twenty-seventh Guv.'

'October twenty-seventh,' repeated Jarvis. 'That's in just under three weeks' time. Now, we don't know who this group is; we don't know why they want to get a game abandoned, nor do we know what they hope to achieve.' He stopped talking and looked around the room. 'Well, any thoughts so far?'

The room remained silent and then Neal White piped up. 'Surely we've got enough to nick Evans for conspiracy now, Guv?'

Jarvis shook his head. 'Who'd testify? Fitchett? He's shitting himself at the thought of what would happen to him if he actually had to go into court and grass up his mates. No, the plan at the moment is to run with it until we can get something more concrete.' He paused, glanced down at the floor for a moment, scratched his head and then looked up. 'But personally, I think the whole thing is bollocks.' He walked over to one of the desks and sat down on it.

'What makes you think that, Guv?' asked Steve Parry.

Jarvis stood up again and began pacing backwards and forwards across the front of the board. 'Instinct,' he said. 'Something's not right. It just doesn't add up. What would any political group have to gain from stopping a game? The Italian public would go mental and any support they hoped to gain, for whatever reason, would vanish. And if it didn't work, well all you'd have then is a load of English lads getting battered and the locals cheering on the police. Again, if your group is anti-establishment, that's totally counter-productive.' He let out a sigh. 'No, I just don't buy it.'

'So what d'you think is going on?'

Jarvis looked up at Harris. 'I still think he's going to use this trip as a front to bring drugs back across the Channel.' He stopped pacing and looked at the men in the room. 'Think about it. He's sending out possibly as many as twenty cars. All he has to do is stash stuff in them while everyone is at the game and then they'll drive them back to England for him. It's simple.'

Steve Parry rubbed his chin thoughtfully and smiled. 'It makes sense I suppose. But surely he wouldn't run the risk of anyone getting tugged on the way back?'

Jarvis shrugged. 'Why not? He's got nothing to lose, has he? So, a few of his mates get sent down and he's lost a motor. The chances are it'll be registered to someone else and so we won't be able to get near him. And no one's going to grass him up, are they? Even if we can trace it back to him, we'd never be able to get him on anything, would we? He won't have been anywhere near it for days or even weeks.'

'And besides ...' interrupted Williams excitedly, 'the chances of anyone getting stopped and given a good going over these days are slim. Customs are too busy looking for illegal immigrants.'

'Well, if you're right, Guv,' said Harris thoughtfully, 'it's bloody clever. He'll make a fortune – and for what? A few hundred quid and some match tickets.'

They all turned round as the door opened and Terry Porter walked in. Jarvis walked over, shook his hand and then looked around at the others. 'Do you all know DS Terry Porter? He's been working undercover with the Selector for a while.'

The others introduced themselves and then Jarvis went on. 'OK, at the moment we're waiting for the DCI to clear this operation with the spooks and the top brass. If they give us the go ahead, then we have to convince the Italians.'

'Not to mention Gary Fitchett,' said Williams. 'He's hardly the most willing informant I've ever met.'

Jarvis gave a wry smile and stole a glance at Porter, who remained leaning against the wall by the door. 'Al, get a plan set up to go with this. Travel, communications, everything. Neal, you give him a hand. Steve, you and Phil get working on some of the photographs we took in Great Portland Street. Let's try and put names to faces, see who we're dealing with.' The room began to buzz as the four men got busy. Jarvis nodded to Terry Porter and they walked over towards his office.

'Fucking hell, it's risky. You know that.'

Jarvis nodded across the table. 'Yeah, I know Terry. But no one's sussed you yet and only Fitchett will know who you really are and we'll be all over the two of you like a rash. But without someone with him, this operation is sunk and all we'll have is a damage limitation exercise for the Italians. I want more than that.'

Porter shrugged his shoulders. 'It's not just that though, is it? I mean, I'm black, or at least I was when I looked in the mirror this morning.'

Jarvis sat bolt upright and feigned a look of shock. 'Christ, I hadn't noticed.' He paused for a moment before standing up and beginning his customary pacing. 'Look Terry, I'm not saying you won't get grief because you probably will. But you know as well as I do that most of that BNP, Combat-18 stuff is media bollocks.'

'Yeah, I know that Guv, but...'

Jarvis stopped pacing and held his hand up. 'You're the only one I can send, Terry. You know Fitchett and he knows you. Or at least he thinks he does. What's more, you know the scene at the moment: who's active, who isn't. No one else available has that kind of insight and it's vital.' He sat down again and looked across the table. 'I can't make you go and I certainly wouldn't want to. But this is potentially a huge operation and the biggest chance we'll ever have to put Evans inside.' He left the rest hanging to put all the pressure on Porter. It was a cynical ploy, but it rarely failed.

Porter took a deep breath and then slowly exhaled. 'OK, if you can get him to agree to it, then I'll do it.'

Jarvis smiled and was about to speak when the phone interrupted him. He listened intently for a moment and then put it down. 'That was the DCI,' he said excitedly. 'It's all systems go.'

Three hours later, Jarvis was back in the interview room, waiting for Fitchett to be brought up. He was trembling with excitement. It had taken the DCI less than two hours to get his plan agreed, although the Italians, rather sensibly in Jarvis's opinion, had insisted that one of their officers accompany the team during the surveillance operation. They had also made it quite clear that they reserved the right to pull the plug on it at any time. Even the top brass and Special Branch had been receptive to the idea, although Jarvis had the sneaky feeling that if anything went wrong, responsibility would fall firmly on only one pair of shoulders and they belonged to him. The final piece in the jigsaw was Fitchett. Jarvis would have to convince him to play his part in it, even if it meant promising him things he could never deliver. The ace up his sleeve was Terry Porter. But as yet, he didn't know how he was going to play that particular card. He was still pondering that when the door opened and Fitchett walked in with Phil Williams. He sat down with a thump and immediately lit a cigarette. He was a mess. Tired, unshaven and in the same clothes as yesterday. From the look of him, he'd probably slept in them.

'Afternoon Gary. Nice to see you again.'

Fitchett stared at the wall and said nothing.

Jarvis leant forward onto the table and asked the question in a calm, relaxed voice: 'Have you decided yet Gary?'

Fitchett remained quietly smoking, his eyes fixed on the wall.

'Will you go to Italy?'

Still no response, something that was beginning to irritate Jarvis, but he continued speaking in the same even-tempered tone. 'Listen Gary, it's up to you. Either you go to Italy to help us out or I put you inside this afternoon. Which is it to be?'

Still no response.

'So, the silent treatment is it?' asked Williams.

Fitchett exhaled deeply, the cloud of smoke spreading across the wall of the interview room. 'I want to see my solicitor' he said without looking round. 'I'm getting set up here and you're right out of order. It's a fucking outrage what you're trying to get me to do.'

'OK Gary,' said Jarvis calmly, 'that's your right. But you know that all this will work against you when you get to court. I mean, I'll have no inclination to help you out if you cause us any more grief, will I? Especially now that we have so much stuff on you and your crew. That means you'll be in a cell for a good few years. Locked away for up to eighteen hours a day. Could you stand that Gary?'

Jarvis watched for a reaction but there was none. He was pushing his luck, but he had no choice. Unless he could get him to play ball, they'd have nothing.

'You see Gary, we're the ones doing the favour here. It's not the other way round. If you help us, we'll help you. If not ... well, we'll settle for what we've got. You and your lads.'

Fitchett took another drag from his cigarette and slowly turned round to face Jarvis. The expression on his face was one of disgust. His eyes glittering with loathing. There was an arrogance about him now that only came from people who believed they had nothing left to lose. 'What other stuff?' he sneered.

Jarvis picked up his notes and pretended to read through some of them before speaking. 'We have received a quantity of information relating to the activities of the hooligan group known as the Selector which we have no doubt will lead to a number of arrests over the coming few days.'

'Where from?' Fitchett sneered.

Jarvis scratched the side of his mouth. Now or never: 'Well, you're the one in an interview room, Gary. Work it out for yourself.'

Fitchett let out a loud laugh and turned back to the wall. 'You're bullshitting,' he said. 'No one would ever believe I'd grass my own lads, no one. You've got fuck all new or you'd have dumped it on me by now.' He stubbed out his cigarette and lit another.

The atmosphere in the room was getting oppressive and Jarvis waved his hand in front of his face to move the smoke away. 'OK Gary. If you think I'm bluffing, I'll prove it to you.' He leant across to Williams, whispered something in his ear and the young DC got up and left the room.

Fitchett continued to chain-smoke as Jarvis stared at him. 'I don't get you Gary,' he said, almost sympathetically. 'Here I am offering you the chance to help yourself and you throw it back in my face. I just don't get it.'

Fitchett let out a grunt and then suddenly spun round. 'What bit of it don't you get?' he smirked. 'Let's see shall we ... the bit where you raided my house, the bit where you got me sacked or what about the bit where you got me to walk into a room full of lads and then tell you what went on? Or maybe it was the bit where you want me to take an undercover copper to Italy?'

Jarvis watched impassively while he ranted on. He was almost relieved to get some kind of response out of him.

'Or what about the bit where I'm left freezing my bollocks off in a cell all morning and can't call anyone to tell them where I am? What about that? And where's my fucking solicitor, you wanker?' He stubbed out his cigarette, sat back in his chair and folded his arms.

Jarvis noticed him glance briefly at the window above the door and smiled. 'Feel better for that do we? Got it off your chest now?' asked Jarvis facetiously. He paused for a moment and then leaned forward. 'Listen Fitchett, don't forget that we raided your house for a reason. And you may have walked into a room full of faces – that's exactly what you are and that's exactly why you're here.' He was about to go on when the door opened and Williams walked in. Behind him walked Terry Porter.

Fitchett looked up, the expression on his face changed to one of outright horror. 'Nick! What the fuck have they got you for?'

Jarvis stood up and looked down at Fitchett. 'Sorry to disappoint you Gary. But this is Detective Sergeant Terry Porter. He's an undercover police officer.'

Fitchett stood up and stared at the man who, up to ten seconds before, he had thought of as a trusted friend. His face showed every emotion possible, from fear to fury. 'But you ... you were with us when ... you dragged me out...' He sat down with a thump and put his head in his hands. 'I don't believe it, I don't fucking believe it.'

Jarvis looked at Porter. He looked not a little gutted. Suddenly, Fitchett was up and diving across the room at Porter, sending the table and chairs crashing against the wall. 'You bastard,' he screamed. 'You fucked us over.'

Porter side-stepped, but not before Fitchett had struck him on the side of the head with a right hook. He was about to spin round when both Jarvis and Williams sprang into action and threw him to the floor. Williams grabbed his right arm, twisted it behind his back and shoved it up toward his shoulders. Fitchett let out a yell and then went limp as all the energy seemed to drain out of him.

'Ay, come on Fitch, fair's fair,' said Porter, rubbing his head vigorously. 'I've got a job to do.'

Williams relaxed his grip and Fitchett rolled over onto his back and began to rub his shoulder. His eyes were fixed on Porter. 'You're scum,' he said, his voice full of venom and hate. 'People slag us off, but you're the worst kind of scum. I trusted you.'

Porter shrugged his shoulders. 'Maybe so, but at the end of the day I'll be going home tonight and you'll be in a cell.'

Fitchett shook off Williams and stood up. 'Yeah, but at least I'll be able to sleep.'

Jarvis looked at Porter and motioned for him to leave the room. He nodded and walked over to the door. 'See you, Fitch,' he said as he left.

The response was as expected. 'Screw you, filth.'

Jarvis sat in the interview room and cursed to himself as he waited for Williams to bring Fitchett back from the toilet. Telling Fitchett Terry Porter's real name had been a bit careless. Still, it had certainly had the desired effect and, in any case, Porter was out of it now. A large envelope and a tray of tea sat on the table in front of him, but he'd drunk his already. He was about to drink Williams's as well when the two men walked back in. Fitchett sat down with his customary thump and Jarvis pushed a cup over to him. He picked it up and took a long, slow drink.

'All right Gary, now you know the score. We can put together enough stuff on you to put you away for a fair while. Not just you either; but almost everyone in your crew.' He picked up the envelope and pulled out a pile of photographs. After looking at the first one for a moment, he pushed it across the table. 'We know this one already don't we? Alex Bailey. Or what about this one; Barry, or Baz, Easton.' He began flicking the pictures across the table so they stopped right in front of Fitchett. '... Steven Brown, Gareth Miller, Kelvin Tatchell better known as "Pillow" ...' Jarvis left a pause and then asked, 'Do I need to go on Gary? I've got another fifteen or so yet?'

Fitchett sat there and looked at them. One by one his mates, people he knew and trusted, were having their lives turned upside down and they didn't know a thing about it. It was all over now. He knew that. All he could do now was what was best for himself. He let out a deep sigh and glanced up from the photographs, his face reflecting the fact that he'd all but given up. 'All right, I'll do it.'

Part Three

Chapter 12
Sunday, 24 October
06.10

The bedroom was in half-darkness, what light there was provided by the glow of the street light outside forcing its way through the tightly closed curtains. Fitchett lay on the bed and stared at the ceiling, while the events of the previous week danced around the shadows in front of him. He'd given up trying to sleep about three hours ago; now he was just reliving his nightmare. Well, nightmare was an understatement: it was worse than that. Much worse. At least if you have a nightmare, you'll wake up one day and it'll be finished. He reached over, took a cigarette from the packet on the bedside table and stuck it in his mouth. The thought suddenly struck him that someone might be looking at him while he lay there. Well, why not? From the moment he'd walked back in two weeks ago, he'd felt as if he were being watched. The phone was tapped, he knew that much, but what else was in there? Had they put cameras in? Or bugs? After all, it hadn't felt right since he'd got back on that Friday. After that bastard Jarvis had finally let him go after giving him what he'd called a 'debriefing'. Debriefing, what a fucking joke that was. All he'd done was promise that they'd be keeping an eye on him every step of the way and that no one would ever know that he'd helped them out. Then he'd given his word that he'd do all he could for him when this was all over. Lying bastard. The word of a copper, what was that worth? He put his hands behind his head and rocked the still unlit cigarette backwards and forwards between his lips. What choice had he had? They had him by the nuts, he knew it and they knew it. He had to co-operate, because he needed all the help he could get. Real or imaginary. He glanced around the room: if they were watching him, where would they have hidden the cameras? He shook his head. 'You're getting paranoid, mate,' he said out loud to himself.

What a day that Friday had been. By the time the coppers had finished with him on the Thursday it had been too late for him to get home, and so he had been forced to spend another night in the cells. But at least they'd left the door open this time and they'd even given him some stuff to have a shower and a shave. First thing in the morning, he'd been out of there and on the first train back to Brum. He'd felt relieved to get into New Street, but the feeling of unease had returned as soon as the taxi had turned into his road and had got worse as soon as he walked through his front door Was it unease or was it guilt? He still hadn't worked that one out yet. He sat up and looked at the clock; it was only 6.18, too early to get up, and so he dropped back down on the pillow and finally lit his cigarette. He formed the first mouthful of smoke into a perfect ring and watched as it drifted upward and into the still dark corner of his bedroom.

Guilt or unease, once he'd sorted himself out, he'd finally rung a few of the lads and told them exactly what Jarvis had told him to say: that he'd been charged in connection with the fight in Camden High Street and was out on bail pending further enquiries. However, he'd kept the conversations short so that no one dropped themselves in it. After all, the coppers were listening to everything and, if nothing else, he owed his lads that much. He had purposely avoided calling Alex. He had tried to work out what he would say, but hadn't known if he would be able to handle it. But when the door bell had rung at about six o'clock that night, it was his friend who'd been standing there. They'd gone to a pub and talked about what had happened, but Alex had seemed different; almost frightened or even suspicious. Fitchett hadn't been able to work out which. After a couple of hours, Alex had said that he was staying away from football for a while to keep his head down. He couldn't risk going inside and he wouldn't risk losing his wife.

It was a side of his friend Fitchett had never seen before, and he'd found it quite unsettling. If he hadn't known better, he might even have said that the police had got to his friend rather than the other way round. Maybe they had: how was he to know? He took a final drag from his cigarette and then lit another from the stub. When they had left the pub, it was on good terms, but it had been obvious to Fitchett that it was the end of their friendship. To be honest, they had little in common other than football, and without that ... well.

Fitchett drew a mouthful of smoke and blew another perfect smoke ring. Poor Alex, he hoped the coppers would leave him out of this when it was all over. He wasn't really even a fighter, he was the brains. The man who put it all together and kept his head while the rest were all over the place. Lads like him were vital in a good crew – and they'd been a good crew. The best. They'd never run from anyone. Not even Portsmouth when he'd got battered, and Nick ...

Fucking Nick, or Porter or whatever his name was. He took a drag on his cigarette and held it in for a while before opening his mouth and letting it drift out. He wondered for the thousandth time how they had fallen for it. How they had let some copper crawl his way into their mob. Looking back, it all made sense. Fitchett had never seen him do any real fighting, just loads of running about and shouting. It looked good but was all bollocks. Yet they'd fallen for it because of what had happened in Portsmouth.

And now ... A long shaft of ash slowly folded over and then fell on to his chest. He studied it for a while before blowing it off onto the bed. 'What a wanker,' he said out loud. And now he was off to Italy, with an undercover copper in tow. It was almost funny. He stubbed out his cigarette and after a glance at the clock, lay back on the bed. Six twenty- two.

Christ, he was going to Italy this afternoon. The call he had been dreading had come on Friday night. Evans had told him to bring his minder and meet him at Dover train station at two o'clock Sunday. That was today. It had been a brief conversation, almost one-way in fact. All Fitchett and his minder had to take were enough clothes to last them for the week, their passports and their driving licences. Everything else was taken care of. And then, after a brief chat about this and that, he'd gone. Fitchett had then rung Jarvis, told him what had happened and had then gone out and tried to get drunk, without success. And now time was pushing on. His train left New Street at 09.03 and Nick – or was it Porter? – would meet him at Euston. They were then being driven part way to Dover, so that the coppers could go over everything, and then getting on a train at the station before. From then on, everything depended on what happened with Evans. One thing was for sure though, it was going to be quite a few days. He looked around at his bedroom and wondered just when he'd see it again.

Just after eleven o'clock, he was walking out of Euston station and heading towards Stephenson Way, where he had arranged to meet the police. Even on a Sunday morning Euston was busy and he hadn't wanted to run the risk of meeting anyone he knew. He crossed the zebra crossing almost without looking and thought about the journey down. It had, to say the least, been an anxious trip. Not only was he worried about bumping into someone, but he was also getting increasingly frightened about the whole idea. He had thought about turning up and telling the coppers that he wasn't going to help them, or even doing a runner, but in the end he had dismissed both of these ideas as pointless. He had no choice really. He had hated being locked up even for a few short nights and had to do what he could to stay out for as long as possible. If helping the coppers would go some way to reducing his time inside, then it was a price he was prepared to pay.

Turning the corner, he spotted Porter leaning against a car smoking and, after a brief glance over his shoulder, walked towards him. As he approached, Porter stood up and faced him, but he walked past and carried on to the end of the road. He then turned and, after a pause and a good look around, walked back, handed Porter his bag and climbed into the back seat where Jarvis was waiting with a smirk on his face.

'Bit cloak-and-dagger there, Gary.'

Fitchett gave him a glare. 'Yeah, well let's get this over with, shall we?' he muttered.

Porter slammed down the hatchback and climbed into the front passenger seat. He turned round to face the men in the back. 'All right Gary? Looking forward to it?'

Fitchett looked back at him. 'Well you wouldn't be my first-choice companion, put it that way.'

Jarvis tapped Williams on the shoulder. 'Let's go Phil,' he said and within a few minutes they were struggling through the North London traffic heading for Dover.

'Fitch!' The brash Cockney accent cut through the cold October air and Fitchett turned to see Billy Evans walking along the platform towards him. He was, as usual, immaculately dressed and his face wore a beaming smile. They shook hands and exchanged pleasantries. Evans glanced around the platform. 'Where's Alex?' he asked curiously.

'Alex hasn't come,' said Fitchett. 'You know he won't have anything to do with stuff like this.'

'Oh, right,' replied Evans, 'so where's your lad?'

Fitchett nodded towards the toilets. 'Having a slash. He'll be out in a minute.'

Evans nodded. 'We'll have a laugh on this trip, mate,' he began excitedly. 'There's plenty of lads on the way already and we're the last to set off by car. I thought we could go down together, in convoy. I've got Hawkeye waiting in the car outside.'

Fitchett nodded as Porter came out of the toilet. Evans's face registered a brief look of surprise but quickly broke out into a grin. 'Terry, Billy. Billy, Terry.'

Porter held out his hand and Evans took it tentatively. 'A word,' he said and, grabbing Fitchett's arm, pulled him over to one side. 'Are you off your fuckin' chump or what? Why've you brought a fucking darkie along?'

Fitchett shook him off. 'He's one of my top lads, Billy; he's fucking sound,' he replied, surprising himself with the venom in his voice. 'If you've got a problem, then we'll fuck off back to Brum right now.'

Evans held up his hands. 'Alright, calm down fella.' A smile spread across his face and he put his arm on Fitchett's. 'Look,you know me, I ain't got a problem at all, but there's a few lads going on this trip who might have. Know what I mean? I just don't want any strife, that's all.'

Fitchett pushed him away and pointed aggressively at Evans's chest. 'There won't be any, not from us. Just keep them out of our way and everything'll be fine. Terry knows the score, believe me.'

Evans took a step forwards and put his arm round Fitchett's shoulder. 'Look, forget it, I shouldn't have said anything. It'll be cool, all right? I just expected you to bring Alex, that's all.'

Fitchett nodded and then walked over and picked up his bag. 'Well,' he said brightly, 'are we going to spicville or what?' He stood there, looking at Evans who, after a brief pause, let out a muted laugh.

Evans hadn't expected this and it was a problem he didn't want. If it had been anyone else, he'd have told them to sod off, but he knew Fitch better than most of the others and that counted for a lot. He'd have to deal with the problem of Terry when it arose. And he had a sneaky feeling it would.

'Come on then,' he said, 'let's get going. We've got a boat to catch.' The three men walked along the platform and out of the exit to find Hawkeye sitting in an almost new black Mercedes C200 Estate. He too was disappointed that Alex hadn't come, but if he was surprised that Fitchett had brought a black lad along, he didn't show it. In fact, he welcomed Porter like a long-lost friend, before driving out of the station and heading into town. As they travelled, conversation in the car avoided the trip ahead and centred around the football of the day before. But the unease was growing in Fitchett and he stayed out of it. He had surprised himself at the station, arguing like that, it had come too easy. But he doubted he could carry it on for long.

'You're quiet Fitch.'

He looked up to see Hawkeye staring at him in the rear view mirror 'Sorry Hawk, miles away. I was just wondering how the fuck Billy can afford this car.'

The two men in the front laughed. 'It's off the lot Gary, like all of them. You wait till you see what I've got for you to travel in.'

'Oh aye. A fucking Skoda, I suppose,' said Porter. Evans gave a chuckle. 'I only deal in the best, Terry mate. Only the best. Here we go.'

The Mercedes swung into a car park and Hawkeye threaded his way through the parked cars until he came to a dark blue Lexus. 'Here we go,' announced Evans triumphantly. 'This is yours for a few days. It's fucking lovely. I almost kept it for myself.'

The four men climbed out of the Mercedes and walked around the large saloon. 'Jeeesus,' Fitchett gasped. 'How much is this worth?'

Evans sniffed and adopted the mannerism of a typical car salesman. '1997 Lexus GS300 Sport. Low miles, every toy you could ever want, it's yours for £26,000.'

'Twenty-six grand!' exclaimed Porter. 'That's almost as much as I earn in two years!'

'That's not far off what I paid for my fucking house,' added Fitchett quietly.

'Well, if you want class, you pay for it,' Evans said proudly, rubbing his hands together like an excited schoolboy. 'And this is pure class.' He pressed a button on the keyring and the car gave a beep and a flash of its indicators. 'Get in, get used to it.'

Fitchett climbed into the driver's seat and placed his hands on the steering wheel. He was used to nice cars, but this ... well, this was something else. An array of switches and dials spread out in front of him and he wondered how he would ever get used to which was which.

'Why are you letting anyone, let alone Fitch, drive a car like this to Italy?' asked Porter. 'That's a bloody long way.'

Fitchett cringed, but Evans answered simply: 'Don't worry about that. I'll be well sorted out. Just don't smoke in it that's all. I know you northerners can't go more than ten minutes without a fag, but it takes me ages to get rid of the smell.'

'Best have one now then,' said Porter and pulled out a packet.

Evans looked at his watch. 'Just a quick one then; I need to go over everything first.'

Porter nodded and offered the packet around. Fitchett and Evans declined but Hawkeye took one and he and Porter wandered off a little way and were soon engrossed in conversation.

'You sure about this, Fitch?' asked Evans. 'I know what you said but, well, you know what the right-wing lads can be like...'

Fitchett nodded. 'He's sound Billy. Trust me.' He almost gagged as he said the words. 'It won't be a problem.'

Evans cocked his head to one side and gave him a thin smile. 'OK mate, it's your skin.' He handed Fitchett the car keys and then reached into the car and pulled a large envelope out of the glove box. 'Here's the documents for the car. It's registered in my name and you're travelling on my insurance – so no speeding, crashes or doing runners from service stations on the way.'

Fitchett nodded, as he continued. 'In the envelope there's a ticket for the two forty-five ferry to Calais, two tickets for the match and five hundred quid for juice and spends. You can exchange that on the boat. I've also planned out a route, but Hawk and me will be travelling with you so you shouldn't get lost. There's a map book on the back seat if you need it. Anything else?'

Fitchett shook his head and then looked across at Porter as the shrill noise of a mobile rang out. They watched as Porter had a brief conversation and then stuck the phone back in his pocket. 'Bloody wife,' he called out before returning to his conversation with Hawkeye.

Evans's eyes remained fixed on Porter for a moment and then he returned to the business in hand. 'OK then. Just in case we do get split up, there's a service station just before you hit the Rome ring road. We're all due to meet there at seven o'clock on Tuesday night. That gives us loads of time.'

Fitchett took the envelope and had a brief look inside. 'How far is it anyway?'

Billy shrugged his shoulders. 'About a thousand miles or so. With two people sharing the driving, that's a piece of piss.' He looked at his watch. 'It's five past two, we best get moving if we're going to make that boat. Oh yeah, one last thing ...' He called the others over and held out his hand. 'I need your mobile.'

Porter looked at him, hesitated and then reached into his pocket and handed over the phone.

'I'll give you it back when we get home.'

Hawkeye clapped his hands together. 'We best be off then. Are you following us down?'

'Yeah, if you like. We'll have a beer or two on the boat.'

Fitchett threw the keys to Porter. 'You can drive.' They climbed into the car and, within three minutes, the Lexus and the Mercedes were gliding out of the car park.

Fitchett stared out of the window as Porter drove the car towards the docks. Despite his calm exterior, he felt a bag of nerves. A few beers on the boat would do him good, let the copper drive for a while. The lights at a pedestrian crossing turned amber and Porter slowed the car to a stop as the Mercedes continued into the distance. He put the car in neutral and turned to face his passenger. 'Right, if we're going to spend two days in this car together we need to get a few things straight.'

Fitchett looked at him, his face devoid of any expression. 'Like what exactly?'

'The first is that you were told not to use my real name.'

Fitchett lowered his eyebrows and glared at him angrily. 'Fuck you. The bloke I thought you were died the second you walked into that interview room. Better I call you by your real name than what I'd like to call you.'

Porter held up his hand and pointed at him aggressively. 'Don't fuck me about, Gary. It's too dangerous. For both of us.'

Fitchett's expression turned from anger to disgust. 'What else?' he snapped.

'What?'

'You said a few things ...'

'Yeah. I'm not your fucking chauffeur, right?'

Fitchett gave a sniff and returned his stare to the windscreen. 'They're green.'

'What?'

'They're green.... The lights.'

The blast of a car horn sounded out and Porter gestured to the driver behind before angrily pulling the lever back into drive and gunning the throttle. The Lexus leapt forward at an alarming rate, pushing the two men back into their seats.

'Fucking hell!' shouted Fitchett. 'Be careful, you cunt. You'll fucking kill us both.'

Porter lifted off the throttle and the car slowed down to a speed approaching the legal limit. 'Jesus Christ,' he laughed. 'That was fun.'

Fitchett glared at him for a moment and then looked out the side window. 'You fucking idiot,' he muttered, before the car settled into silence.

Jarvis answered the phone on the second ring and, after listening intently to what was said, barked a simple 'Cheers,' and snapped it shut. He waited for a moment and then said 'Bollocks,' before adding, 'Both cars are registered to Evans. Why would he do that?'

Williams gave him a quick glance and then returned his eyes to the road and the back of the Lexus about fifty yards in front. 'What d'you mean?'

Jarvis rubbed his chin thoughtfully. 'When you sell a car to a dealer, you have to send off a part of the log-book to register the sale with the DVLA. But the dealer doesn't register the car. He hangs on to the rest of the log-book and changes the name and address when he sells the motor on. So why would Evans actually register these two in his own name?' '"Maybe he's keeping them for himself? Or maybe he hires them out?'

'A twenty-five-grand Lexus and a top-of-the-range Mercedes, it'd be a bloody odd hire firm.'

Williams shook his head. 'No, there's loads of firms like that around, Guv. They do weddings, corporate stuff, things like that.'

Jarvis let out a sigh and scratched the back of his ear. 'Well, it's a new one on me. But it still doesn't answer the question: if he's going to smuggle drugs back, why would he use his own motors? It doesn't make sense.'

His phone let out another ring, and again he answered it on the second ring. He listened for a while and then threw the phone down into his lap before picking it up again and shutting it. 'That was Steve Parry: they think they saw Evans take Terry's phone off him in the car park.' He sucked in a mouthful of air and then blew it out. 'If they're right, then we could be in trouble. Not only have we got no way of contacting our man, but if Evans has got his phone, all he has to do is switch it on, look at the stored numbers and fuck knows what he'll find.'

Williams looked across at Jarvis in between dodging the ferry-bound traffic. 'He wouldn't be that stupid, would he, Guv?'

'Who, Evans?'

'No, Terry. Surely he wouldn't store numbers on his phone that could drop him in it?'

Jarvis turned to the front and watched as the Lexus joined the queue of traffic entering the port and slowed to a halt. 'I bloody well hope not,' he said. 'Or he's in the shit.'

Chapter 13
Sunday, 24 October
17.00

Terry Porter pulled the Lexus out of the confines of the docks and followed the black Mercedes as it headed for the motorway. The ferry had been negotiated without any problems, and in fact he had quite enjoyed it. They had been four of about three hundred or so England fans heading for Rome by road and the atmosphere on board had, to say the least, been jovial. Evans had seemed to know everyone on board personally and Porter had kept a wary eye on him throughout the trip. He needed to know as much as he could about him but, aside from the fact that he had a liking for duty-free Bacardi and sexist jokes, he'd learnt nothing of value. 'Did you spot anyone else you knew on the boat?' he asked without looking away from the road.

Fitchett looked up from his magazine and shrugged. 'A few.'

'Well, were any at the meeting you went to?'

'Not that I remember.'

Porter sighed out loud. 'Is this what it's going to be like all the way down?'

'What d'you mean?'

'You being a miserable fucker.'

'Well you won't have to put up with me all the way, will you? First chance I get, I'll jump in with Billy and you can have Hawkeye in here.'

Porter flashed a glance across the car and raised an eyebrow in admonishment. 'Oh no. You can forget that. You're not going anywhere. I can't drive all the way on my own, can I? And besides, I want to keep an eye on you.'

Fitchett gave him a glare and then returned to his magazine, the aggressive rustling of the pages an indication that the conversation was over. Porter let out a heavy sigh and decided to let him sulk. He had other things on his mind at the moment and dealing with a moody passenger was not one of them. He was certain he'd noticed Evans staring at him a few times on the boat, so clearly he was still cautious. And with him in the car in front, there was no way he would be able to meet up with the team during the journey.

At least he had managed to have a quick word with Steve Parry in the toilets during the crossing. He had told him that Evans planned to do the trip in one hit and that they were meeting up with everyone else at a service station just outside Rome. But after refusing the offer of a replacement phone in case Evans found it, someone else had come in and Steve Parry had left. Still, at least he now knew that Jarvis was also on board and that they had two cars following him to the outskirts of Rome, where they were due to meet one of the local coppers. That should prove helpful. But for now, he would just have to try and work out a way to speak to them when they stopped for fuel, food or coffee. At least, with so many English cars heading for Rome, they wouldn't stand out.

A hundred yards behind them, Jarvis was busily writing down the message being relayed to him over the phone. 'I don't believe it,' he muttered as he clicked his phone shut.

Williams stole a brief glance at his DI. He'd never driven abroad before and wasn't finding it as easy as he had thought he would. The thought of crashing his Guv'nor – and the repercussions for the operation – scared the hell out of him. 'What is it, Guv?'

Jarvis looked across at him, the expression on his face one of total bewilderment. 'They've just done a PNC check of all the cars on the boat: six of them belonged to Evans.'

'So?' shrugged Williams. 'We spotted at least three of the faces we saw going into the hotel in Great Portland Street. Chances are there were more.'

Jarvis shook his head. 'No, that's not what I'm saying. Six cars, all registered to Evans. Why would he use his own motors to smuggle stuff back to England? It doesn't add up.'

Williams gave another shrug of his shoulders. 'Maybe you're wrong Guv ... about the drug thing, I mean.'

Jarvis rubbed his hand down his face; it felt greasy. He guessed it was from standing out on the deck talking to Steve Parry and the others instead of staying in the warm where he might be recognised. 'So you think that this whole riot thing may be right after all?'

'Well, why not? Can you think of anything else?'

Jarvis looked out of the window. It was starting to get dark. 'No, to be perfectly honest, I can't.' He picked up the phone and rang Steve Parry. He was in a second car about a hundred yards behind them and had Neal White for company. After passing on the news about the cars, he had a brief discussion about the possible reasons for the trip and, after asking the others to give it some thought, hung up. He looked out of the window and rubbed his eyes. He suddenly felt shattered.

'I'd better get some sleep,' he groaned. 'God knows how this trip is going to pan out. Two days in a poxy Vauxhall and the villains get a Mercedes and a Lexus. And they say crime doesn't pay.' He climbed into the back seat and draped a blanket over himself.

'Guv, before you crash out ...?'

'What?' he said without opening his eyes.

'There's one more thing that doesn't add up.'

Jarvis opened one eye and stared at the back of Williams's head. 'What's that?'

'Well, it's been nagging me since we left Dover...'

'For fuck's sake Phil, spit it out.'

'Well, if there are four of them, why go in two cars? Why not just go in one?'

Jarvis opened his other eye. 'Comfort,' he replied. 'It's bad enough having to do a thousand miles in two days with just one other person in the car. With four, it'd be a nightmare. And then you've got to turn round and come back.'

Williams shook his head. 'You ever been in a Lexus, Guv? They're bigger than my front room. Come to think of it, they're quieter and more comfortable as well.'

Jarvis sat up. 'So, what are you saying?'

'That's just it, I don't know.'

Jarvis looked at the young DC and then lay back down. 'Well, that's a lot of use then ain't it? If you come up with anything, tell me when I wake up.' He settled down and, within a few minutes, had fallen into a restless and uncomfortable sleep.

Chapter 14
Tuesday, 26 October
11.20

Jarvis awoke and stared at the roof of the car. He felt like he'd been in there forever, but since leaving Calais it had been just two nights and about nine hundred miles. He lay there for a while and reflected on the events of the past two days; the seemingly endless motorways and the long stops for fuel and food. And all the while keeping watch on the Mercedes and the Lexus. Wondering what was going to happen when they got to Rome and what all this was really about. What a journey. He certainly wasn't looking forward to doing it all again on the way home. He suddenly realised that the car wasn't moving, and sat up to find it empty. The sun was streaming in through the windows, but when he jumped out it was bitterly cold and he noticed for the first time that he was in a rest stop next to the motorway. The only other vehicles around were HGVs and a dozen or so British-registered cars obviously on their way to Rome, judging by the England scarves and flags hanging out of the windows. He let out a yawn and then rubbed his eyes to wake himself up.

'Oh, you're awake at last.' He turned to see Phil Williams walking towards him with a tray of steaming coffee and rolls.

'What time is it?' he asked, arching his back to relieve the stiffness. Williams put the tray on the roof of the car and took a sip from a steaming cup. 'It's about twenty past eleven,' he said wearily. 'They stopped for something to eat at a service station a few miles back. Steve and Neal are keeping an eye on them and we'll pick them up when they leave.'

Jarvis looked around again. He needed to go to the toilet and freshen up a bit. He looked at Williams and furrowed his brow. Something wasn't right. 'You've shaved! Where the fuck ...?'

'There's a truckers' washroom in there,' he said, nodding in the direction of a small brick building. 'That's where I bought this lot.'

'Jesus, I didn't even hear you get out of the car. I must have been in a coma. Anything else happen?'

Williams shook his head. 'Nothing much, this is their first stop since breakfast. You had another call from the DCI though. He wants you to call him as soon as you can. And we'll need to get some juice soon. The next station is about twenty kilometres up the road.'

Jarvis took a deep breath of fresh air. It felt exhilarating. He took a coffee and bit into a roll. 'Where are we anyway?'

Williams put down his coffee and reached into the car for the map. 'We're here,' he said, pointing at a nondescript red line. 'On the A1 near a place called Orvieto.' He moved his finger along the line and settled at a point just outside Rome. 'There are five service stations between here and Rome. This one here is the last one, so it would make sense for the meet to take place there. That's only about seventy or eighty miles from here.'

Jarvis let out a sigh and swallowed another mouthful of coffee. 'Thank fuck for that,' he said. 'Give Al Harris a call and find out where we're supposed to be meeting this Italian copper. And you'd better get his name as well. That'd be handy. Get him to tell the boss I'll call him in about thirty minutes. I need a slash and a shave before I do anything.' He reached into the boot, grabbed a towel and his wash-bag and headed for the brick building.

When he came out, Williams was standing by the car with the phone in his hand. He looked across at Jarvis and held it up, motioning him to get over as quickly as he could. Jarvis thought about jogging but decided against it. He was too tired, but at least he felt clean now. If he could, he'd get a shower in the local nick later on. Williams was getting more animated by the second, and so, reluctantly, he broke into a trot, arriving at the car probably twenty seconds faster than if he'd walked.

'It's the DCI,' said Williams, a slight trace of urgency in his voice.

Jarvis took it and made a silent screaming face. 'Yes Guv?' He listened attentively for a while and then broke into the conversation. 'Look Guv, I know all that. But if we hand them over to the Italians we've got nothing ... Yes, I know that, but what do they say? ... Well do we know where we're meeting him? ... OK, well we'll just have to see what happens then, but it'd be a bloody farce if all this work went to waste ... Well it'd be a waste as far as I'm concerned – and how would we get Terry Porter out at this stage? ... OK Guv, well look, I'll see what this Italian guy has to say and wait to hear from you.'

He snapped the phone shut and threw it into the car. 'For fuck's sake!' he barked, and thumped the roof of the car, more in frustration than anger. Williams looked at him, but said nothing. He knew from experience that Jarvis would tell him what had happened, because it helped him to think. He didn't have to wait long. 'You're not gonna fucking believe this,' he burst out angrily. 'The DCI has had a call from the Home Office. They're getting twitchy about all of this and are considering pulling the plug. We may have to hand the whole operation over to the Italians and let them deal with it. Can you believe that?' Jarvis kicked out at the front tyre. 'Bollocks!'

Williams gave him a second to calm down and then spoke up. 'Well, what's happening now?'

Jarvis leant on the car roof and put his head in his hands. The pressure was clearly getting to him and Williams wondered just how he would react if they were pulled out. 'They're speaking to the Italians at the moment to try to find out what they want to do.'

Williams smiled. 'Sounds like a buck-passing exercise to me, Guv.'

Jarvis looked up. 'That's exactly what it is, and there's fuck all we can do about it.' He rubbed the back of his neck and looked skywards. 'Shit, I don't need this.' He let out a sigh and took a drink from a half-empty cup of coffee. It was cold and he spat it out on to the road with a curse. 'Do you know where we're meeting this copper?'

Williams nodded and picked up the map. 'His name's Fabio Casoretti or something and he'll be waiting for us at a junction on the motorway here, at a place called Magliano Sabina.'

Jarvis let out a sigh and scratched his head. 'Well let's get down there then and see what he's got to say. I'll give Steve a call and tell him what's happening. He'll have to track them until we find out what's what.'

'Well, that shouldn't be a problem,' said Williams as he began sorting out the empty cups. 'Half the motors on the motorway seem to be English, and they're all heading in the same direction. I've already seen a few of them about ten times, so the chances are Evans won't even notice Steve.'

Jarvis threw his wash-bag into the boot and slammed it shut. 'I bloody hope not,' he muttered, climbing into the front passenger seat, 'or we'll be in the shit.'

Terry Porter walked out of the toilet and crossed the foyer of the service station to the small shop. Through the windows, he could see Gary Fitchett and Hawkeye leaning against the Lexus, smoking. They had been joined by a man in an England shirt and were watching a game of football that had begun among the England fans at the far end of the car park. There were about fifteen people on each side, and even with his restricted view, it was clear to Porter that skill was in short supply. He guessed all the lads were killing time and staying out of Rome until later on, to avoid the attentions of the local police. A sensible move, judging by what he could make out from the front of the Italian papers on display in the shop. They were covered in photographs from the last England visit to Rome, in 1997, when the riot police had given a good number of the England fans a serious hiding. 'I'm going to be smack bang in the middle of that lot tomorrow night,' he thought.

He paid for four cans of Coke and was about to walk out to the cars when he noticed three pay phones on the wall by the main door. He stared at them for a brief second and then turned away; it wasn't worth the risk. And besides, even if he did manage to get through to Jarvis and the others, he had nothing much to say. What time he had spent with Evans and

Hawkeye had involved conversations about previous trips abroad with England and the poor management of the national side. No politics, no drugs, not even any criticism of the police. He wasn't even certain that Hawkeye knew anything, anyway. Truth to tell, he was intelligent in a streetwise sort of way and was even quite a nice bloke, but he was hardly *Mastermind* material. Porter had been working undercover for long enough to know that people like him were fighters, not planners. Evans, on the other hand, well, he was a different beast altogether. There was something about him, an arrogance that Porter had rarely come across before. He certainly knew the score as regards the hooligan hierarchy but it was more than that, as if he almost believed he were untouchable. He had tried to get more information about him from Fitchett, but he'd been no help at all. Whatever he knew, and he was sure it was more than he had let on, he was keeping it to himself.

Porter pushed open the door and walked out across the car park to the waiting cars. The guy in the England shirt had wandered over to the football game and was now cheering on the players. Porter gave a brief nod in Fitchett's direction and handed him and Hawkeye a can each. He looked around. 'Where's Billy?'

'He'll be back in a minute, he's just making a call,' replied Hawkeye. 'Probably using your phone, knowing him. He's a tight cunt.'

Porter opened his can and took a long drink. It was freezing, but the jolt it gave him was just what he needed to wake him up. 'Well he can't be that tight,' he said. 'This lot must be costing him a packet.'

Fitchett sucked in a mouthful of air through his clenched teeth, but if Hawkeye noticed, he didn't show it. He simply laughed out loud. 'Don't you fucking believe it, mate. One thing I've learnt about Billy, he never does anything for free.'

'Is that right?'

'Oh yeah. Billy'll be making out of this trip, have no doubt about that. He ain't no charity.'

Porter took another drink from his can, pulled out a packet of cigarettes and offered them round. Hawkeye took one, but Fitchett looked at them like they were poison. 'So what's he up to then?'

Hawkeye shrugged his shoulders. 'Fuck knows. It don't do to ask too many questions where Billy's concerned. Besides, whatever he does is nothing to do with me. I'm just here for a laugh, a few beers and a ruck. A bit like Dublin, really.'

Porter took a drag from his cigarette and glanced at Fitchett. He was clearly getting angry at the way this conversation was going and after opening the door of the Lexus, dumped himself inside and turned on the radio. 'Oh, so you were in Dublin then?' Porter continued. 'That must have been the dog's bollocks.'

Hawkeye took a drink and nodded furiously until he had swallowed it. 'Yeah, it was fucking top. We spanked some Irish arse over there, I'll tell you. The Micks we were dealing with were a bit of a pain in the arse but...'

Fitchett jumped up out of the car and interrupted the conversation, or was it interrogation. 'Here's Billy!'

Porter gave him a vicious glare and then turned to see Evans walking back across the car park towards them. He had a mobile in his hand and Porter was relieved to see it wasn't his. The thought that he might take a look at the stored numbers had occurred to him as well, and although he had given everyone on there a false name, if he had called one it wouldn't have been difficult to work out who they really were. As he approached, he ended the call and stuck the phone back in his pocket. 'All right lads?' he asked.

'I need a kip and a few beers, I know that,' replied Porter.

Evans nodded as he took the can Porter held out for him. 'Yeah, I know what you mean, Terry. Still, it won't be long now. That was one of the wops on the phone. There's been a change of plan.'

Porter took a drag from his cigarette and, in as indifferent a voice as he could manage, asked, 'Anything we should know about?'

Evans lowered the can from his mouth and looked at him. Suddenly, the humour had gone from his face and his eyes were blazing. He moved forward until he was barely a foot away, his finger pointing aggressively at Porter's chest. 'There's nothing you need to know about,' he hissed. 'Nothing at all. The only reason you're here is to keep an eye on your man, you leave everything else to me. Besides, if I had my way ...' He let the sentence drop.

Porter stood up straight and turned to face him. 'If you had your way, what?'

Evans left a pause and then laughed out loud. 'Forget it,' he said, slapping Porter on the arm and looking around. 'Who flashed the ash?'

Porter waited for a second and then relaxed. That had been the first time he had seen Evans do anything other than laugh and joke, and the transformation had been startling. He pulled out his cigarettes and Evans took one gratefully, lit it, and then looked at his watch.

'Right, it's twelve thirty. We've got just under a hundred miles to go and we need to be there at about three, so we best get our arses in gear.' He lit his cigarette, took a deep drag and then leant into the Lexus, where Fitchett was still fiddling with the radio. 'Are you fit, fuck-face?'

Fitchett climbed out and scratched his backside. 'Yeah. Let's get this over with then. You can drive Terry, keep you from getting bored.'

Evans rubbed his hands together and then flicked his cigarette away. 'Right, let's go then.' The four men climbed into their respective cars, and within a few moments were back out on the motorway heading for Rome.

Jarvis was half asleep when the phone rang. It was Steve Parry, telling him that the two cars had left the service area and were heading towards Rome.

'OK Steve,' Jarvis sighed, 'we're not far from where we're meeting our Italian, so we should know the score fairly quickly. I'll give you a call if we find anything out.' He listened for a while and then let out a laugh. 'Yeah, I know, I'll keep an eye out for you. Oh, while I think of it, make sure the phones are charged up. I've a funny feeling we'll be spending some time walking around the delights of Rome tonight.' He said his goodbyes and turned the phone off as Williams nodded towards a road sign.

'Here we go Guv, our boy should be waiting around here somewhere.'

Jarvis stared at the blue motorway sign as it rushed past. His whole operation could fold in a matter of minutes; everything depended on what the Italian police had decided. He stifled a yawn and stretched his arms. 'I tell you what Phil, when we get home I'm going on three weeks' leave to catch up on my sleep. I don't know how you do it.'

Williams let out a chuckle. 'It's called youth, Guv.'

'You cheeky fucker.'

Williams indicated and took the car up the slip road.

'Best keep out of sight of the traffic,' said Jarvis. 'Our Italian could be in a patrol car and we best not take the chance that anyone will spot us.'

Williams nodded and slowed as the car reached the junction with the main road which crossed the motorway. 'Is that them?' asked Williams. He pointed to a green Fiat parked by the side of the road. Two men wearing jeans and leather jackets were leaning against it smoking. One was quite tall and slight, the other was more stocky. Jarvis was unsure if he were muscly or just fat. Typically, they both had thick black hair.

'Fuck me, even you could spot them for Italians Phil.'

If Williams spotted the sarcasm, he didn't show it. 'Well, d'you think that's them, then?'

Jarvis gave him a blank look and answered tetchily, 'How the fuck do I know? Drive over and find out.'

Williams pulled the car over in front of the Fiat and after climbing out, walked over to the two men. As the three of them shook hands, Jarvis got out to join them.

'Guv,' said Williams as he approached, 'this is Fabio Casoretti and Paolo Tessoni, from the state police.'

Jarvis held out his hand. 'Hello, I'm Detective Inspector Paul Jarvis.'

'Yes, I know,' said the shorter of the two men in almost perfect English, 'I've been waiting for you.'

Jarvis rubbed his hands together. He had no jacket on and was feeling the cold. 'Shall we ...?' he said, gesturing in the direction of the Fiat.

'Ah, no. If it's OK, I will come with you. Paolo has got to get back to Rome. You must understand we are under a little pressure at the moment ... the game ...'

Jarvis smiled. 'Of course, please ...'

Fabio rattled off something to his colleague, grabbed a briefcase from the Fiat and walked over to the Vauxhall. 'OK,' he said, as the Fiat roared off and disappeared down the slip road and onto the motorway, 'we must go over a few things, yes?'

Jarvis held up his hand. 'Hold on.' He felt uncomfortable saying a strange, foreign name and so made a conscious effort to avoid using it. 'The first thing we need to do is find out what's happening. My guv'nor, I mean superior, has told me that they are waiting to hear what you ... I mean the Italian government, want to do about this operation.' He paused for a while and then added: 'Are you going to arrest these men or not?'

Fabio looked at him and smiled. 'It's cold and we should have some coffee. Let's drive and I will tell you as we go.'

They climbed into the car and Williams was soon speeding southwards on the motorway. Fabio was in the front and Jarvis was squeezed in the back among all their junk. The Italian twisted round to face the back seat. 'You asked me if we will arrest your men, the answer is no. Not unless they break the law.'

Jarvis shut his eyes for a second and sighed. 'That's good news,' he smiled.

Fabio smiled back. 'I understand you must be worried, but there is no need. You see at the moment, all we have is a group of your English hooligans, nothing more. On the face of it, they are no different from the hundreds of others you and your Unit have told us are coming – and we are more than ready for them.' He gave a broad grin and then continued.

141

'Your officer, Harris, said that there were about twenty cars coming. That's forty men yes?'

Jarvis rubbed his chin and then gave a nod. 'Yes, we think about forty in all, but there may be more. To be honest, we're not sure if others are coming by train.'

Fabio shrugged. 'No matter, we will keep an eye on your targets – and if their numbers get out of hand, they will be dealt with. And you say you have a man undercover?'

Jarvis nodded. 'Yes, he's in one of the cars we've been tailing. If anything happens, he will of course identify himself to your men.'

'Good, very good.' Fabio turned back in his seat and stared out of the window. Without turning back to Jarvis he began speaking again. 'Do you still think there is something else to this?'

Jarvis shook his head and leant forward. He wasn't about to have a conversation with the back of the seat. 'Well, you should know all there is to know by now. But at the moment, my idea that they're planning to smuggle drugs back to England looks a bit off.'

The Italian twisted round. 'Off?'

'Wrong.'

'Ah, well we will keep an eye on them in any case. They will not do much we do not know about.' He paused for a moment and then added, 'So it looks like the riot will go ahead maybe.'

'That's up to you, isn't it?' said Jarvis snappily. He was getting slightly irritated by the man in the front seat and wondered if he knew that he was talking to a senior ranking officer.

Suddenly, Fabio spun round, almost bumping into Jarvis who fell back into his seat with surprise. 'If, as you say, this group are involved with some kind of political plot, then that is very serious. We have been talking to some of the Ultras as well as a few of the political activists but they know nothing. But we must find out who is behind this. We must.'

Jarvis nodded and went to speak, but Fabio held up his hand to stop him. 'It is no secret that Italian politics can be very disorganised, Paul, but we are very wary of the extreme right here. If it is them ...'.

'Well, my money would be on the right every time,' interrupted Williams.

'As would mine,' said Fabio turning his head towards the driver. 'And if they are growing in Italy, then many people will be concerned, which is why we must stop them.' He turned back to face Jarvis and gave him another grin. 'We just have to hope that your hooligans can help us do that. Then we will arrest them all.' Jarvis relaxed back into his seat. He was beginning to warm to this man.

Chapter 15
Tuesday, 26 October
15.00

Terry Porter slowed the Lexus to a crawl and steered it in to a parking bay three away from the Mercedes. 'Well, that's it, what a bloody journey.' He turned off the engine and looked across at Fitchett. He was white as a sheet. 'You all right?'

He flicked a nervous glance across the car and said, 'Yeah, I just need some fresh air and a fag, that's all.'

Porter reached over and held his arm. 'Listen Gary, all this will be over with soon. You're doing OK, so don't worry.'

Fitchett pulled himself away. 'You think I give a fuck about you?' he hissed. 'I'm shitting it at what that lot'll do if they suss what I've done. They'll do for me, no messing. And you.'

'They won't, there's no way they can. Don't forget, I'm in the middle of this as well – and it may have escaped your attention that I'm hardly a white Anglo-Saxon. I've got all that shit to deal with as well.'

'Oh, and I haven't? Remember, I fucking brought you. And besides,' he added, looking around nervously, 'it's your fucking job.'

Porter stared at him and shook his head. 'Why do you do it, Fitch?'

'Why do I do what?'

'Why do you travel with these wankers? You're no racist, nor are half the blokes here. So why do it?'

Fitchett looked out of the window. 'It's no different from being at home. You know what football is all about for lads like these. You should do, you've been in the middle of it for long enough.'

Porter shook his head. 'You're full of shit. This is nothing like it is at home, that's just gang warfare. This is more than that, so what is it? Come on. Tell me?'

Fitchett turned away from the window and looked around. 'It's the crack. That's all.'

'That's bollocks, Fitch, and you know it. If that's all it was, then you'd be sitting in a bar getting pissed and having a laugh. This is nothing like that. This is just hatred and violence. No, it ain't even that. It's just bullying.'

Fitchett turned back to his window. 'Yeah, maybe it is. And you know why? 'Cause everywhere I've ever been with England, I've been treated like shit. Well, fuck that. You might be happy to let some country take the piss with your own, but I'm fucked if I am. And none of these lads are either. If they hate us so much, let's give them something to hate us for.'

'What the fuck are you on about? All this we're-doing-it-for-England bollocks. I'm as English as you are and there's no way these cunts represent me.'

Fitchett looked at him, a slight sneer on his face. 'That's the fuckin' truth.'

Porter slowly shook his head. 'Maybe I had you all wrong all along. Maybe you're no better than some of those bastards out there.'

'Don't compare me to those right-wing twats,' Fitchett replied angrily. 'If you know anything about me, you know I ain't nothing like that. I don't care if your skin's black, brown, yellow or white, as long as your heart is blue. But if you think being proud of my country makes me a racist, then yeah, that's what I am.' He gave Porter a look of disgust and shook his head. 'Why the fuck am I explaining myself to you?' He grabbed the door handle and climbed out.

'That's all I need,' thought Porter as he watched Fitchett storm off across the car park, 'him to bottle it now.' He opened the door and stretched his arms above his head before lifting himself out and lighting a cigarette. He took a long drag and looked at Fitchett, who had wandered over to the Mercedes and was talking to Hawkeye. Poor bastard, he almost felt sorry for him.

'All right Terry?' He felt an arm on his shoulder and turned his head to find Evans standing behind him. 'Jesus!' he said, 'you scared the shit out of me!'

Evans laughed, but his hand remained on Porter's shoulder. 'Listen, sorry about what happened back there. I was bang out of order.'

Porter held up his hand. 'Forget it, you don't have to explain yourself to me.'

'Well I don't want you to think that I'm a ...'

Porter stopped him. 'Look Billy, I don't give a fuck. Honestly.'

Evans lowered his arm and gave a single nod of his head to accept the sentiment. Porter looked around; the car park was about two-thirds full, mostly with cars bearing British plates, but there were a few coaches, some minibuses and a number of lorries. Yet another football game was under way on the grass and about thirty men were watching and screaming abuse at the players. The atmosphere was good-natured, like a fun-fair without the music.

'I see the filth are here,' said Evans, nodding towards the exit, where two police cars sat next to each other.

'Well there's a surprise,' laughed Porter. 'I wonder what they're up to.'

Evans gave them a smirk. 'Don't worry about them, they've got nothing better to do that's all. Not yet, anyway.'

A voice shouted out and they turned to see a small group of men walking toward them. 'Billy, you old cunt. So you made it then?'

Williams avoided the car park and headed towards the petrol station, where Steve Parry and Neal White were waiting for them. After introducing Fabio, and a brief chat about their respective journeys, Parry pulled out a notebook.

'Guv, we had a walk round the car park about ten minutes ago. There's some serious lads in there. Most of the ones we saw at the meet in London are here already, but there are still a few missing.' He stole a glance at his watch. 'Mind you, it's only three thirty now; they've not got to be here 'til seven.'

Jarvis nodded and looked around nervously. He was well aware that, of the five of them, he was the only one likely to be recognised by anyone other than Terry Porter or Fitchett.

After all, he and Billy Evans were old friends. 'We're wide open here, let's get out the way. Phil, take Neal and get over to that car park. Get every number of every car in there and run a check on it with London. Let's find out who we're dealing with.'

The two DCs went to move but he called them back. 'Be careful. I don't want to blow this now, all right?'

'No worries Guv,' said Williams with a grin, and the two of them jumped into the Mondeo and headed for the car park.

The others climbed into the Vauxhall and Fabio directed them over a bridge towards the service area on the other side of the motorway. A small building sat at one end of the car park and Fabio directed them over to it and took them inside. It was, in effect, a small police station for the traffic patrols and contained everything they could possibly need, including a cell and, most importantly of all, a shower. However, it was the smell of hot coffee which drew the biggest reaction. Primarily from Steve Parry, who hadn't had a hot drink for ages.

'Help yourself,' said Fabio. 'You should take a shower as well. You look like you need it.'

Jarvis looked down at himself. He felt rotten, and could only imagine what he actually looked like. 'Yeah, I think I will.'

Across the motorway, Porter was beginning to feel very uneasy. The group of men standing around the Mercedes had now grown to around twenty, and as each one had arrived Evans had introduced them to everyone else. But only a few had shook his hand and it was clear that his was not a face some of them welcomed. He had even caught a few comments but hadn't reacted. He'd simply carried on smoking and listening as the others discussed their trip down. If Evans was aware of the growing tension, he certainly hadn't said anything. He was too busy holding court. Waving his arms about and punctuating his conversation with loud belly laughs. Clearly, being the centre of attention agreed with him.

A loud blast on a car horn made them all turn to look as a dark green Mitsubishi Shogun slowed to a stop in the middle of the driveway two rows along from where they were standing, the driver seemingly unconcerned that he'd just blocked access to that part of the car park. Evans walked through the parked cars and warmly shook the hands of the two smartly dressed men who got out. Like most of them, they were in their early thirties and wore an expression of arrogance that seemed strangely disconcerting. After a brief conversation and yet more laughs, the three men left the Shogun and headed for the growing throng. They looked the picture of respectability, but as they approached, one of them noticed Porter and, in an instant, the smile vanished from his face. His eyes were fixed, glaring at the only black face for miles. 'Here Billy, who brought the fucking nigger?'

Porter stood up, let out a deep breath and then looked around. 'Who me?' he said, pointing at his chest comically and raising an eyebrow in mock surprise. 'You mean me?' Half the group burst out laughing, the others merely smiled, but Porter was well aware that all of them were easing back from him. This wasn't good.

'Oh, a fucking comic,' came the reply, and then they were running, covering the last few yards in an instant and lungeing through the crowd at him. He lifted himself up on his toes and began winding himself up for the attack, bobbing around like an amateur boxer on acid. His eyes focused on nothing but the eyes of the two men heading directly at him, their faces showing only rage and hate. The first one flew at him, but he side-stepped and used the momentum to throw the body past and into the side of the Mercedes. But the second was too close and, before he could spin around, a punch drove into his back like a sledge hammer, sending shockwaves up his spine and forcing every ounce of breath out of him with a gasp. And then another blow, this time the killer: a steel-capped shoe smashed into his knee and he was down, curling into a ball to avoid the blows and minimise the damage.

But no more came. Just shouting and the rapid-fire scraping of feet on hard tarmac. He waited a second and then lifted his head to see Fitchett standing over him, his right fist clenched in anger and his left arm pointing at his two attackers as they were dragged away shouting and spitting, like two demented banshees. Porter uncurled himself and tried to stand up but his leg collapsed under him and he fell back down, the thump sending another sharp pain through his back. He was in agony, but that was nothing to the shock and humiliation he felt. He reached down and felt his knee, more to disguise his embarrassment than anything else, and noticed for the first time a tear in his jeans. He pulled the material apart and stared at the small pinpricks of blood peppering his skin. That would sting like crazy later on.

'Bastards!' he barked and tried to stand again, this time making it halfway before a pair of arms lifted him to his feet and helped him over to the Mercedes.

'Get in the motor!' He looked around and realised it was Fitchett who had lifted him up. 'Get in the fucking motor, the pigs are over there, for fuck's sake.' He put his hand back and realised the door of the Mercedes was open, so he sat down and swung his legs inside, pulling the door closed behind him with a silent thump. Within seconds, a body leant against the window, instinctively shielding it so that no one could see what was happening inside.

'You all right son?' He looked up to see Billy Evans leaning over the door on the other side of the car. Porter rubbed his head. The pain was easing slightly and his initial feelings had passed. Now he just felt shocked and aggrieved. It had happened so fast, come from nowhere.

He looked across the car at the face leaning in looking at him. 'Yeah, I'm OK. Nice lads, friends of yours?'

Evans gave him a wry grin. 'Pair of wankers. I'll have a word, that was bang out of order, that was. You don't fight your own, not on an away trip.'

Porter gave him a frown. 'Even if they're a nigger?'

Evans paused and turned towards the back seat as Fitchett climbed in and sat behind Porter. 'I fucking told you, Fitch,' he said angrily, 'and don't you say I didn't.' He pushed the car door shut and walked off.

Fitchett watched him go and then leant forward against the front seat. He looked almost ashamed. 'Sorry,' he mumbled, 'I should have warned you about those two. They're nasty bastards.'

'Know them, do you?' asked Porter, vigorously rubbing his knee in an effort to get the blood flowing around it.

'For years. They're Leeds, Service Crew.' He stopped talking for a second and then turned his head away to stare out of the window. 'Listen, you'd better be ready for more of that. I've got a nasty feeling about this.'

Porter stopped rubbing his knee and turned to look at him, but his back let him know it wasn't such a good idea and he returned to his original position. 'And you think I haven't?'

Fitchett started to speak, but was interrupted by Hawkeye wrenching open the door and thrusting his head into the car. He looked remarkably clean but was almost scarlet with rage. 'You all right Terry? Fucking Yorkie bastards! You can't take the wankers anywhere. Listen, you give me the nod, we'll do the cunts later. They're fuck all.'

Porter climbed out and stood up beside him. 'Forget it, Hawkeye,' he said, shaking his head. 'Just forget it.' He looked over to the service area and started limping towards it. 'I need a slash.'

He had only gone a few steps when Hawkeye appeared beside him, closely followed by Fitchett, who looked remarkably sheepish. 'Come on you fucking cripple, we'll hold it for you. I want to see if all those rumours are true.'

They all laughed out loud and set off towards the service area, but Porter was worried. His knee was struggling to take his full weight – if anything happened and he had to run for it later on, he was going to be in big trouble.

Jarvis walked out of the shower room, rubbing his hair with a towel. 'Jesus Christ, that feels good.'

'It's all right for some,' moaned Steve Parry. 'My gear's in the car on the other side of the bridge.'

Jarvis smiled. 'Rank has its privileges, Detective Sergeant.'

Parry handed him a cup of coffee and doffed an imaginary cap. 'Hope that's all right, your Lordship.'

Jarvis was about to reply when Parry's mobile rang. 'Yes Neal... No, he can't, he's drying his hair ... Yes, that's right, he's drying his hair.' He looked across at Jarvis but the smile on his face suddenly changed to one of panic. '... What! Hang on, I'll tell him.' He put his hand over the mouthpiece and lowered the phone from his face. 'Guv, it looks like we could be in trouble. Neal thinks two of the crew just attacked Terry Porter and gave him a kicking.'

Jarvis ran over and grabbed the phone from his DS. 'Neal, tell me exactly what happened.' He listened while Neal White ran through what he had seen and, after thinking for a moment, asked, 'Have you got those numbers yet? ... Then get them over here now. We'll fax them through to London from this office. Forget Terry, you just leave it to me.' He cancelled the call and looked across at Fabio who was watching them from the other side of the office. 'Will you contact your lads and ask them to keep an eye on our targets?'

Fabio nodded. 'Of course.' He pulled a radio out of his pocket and went to speak but Jarvis suddenly held his hand up to stop him.

'And can your lads pull our man out for a while?'

The Italian looked puzzled. 'But why?' he asked.

'We have to speak to him and try and find out how he is and if he knows anything.'

Fabio gave him another nod of his head and lifted the radio to his mouth. 'Which one is he?'

Jarvis gave Steve Parry a fleeting glance and then said, 'You can't miss him. He's the only black face in the car park.'

'Heads up lads! Old Bill.' Hawkeye nodded to his right and Porter turned his head to see that the two Italian police cars which had been sitting idle at the far end of the car park were now threading their way through the rows of parked traffic. He immediately noticed that the men inside the cars were looking directly at the three of them and, judging by the movement in the cars, were about to pull over and get out.

'Careful lads, stay cool.' Porter stood up straight and made an extra effort to disguise his limp, but he was suddenly more aware of the tear in his jeans and unconsciously reached down to touch it. Fitchett grabbed him and pulled him up. He was tense. Too tense. They carried on walking and, as he feared, the two cars stopped and four policemen got out. They looked at the three men for a moment and then one of them put on a pair of sunglasses and walked over. He nodded to Porter.

'What happened to you?'

'I fell over, playing football.'

'I don't think so. You were fighting over there.'

'What me? No officer, I fell playing football ... honest.'

The policeman stood there for a moment, a long black stick in his hand. He looked an evil bastard and Porter could feel Hawkeye and Fitchett tensing up. Getting ready, just in case. He felt strangely comforted by that. The policeman suddenly reached up and took off his glasses and instantly the mood relaxed. They could see his eyes, the windows to the soul they called them, and now he wasn't an evil bastard at all. Just a bloke doing a job.

'Your leg is hurt?' The three of them looked down at the torn jeans and the graze peeking through.

Porter took a step back and held up his hands. 'No, it's OK, don't worry.' But the policeman moved forward and took his arm.

'No, you come with us, we will 'er ...' he smiled as he struggled for the right words. 'Erm, doctor yes? Over the bridge.'

Porter turned and looked at Hawkeye, who flashed a look at the two police cars. They were clearly getting agitated by the time this was taking.

'You better go Terry. Just get them to bring you back sharpish, that's all.' He patted him on the shoulder and took a step backwards.

'Don't worry, I'll go with him.' Porter turned as Fitchett moved forward and placed an arm around his back. 'Just to make sure he comes back.' The policeman looked puzzled for a moment and then Porter suddenly realised what was happening.

'It's OK,' he said, barely disguising the sense of urgency in his voice. 'That's OK.' He caught the eye of the Italian policeman who nodded and ushered them over to the two cars. Within a few moments, they were out of the car park and heading across the bridge. Hawkeye watched them go, and then turned and walked briskly back towards the others.

Jarvis handed Terry Porter a cup of coffee and gave him a nervous grin. He looked a sight. Dirty, unshaven and sitting on a table with his trousers round his ankles as Neal White knelt in front of him and cleaned the wound on his leg.

'I wish I had a camera. I could make a bloody fortune with a picture of that.'

The others burst out laughing, but Jarvis just smiled. He hadn't really considered the full implications for his man and he suddenly felt very guilty. 'Look Terry, if it's getting too heavy then you're out mate. You can't play games with this lot, it's just not worth the risk.'

Porter looked up at him and grinned. He heard what Jarvis was saying but knew what he was really doing, applying pressure. Putting the onus on him, absolving himself of responsibility if anything happened, he'd done it before. Porter shook his head and took a mouthful of coffee. 'Forget it, we've come all this way and I'm not pulling out. Not yet.'

Jarvis nodded and smiled. He looked across at Fitchett who was leaning against the wall by the door. 'You OK?'

Fitchett grunted and folded his arms as Neal White stood up and admired his handiwork. A tight, white bandage covered the wound, but on Porter's black leg it looked quite hilarious. He stood there and looked down at it.

'A few more of them and I'll look like a bloody piano.' His knee still felt dodgy, but better than before. He tested his weight on it a few times and, when he felt satisfied, pulled up his trousers and sat back down on the table. 'Listen Guv, the truth is I've got nothing to tell you. He's given nothing away at all.'

Jarvis let out a sigh and closed his eyes for a moment. 'So what are you saying then?' Porter shrugged his shoulders. 'It looks to me like they're going in to kick this off, just like he's always said.'

Jarvis walked around the room for a moment and then looked at Fitchett. 'Well?'

'Well what?'

'What do you think?'

Fitchett gave his customary shrug. 'I don't know, but I'll tell you this much: it took about twenty people to kick things off in Dublin, if that. There's thirty-eight over there and a lot of them are still pissed about what happened down here in ninety-seven. You think about that.' He leant back against the wall and looked up at the ceiling.

'There is one thing you should know, Guv,' chimed in Porter. 'Thanks to dick-head here, they're using my real name.'

'What! Why did you do that?' groaned Jarvis.

Fitchett shrugged his shoulders. 'Why not?' he replied, without looking down from the roof.

Jarvis watched him for a second, before shaking his head and turning to face Fabio. 'OK my friend, this is your call. As far as I'm concerned, we have to go with the idea that they will try to stop the game. But we still do not know why.'

Fabio pushed himself off the wall, walked over and looked at Porter. 'Are you OK?' Porter nodded. 'And you will go back in?' Another nod, slower this time. 'And you?' He turned his head towards Fitchett, who shrugged and lit a cigarette.

'Do I have a choice?'

The Italian took a deep breath and stood up to his full height. 'Then I will get my men to take you back over the other side. But as soon as you have anything which may help us, you must get out. It is very dangerous for you.'

Porter jumped down off the table and grimaced as his leg felt the jolt. 'I'll be OK.'

Fabio nodded and spun away as the fax machine began churning out a sheet of print. He took a brief look at it, gestured to Williams that it was for him and picked up the phone. 'I will call my superiors and I suggest you do the same, Paul. But from now on, whatever happens, we make the decisions. This is our operation now.'

Chapter 16
Tuesday, 26 October
18.00

Terry Porter followed Gary Fitchett out of the patrol car and, without thanking the driver, closed the door and limped across the car park in the direction of the parked Lexus. Within a few moments, Hawkeye and Billy Evans appeared in front of them, both of them looking remarkably concerned.

'You sorted?' asked Evans.

'Yeah, they were all right. Just cleaned it up and stuck on a bandage. Bloody wops, only one of them could speak any English.'

Evans looked at him for a moment and then smiled. 'You OK, Fitch?'

He nodded slowly. 'Poxy spics, fucking place stank of garlic.'

Evans pulled out a packet of cigarettes and offered them around. They all lit up and stood there for a moment, before Evans took Fitchett's arm and led him away. Porter watched him leave and had begun walking to their cars with Hawkeye when the noise of Evans shouting made him turn back. He made a move to hurry over when Hawkeye grabbed him.

'None of our business, son. Just let them sort it out.' He led Porter over and sat him in the Lexus. 'It's getting dark, Terry lad. We'll be off soon.'

'Why? Where we going?'

Hawkeye looked down at him and grinned. 'You'll find out soon enough.'

Jarvis was angrily pacing up and down the small room, a mobile phone pressed tightly to his ear and a long fax hanging out of his other hand. 'Look Guv, I just don't know. At the moment, it looks like I was wrong. From what we know at the moment, and to be honest that isn't much, they'll kick something off tomorrow night inside the ground.'

He stopped pacing and looked at Phil Williams, who was the only other person in the room. The others had left after Porter and were now helping Fabio keep the car park under observation. '... Well he was happy to go back in and the Italians are all over them. If anything happens, they'll get him out ... How can they make a mistake, Guv? He's the only black guy over there.' He sat down on a chair and rested his chin in his hands, his eyes fixed on Williams, who pointed an imaginary gun at his temple, as if to shoot himself.

Jarvis simply looked back, unsmiling. 'Guv, are you going to order me to pull him out?' There was a long pause and then he relaxed. 'Yes Guv. I'll wait to hear.' He closed the phone and put it in his pocket. 'Fucking hell,' he groaned. 'Talk about covering your own arse.' He sat up and rubbed his hands over his face. 'If he had his way, we'd be over there pulling Terry out right now. Thank Christ the Home Office or something have told him that the Italians have asked for him to be left in as long as possible. If there is something set up, they want to know who the contacts are – and he's the only one who can find out for them.' He slapped his knees and stood up and walked over to the kitchen area. 'I need caffeine.'

'Well, what's happening now?'

Jarvis looked at Williams over his shoulder as he poured himself a coffee. 'Nothing ... yet. The DCI can't, or won't, make a decision. He's waiting for something to happen here.'

He picked up his cup and sat down. 'I'll tell you what though, I wouldn't like to be in Terry's shoes at the moment and I'm certainly not leaving him in there a second longer than I have to. Not even Evans is worth that.'

They sat for a moment and then Williams walked over; picked up the fax and studied it for a moment. 'This still doesn't make sense to me.'

Jarvis looked up from his cup. 'What?'

'Well, out of all the cars in the car park, we now know that at least seventeen are registered to Evans, right?'

Jarvis nodded.

'But why use cars we can trace back to him? And have you seen them? On here it just says BMW, Mercedes or whatever.

But they're top-of-the-range jobs. Not rubbish. I just don't get it.'

'And you think I do?' He stood up and walked over to where Williams was standing and took the fax from him. After a quick glance at it, he suddenly gave Williams a slightly quizzical look. 'Could we have been looking for something that doesn't exist?' He handed Williams back the fax and swallowed a mouthful of coffee. 'What if everything Evans told Fitchett is the truth and he really is being paid to take this lot into the city, get things kicked off and then get them all out and back home quickly. That's what they did in Dublin, and we never managed to tug anyone for that.'

Williams looked down at the list and shrugged, as Jarvis went on. 'That's why he's using cars from his garage. He knows they're decent motors and so they'll be quick and reliable. But they're incidental.' He put down his cup and began pacing around, talking more to himself than Williams, who simply stood and watched as his DI struggled with the whole concept that he might have been coming at this whole operation from the wrong angle. 'Remember, he recruited all these lads. He knows them all personally, or at least most of them, and if he had any doubts about anyone, they'd have been cut loose by now, even Terry.'

Jarvis stopped pacing and turned to face Williams. His body language had changed: now he was obviously excited. 'But this lot aren't just fighters, they're top boys. They know how to hit a target and then vanish like that,' he said, with a click of his fingers. 'From what Fabio has told us, we haven't even got the benefit of CCTV here, and so it'll be even easier for them.' He began pacing again. Staring down at the floor and grinning as he warmed to the task. 'He's so fucking arrogant, it probably never even occurred to him that we would get hold of this.' He walked over to the table, picked up his cup and sat down again, a smug look of satisfaction on his face. 'No, it pains me to say it, but I'm beginning to think we've been barking up the wrong tree all along.' He swallowed a mouthful of coffee. 'We keep trying to work out what he's up to, but we already know – because he told us. There never were any drugs. This is all about tomorrow night.'

Williams looked at him and shook his head. 'Then I best give this to Fabio,' he said, picking up the fax and stuffing it in his pocket. 'If this is their case, then everything is down to them now.'

Jarvis looked at him, and if anything, the smile on his face widened. 'That's what the man said. It's their operation now.'

Gary Fitchett came storming across the car park and thumped his fist on the top of the Lexus. 'Cheeky cunt!' he barked, before taking out a cigarette and lighting it angrily. Hawkeye gave Porter a wink and walked off, leaving him sitting half in and half out of the car.

'What was all that about?'

Fitchett looked down and shook his head. 'He's getting twitchy, that's all. Giving me the biggie about bringing a ... you know ... sorry ... oh bollocks.' He looked away and sucked furiously on his cigarette.

Porter looked down at the floor. 'So what's happening now?'

'In about twenty minutes, we're all getting picked up by coach and taken to a bar in the city. There's beer and grub laid on, or something. He'll tell us all about it when we leave here.'

Porter nodded. 'Then what?'

'How the fuck do I know? Back here and crash in the cars again, I suppose. Get ready for tomorrow.'

He turned away and leant against the car but Porter grabbed him and pulled him round and down so they were almost face to face. 'Now tell me what really happened over there!' His voice was angry, barely disguising the fear that was beginning to gnaw away at the pit of his stomach.

Fitchett tried to look away, but was too close and gave up. 'Some of the others have been giving it the large one. You need to be careful. That's all.'

He pulled away and stood up, but Porter climbed out of the car after him. 'What d'you mean?'

The two men stared at each other for a moment. 'Are you fucking stupid or what?'

Porter grabbed him by the collar and pulled him towards him. 'What do you mean?'

Fitchett grabbed his arm and shoved him back against the car. He was angry now, the look in his eyes no longer subdued, but raging. Porter took a step back, he'd seen enough of Fitchett in action over the past couple of years to know that, when he got like this, he usually struggled to keep control of himself. He glanced around and when he saw no one was in earshot moved forward and hissed: 'Look, you stupid cunt, you're a black bloke right in the middle of one of the heaviest England crews anyone has ever put together. If you want me to spell it out, then here it is: this lot aren't your greatest fans and they don't fuck about. If they can, they'll do you. Big time. And they won't think twice about it.'

He flashed another quick glance around and then moved even closer, thrusting his finger into Porter's chest. 'Billy wanted to know if I'd back you up if they started and, fuck knows why, I said I would. But if they find out that you're a copper, they'll do me as well and the only way either of us'll get home is in a box. That's if they can find enough bits.' He gave him a final glare and then moved back a step, before taking another swift glance around.

Porter looked at him for a moment and then sat down in the car. He was scared now and his mind was racing. He'd been in plenty of dodgy situations before, but never anything like this. He felt alone, and in big trouble. He was sure that Jarvis and the others were nearby, but he couldn't see them – and that made it even worse.

The sound of singing broke out across the car park and he stood up beside Fitchett and looked across towards it. *'No surrender, No surrender, No surrender to the IRA!'* The right-wing anthem. He turned his head and looked towards the two police cars still parked by the exit. Bad knee or not, he could be there in less than a minute – and then that'd be it. All over. Screw Jarvis, screw Fitchett and screw this lot. He had himself to worry about and he'd had enough.

He put his arm on Fitchett's shoulder and pulled him round. 'Gary, I'm out of here.'

'What? What d'you mean?'

'Fuck this for a laugh, I'm off, it's too dangerous.'

Fitchett spun round and grabbed him. 'You cowardly wanker, you're going to leave me here to face this lot aren't you?'

Porter shook his head. 'No, you're coming with me. Jarvis is still on the other side of the bridge, we can ...'

Two hands shot forward and grabbed his collar, pulling him forward until he could feel Fitchett's breath on his face and he could see every detail of his eyes. 'Oh no. You're not going anywhere, you bastard. Not yet, not until I say so. I swear, you try and dump me and I'll fucking do you myself!'

The sound of approaching footsteps made them both turn their heads. Walking towards them were two men. Like most of the others, they were late twenties, early thirties, slightly stocky and smartly dressed. Their arrogance walked about ten feet in front of them. Porter hadn't seen either of them before, but Fitchett obviously had. He dropped his hands and pushed Porter back against the car before turning to face them.

'Well, well ...' began the taller of the two, 'lovers' tiff?'

Fitchett pulled himself up to his full height and Porter leant off the Lexus and stood up behind him.

'Fuck me, look what we've got here. You remember these two, don't you Terry? They're part of that little firm we turned over in London a couple of weeks ago. I can't remember who it was ... Orient? Or Brentford?' He shrugged his shoulders, a gesture inviting them to say who they were. Demean them a little. They never took the bait and so he went on. '... Rangers maybe? Oh no, I've got it,' he exclaimed with a click of the fingers and a broad smile. 'Chelsea! Yeah, that was it. How's your boy then? Can he see yet?'

The bigger of the two moved forward. 'Yeah, that's right. And you're the mouthy Brummie from the Globe. I see you've brought your pet monkey with you this time.'

Porter looked at the back of Fitchett's head. He was finding it hard to come to terms with the transformation that had taken place in him. Only a few seconds ago they'd been arguing about their very survival, and now he was the old Fitchett. The one he knew from a hundred away trips. Arrogant, cocky, confident. And very dangerous. The tone in his voice was calm and assured, but he was getting ready. Winding himself up. He looked the two of them up and down and started again. But this time his tone was more disapproving and accompanied by a slow shake of the head.

'I don't know, we'll have to have a word with Billy about this, Terry. He told me that the only people coming on this trip were top boys. But these two can't be top boys, can they? Not the way they ran from us.' He moved his head slightly, as if looking over his shoulder, but his eyes remained firmly fixed on the men in front. Just in case. 'If Billy'd told me there were some under fives coming, I wouldn't have bothered.'

The two men let out an ironic laugh. 'That's what we like about you northerners, your sense of humour.'

Fitchett smiled. 'Well, that's why we like taking on the Cockneys. It always gives us plenty to joke about.'

The three of them laughed, and then the bigger of the two Londoners raised his finger. 'Watch your back son. We owe you, big time, and payback's coming. And you,' he said, pointing past Fitchett at Porter, 'you shouldn't even be here. But we'll sort that out later on.'

Fitchett moved forward. 'How about we sort it out right now? I need cheering up.' But without another word, they turned and walked away. Fitchett watched them go for a few moments and then turned round. 'That's all we fucking need.'

Porter grabbed him again. 'Look, we can be out of here in two minutes ...'

Fitchett's face was a picture of disgust. 'You make me want to vomit. You think I'm walking out of here now? So they can say I bottled it? Fucking forget it. I've never run from a ruck before and I'm sure as shit not gonna start now.'

Porter pushed him away angrily. 'Well screw you. I'm out of here.' He bent down and reached into the back of the car for his bag, but as he did so, a boot shot forward and smashed into the side of his damaged knee. He let out a loud yelp and fell face-forward into the car. 'Jesus Christ!' he shouted, grabbing hold of the steering wheel and pulling himself up. 'What did you do that for?'

Fitchett stood over him, his face sneering down, almost manic. 'I told you, you're not going anywhere.' He looked around to see if anyone had seen what had happened, and then smiled. 'Besides, the bus is here. We've got a party to go to.'

The two men ran out of the small brick building and headed towards the Vauxhall Vectra. 'Where are they now?' Jarvis screamed into the phone as Williams dived into the driving seat, started the engine and pulled away even before the doors were closed. 'Right, wait there. We'll be about thirty seconds.' He closed the phone and inhaled deeply. 'Shit, what's the bastard up to now?'

Williams sped across the bridge and then hit the brakes, slowing the car down to avoid drawing attention to them. 'Where are they?' he asked.

'By the entrance I think, over there.' Jarvis pointed towards the petrol filling site and Williams steered the car towards it. They quickly found Parry and White, and Williams pulled in beside them.

'Where's Fabio?' asked Jarvis, after winding the window down.

'Some of their plainclothes lads have just turned up. He's gone to brief them in the cafe.'

Jarvis nodded. 'And what's happening over there?' He looked over to the far end of the car park. It was getting darker by the second and even though it was fairly well lit, they could barely make out any of the cars they were supposed to be watching.

'An Italian-registered coach turned up about five minutes ago and our lads have started to get on board. Evans must be bussing them in to somewhere.'

Jarvis pushed open the door and got out. If he couldn't see them, they sure as shit wouldn't be able to see him. 'Any sign of Porter?'

Steve Parry got out and walked round beside him. 'No – well, not really.'

Jarvis turned to face him. 'What d'you mean not really?'

Parry screwed up his face. 'Well, the Lexus is parked just over there,' he said, pointing vaguely in the direction of the car park. 'Terry and Fitchett were standing next to it and it looked like they were arguing, but we couldn't be sure. Then two of the targets came over and they spoke to Fitchett, but after it looked like it might get nasty, they left.'

'That's all?'

Parry nodded. 'Yeah.'

Jarvis turned back to look at the dark outline of the coach. He could see the lights on inside and people milling about, but couldn't make out anything specific. He sighed out loud. 'Shit, this is a new one. Where'd you think they're going?'

'Fuck knows,' said Parry. 'It could be anywhere.'

The sight of a man approaching caught his eye and Jarvis turned to see Fabio jogging towards them. 'Did you know about this? The coach?' he asked, slowing to a walk and stopping in front of them.

Jarvis shook his head. 'No, this is new to me. I've got no idea what's happening.'

Fabio took a deep breath and turned his head to look at the coach. 'OK. Well, we will follow it and see where they go. I think you should come with me.'

Jarvis nodded. 'Yes. I think that would be a good idea. But we'd best go in one of your cars. It might be suspicious if we tail them in ours.'

Fabio smiled. 'Of course, but I must warn you, there has already been a bit of trouble in the city. Some of your fans were attacked in a bar about an hour ago.'

Jarvis let out a curse and then reached into his pocket as his phone let out a shrill ring. He listened for a while and then closed it. 'It gets worse,' he said. 'Steve, that was Al Harris. He's had the DCI all over him. It seems like there's about four hundred lads already in the city and more on the way, not including our lot. It's looking like it may well kick off again later on. The Italians have asked for more spotters and, as our part of this operation is over, at least for a while, that means you two I'm afraid.'

Parry let out a curse and looked at Fabio, who was shaking his head.

'I'm sorry, I did not know about that. You must understand, there are many departments in the *Carabinieri:* in situations like this, things happen.'

Parry looked at Jarvis. 'And Terry?'

'The DCI wanted us to pull him, but the Italians have insisted he's left in. At least for the next few hours, or until I decide he's in danger:'

Parry let out a low whistle. 'Nice buck-pass by the DCI. Put all the responsibility onto you.'

Jarvis rubbed the side of his head. He hadn't expected anything less. If the next few days were going to see a lot of trouble, everyone would need to cover their arses. His DCI was no different.

Parry swung round and tapped Neal White on the shoulder. 'We best be off then. Can your lads escort us into the city?' he added to Fabio.

'Of course, I will arrange that at once,' he replied and began speaking into his radio.

Parry looked across at Jarvis who had returned his gaze to the coach. 'Be careful, Guv.'

Jarvis looked round and smiled. He walked over and leant forward, his voice lowered almost to a whisper. 'Don't worry. As soon as I know where they're going, I'm gonna pull him out. And I don't give a shit what anyone says.'

A dark blue patrol car came hurtling round the corner and Fabio waved it over. 'Here, these men will take you to where you need to be. Just follow them.'

Parry climbed into the Mondeo and, with a final wink at Jarvis, followed the Italian police car into the darkness. Jarvis watched them go and then turned to Fabio and Phil Williams.

He was getting cold and began rubbing his hands together for warmth. 'Right, this is your operation Fabio, what do you want us to do next?'

The Italian looked at them and smiled. 'We will follow the coach into the city, if that is where they are going of course. When they stop, then we will see ...'

Jarvis nodded and grinned, but inwardly he felt a growing unease. This was all too haphazard. All this 'play-it-by-ear' stuff. That was no way to run an operation like this. And there was the small matter of Terry Porter to consider. 'We must stick together. If things go wrong, then we must do whatever it takes to get our man out from there. He could be in grave danger.'

Fabio grinned. 'Of course. Leave everything to me.'

Jarvis looked at him for a moment and then glanced at the coach. 'As if I have any bloody choice,' he thought. He turned back to face the Italian. 'I have to ask you two questions: when the coach leaves, is there any way we can get into Evans's Mercedes before they come back? We may learn something.'

Fabio rubbed his chin and shrugged before lifting up his hands and raising his eyebrows. 'We can try, but it is a big risk. We do not know if all of them will be on the coach. And if someone sees us ...'

Jarvis turned crimson with embarrassment at his mistake. Shit, he must be tired to make a fundamental error like that, and now he'd made himself look like an idiot. He stole a quick look at Williams but he was still looking at the coach and wasn't listening. Thank Christ for that at least.

'You had another question ...?'

Jarvis lifted up his hand and scratched the side of his head. 'Yes ... sorry. Where can we get something to eat? I'm bloody starving.'

Part Four

Chapter 17
Tuesday, 26 October
19.30

Terry Porter watched as the city of Rome swept into view before him. Tall, brightly lit buildings passed by on either side as the traffic, a chaotic mixture of flashing lights and blaring car horns, battled to get to wherever it was it was going. Ordinarily, he would have been enthralled by such a sight, but not this time. This time he was terrified, and was struggling to stop himself from shaking. In the seat behind him, Fitchett and Hawkeye were, as they had called it, riding shotgun for him while, further up the bus, Evans was walking around, handing out beers and joking with the others. He'd been doing that since they'd set off. Geeing everyone up and getting them in the mood for the evening he had planned for them. And so far, it had worked. Except for him of course; for him, every single second had been a nightmare. He closed his eyes, his leg hurt like hell – and that bastard Fitchett hadn't helped. As they'd walked to the bus, he'd just followed along a pace or two behind to make sure he didn't bolt for the police cars. Thank Christ he'd been the last one on and the front seat had been empty. He couldn't have handled being made to sit at the back. Someone behind him started singing '*No surrender*', and the rest of the bus quickly joined in, following it up with '*There ain't no black in the Union Jack, send the bastards back*'. He sat there and stared out of the window. Ordinarily, he would never take shit like that. He'd have turned round and sorted out the scum responsible. But not this time: there were too many, and his leg was in agony.

A tap on the head made him jump, and he looked up to see Hawkeye leaning over the chair. 'Fuck me mate, you're nervous.'

Porter closed his eyes and gave his heartbeat a few seconds to revert to something approaching normal. 'That's an understatement mate, but it's not the Italians that bother me,' he said, hooking his thumb towards the back of the bus, 'it's these wankers.'

Hawkeye put a hand on his shoulder. 'Don't worry about them twats, we'll look after you. Here ...' He handed across a cigarette and Porter took it gratefully. He felt strangely relieved by this show of solidarity, and wondered what was going on in the heads of the two men sitting behind him. Whatever it was, he'd decided that Fitchett would pay. One way or another. He took a drag from his cigarette and settled back in his chair as the coach pulled up at a set of traffic lights. For a moment, he considered diving for the door, but knew it would have been a waste of time. He could hardly move his leg now and Fitchett would have been on him like a flash. Then what? Fed him to the animals probably.

A loud thump echoed through the bus and Fitchett turned to his left and spotted a small group of Italian football fans standing across the road. They were hurling missiles at the bus and gesturing furiously for the passengers to get off. He stared at them for a split second and then all hell broke loose behind him. A shout went up and the bus almost tipped over as everyone on board dived over to that side, hammering on the windows and screaming at the tops of their voices.

Suddenly, Billy Evans came flying down the gangway and grabbed the microphone on the dashboard next to the driver. 'Leave it, you wankers! Leave it! Sit down, come on for fuck's sake, sit down!' Gradually, the bus fell quiet and, after a reassuring word with the driver, it pulled away and carried on towards the city centre.

Evans climbed up the two steps from where the driver sat and stopped next to Porter. 'Listen, you bastards,' he shouted angrily, 'there'll be enough of that tomorrow. Just fuckin' jack it in 'til we get there, all right?'

'Where we goin'?' came a shout from the back.

'You'll see. Just settle down and have a few beers, we'll be there in a bit.' He stood there while a general hum of calm conversation returned to the coach, and then began to move back to where he had been sitting.

'Ay Billy!' He stopped and looked up as a thick Yorkshire accent broke out above the din.

'What?'

'I don't mind drinking with wops, but I ain't drinking with no blackies.'

The coach fell into silence and Porter tensed himself, unsure of what he should do next.

'Well I don't see why not, we have to drink with you, you fucking pie-muncher!'

Porter turned his head and looked at the reflection in the window on the other side of the bus. Fitchett was standing up and pointing towards the back. Like almost everyone else now, he was laughing.

Another voice broke out, this time southern, and it was one Porter knew. 'Well fuck me! If it ain't the mouthy Brummie. Where's your pet then, Brummie?'

Porter closed his eyes and took a deep breath. He'd fought against shit like that all his life, and the realisation hit him that if he took it now and did nothing, he'd never be able to live with himself. He exhaled slowly and felt the fear drain out of him, to be replaced by anger. Not just at the scum on the bus, but at Fitchett, Billy Evans, everyone. He grabbed the armrest on the chair and pushed himself up. He hadn't joined the police force for this. He'd joined to help people, to be a good person. And here he was, on a bus with a load of racist thugs heading into the middle of God knew what. Well fuck them, fuck them all. Whatever happened, he'd go down fighting.

Leaning on the back of his seat, he turned round and knelt down on the cushion, taking his weight on his good knee. 'You want some of me, you wanker?' he asked, his calm voice totally at odds with the way he felt. 'Then come and fucking get it!' He knelt there and watched as the two men who had attacked him in the car park got up and came walking down the gangway towards him, their faces blank but filled with hate. They were shouting, but he couldn't make out a word they were saying. All he could hear was the steady thudding of his heart as it threw adrenalin into every atom of his body, preparing him for the ordeal ahead. But he was glad. After all he'd been through in the last few days, he needed to hurt someone, make them pay.

They were almost within striking distance when first Evans, then Fitchett and Hawkeye appeared in front of him, throwing punches and pushing them backwards and away from him.

'Sit down Terry you twat! Just sit down!' Hawkeye barked and, turning, pushed him backwards and he fell, knocking his knee. A surge of pain shot through him and he almost screamed out loud.

'For fuck's sake, what is it with you lot!' shouted Evans above the noise. 'We'll be there in five fuckin' minutes!' Porter glanced up to see Hawkeye standing above him. He was looking down and grinning. 'What a pair of cunts, eh? I told ya, stick with me. We'll do them later on. I'll enjoy that,'

Porter gave him a half-hearted smile and then looked down at his leg. The knock on the knee had clearly caused more damage than he had thought and the bandage was covered in blood. He could see it through his torn trousers.

He looked up to see Billy Evans staring down at him, an anxious look on his face. 'Listen Terry, we'll be there in a bit. I know your leg's fucked and all that, but the second that door opens, you'd better get the fuck out of this bus.'

Jarvis leant forward excitedly and stared out of the window as the back of the coach came into view. He felt totally refreshed after eating, and now that the combined efforts of Fabio and the Italian police had brought them back to within sight of their targets, he felt ready for anything. 'Where are we?' he asked, as if knowing would make any difference.

'This is Via Momentana, the Stazione Termini, er ... the train station. It is this way.' Fabio shook his head. 'I feared this, this is a bad area of Rome. We have many problems here.'

'Such as?' asked Williams.

'Drugs, prostitutes, immigrants, you know. It is the same as any city. We have already had trouble with some of your fans near here, the ones who have come by train.'

Jarvis glanced around. 'Is this where my men came?'

'Yes,' nodded Fabio. 'They are working around here with some of my men.'

Jarvis looked out of the window as Rome passed him by. The wide street was lined with cafes, bars and the occasional police car. He let out a sigh. Usually, he'd have been at the forefront of this whole operation, liaising with the Italians and making sure known troublemakers were spotted and taken out, but he'd been so wrapped up in all this, he didn't even know what was happening. 'What are your plans for dealing with the England supporters?'

Fabio turned and gave a broad grin. 'We have asked your Mr Mellor for advice.'

Jarvis and Williams burst out laughing. When trouble had erupted the last time England had played in Rome, the former Tory MP turned radio DJ and supposed spokesman for fans everywhere had been vociferous in his condemnation of the Italian police who, judging by Fabio's smirk, clearly regarded him with some contempt.

When the laughter subsided, Fabio continued, the tone of his voice more serious. 'We are ready for them – and if they behave, then they will be welcome. But if they do not ... then we will deal with them.'

Jarvis sucked on his teeth noisily. 'Do you know how many are coming?'

'We are expecting about seven thousand, but who knows? It is a big game and many will come without tickets. It could be eight, nine, even ten thousand. We will only know tomorrow.'

Williams leant forward. 'Do you know how many are already here?'

Fabio shook his head. 'We think about one thousand, but it could be more. Many are in bars around here, but others are outside the city. We have provided places for them to stay, for camping.'

Jarvis nodded, his professional curiosity satisfied. Once he'd got Porter out, he'd have more time to get involved, do some spotting of his own. He pulled out his phone and rang Steve Parry but, despite leaving it ringing for a while, there was no answer. He cancelled the call and rang Harris in London. 'Al, anything happening?'

'Nothing at all, Guv. Until something happens at your end, I'm in limbo. I've been helping co-ordinate the surveillance of some of the other Cat Cs. The ones not with you.'

Jarvis nodded to himself. There were hundreds of known hooligans in England and, with a game as serious as this one, they all had to be monitored in case they travelled. With five officers tied up on Operation Legion, the Unit must be stretched to the limit.

'How are the mad, bad streets of Rome then?' Harris asked cheerily.

'You tell me,' replied Jarvis. 'All I can see is traffic. Have there been any reports yet?'

'Yeah, it's been all over Sky News. One of their film crews was attacked earlier and had their gear wrecked. Some of the lads they were filming took exception to the attention.'

'Where were they?'

'Near the station, I think. It sounded as if it was really nasty.' Jarvis flashed a look at Fabio as Harris continued. 'And some England lads were attacked in a bar about an hour ago. By a group of Italians.'

Jarvis chewed his lip for a second. 'What time are you going home, Al?'

'Christ, you know better than that Guv! I'm here for the duration.'

'Good, give me a call if anything big kicks off, will you? And tell the DCI I called, as well. He'd best know I'm still alive.'

They said their goodbyes and Jarvis told the other two about the TV crew.

'It happens a lot here,' said Fabio. 'The fans are fearful of the media these days. They do not want to be seen in the papers. It is too bad for them. That is why most of them wear scarves across their faces.'

Fabio's radio interrupted them and he listened intently for a moment before answering and putting it on the dashboard.

'There is more trouble. Near the Via Veneto. There are many bars there and it sounds bad.'

'Is that far from here?' asked Jarvis nervously.

Fabio shook his head. 'No, it is just along here, on our right.'

'Well that looks like where we're going.' The three men watched as the coach indicated right and turned.

'This is Via Saldra, the trouble is further up.' Fabio pointed and then pulled the car sharply into the side of the road as the coach slowed to a halt and its brightly coloured orange hazard lights began to flash. 'They must be stopping here. This is not good for us.'

They watched in silence as the door opened and a man almost fell out onto the pavement and limped towards the back of the bus, closely followed by Gary Fitchett.

'There's Terry!' exclaimed Williams, leaning forward between the two men in the front. 'Bloody hell, he looks in a bad way.'

Jarvis bit his lip, but said nothing. He was too busy watching the front of the bus as the thirty-eight other passengers poured off and made their way towards a large, brightly lit cafe. A few tables and chairs were scattered outside, but they were empty, and the men went straight through them and into the building. 'What is that place?'

Fabio screwed up his eyes and looked through the darkness. 'It's called Bar San Marco: it is just a simple bar but it has a bad reputation. In the past, we have seen a great deal of trouble here with Irriducibili.'

'The what?'

Fabio smiled and shrugged. 'Sorry, Irriducibili. They are the Ultras from Lazio. Like a supporters' group but with more, erm ... passion. There are two at Lazio, the other are the Vikings, but they are not so bad.' He looked back out of the window and looked towards the bar, a thoughtful expression on his face. 'And also when England came to Rome last time, it was very bad around here.' He lifted up his radio and chewed at the aerial for a moment. 'This would begin to make sense,' he said, an excited tone clearly evident in his voice.

'Lazio have had a strong following from the far right for many years now, right back to II Duce ... Mussolini,' he added, for the benefit of the two Englishmen. 'And there has been some trouble with Irriducibili lately.'

Jarvis looked at him. 'Trouble?'

'Yes. In Italy clubs have always erm ... *chiudono un occhio* ...' He struggled for the words, his eyes registering his frustration. '... Not looked out ... You have a saying for it ...'

'Turned a blind eye!' said Williams excitedly.

'*Si*, turned a blind eye. Yes. They have always turned a blind eye to the Ultras, but now it is getting more difficult for them to do that. Their demands are growing and the clubs must follow the rules of the Federazione di Calcio, which say that they must not deal with them.'

'The Feder ... what?'

Fabio looked at Williams. 'Our association of football,' he said patiently.

'Ah, right. But what kind of demands do they make?'

'Free tickets, and travel of course. At some clubs they very powerful and will demand that certain players are sold if they do not like them.'

'And the clubs go along with that?'

'*Si*. The threat of violence is not unknown if they do not get what they want.'

Williams let out a low whistle. 'Wow. I can't see that happening at Chelsea. Ken Bates scares the shit out of me!'

Fabio turned back to face the front and watched as the group vanished into the cafe. 'Maybe that is who is behind all of this. Irriducibili want to stop the match as a protest. So that the game will listen to them. Yes, that could be it.' He looked towards Jarvis for some kind of endorsement, but it never came. He was too busy looking at Porter and Fitchett, who were standing next to the coach. 'Your officer, he looks in a bad way.'

Jarvis turned his head towards the Italian. 'Yes, he is. And I want him out, right now.' He went to jump out of the car but Fabio grabbed him and pulled him back.

'No, not yet,' he said, shaking his head. 'We must know who else is in there first.'

Jarvis looked at him, his face a picture of shock. 'Are you mental, send a black policeman into a pub full of fascists? They've already given him a hiding; this time they'll bloody kill him!'

Before Fabio could speak, he turned and barked at Williams sitting in the back. 'Phil, get out there and grab him before he gets into that bar.' Williams dived for the door and got out.

'No!' shouted the Italian and began speaking quickly into his radio. A voice answered, but Jarvis couldn't work out if there was any urgency in it or not. Italian always sounded like it was being spoken at breakneck speed to him. Fabio threw down the radio and dived out of the car after Williams, who was walking quickly through the milling pedestrians towards the back of the bus. Jarvis watched him for a second and then flung open the door and stood up. He wanted to run down the road after them but held back. If anyone came out and sussed them now, they were all history.

Porter leant against the back of the coach and watched as the final few men disappeared into the cafe. 'That's it, I'm out of here.'

'You what?'

Porter shook his head. 'I'm not going in there, Fitchett. It's too dangerous. Let's get out while we still can.'

Fitchett grabbed hold of his jacket and pulled him angrily towards him. 'Forget it, filth. You're coming in there with me or I'll fucking do you myself, right here.'

Porter tried to shove him off but the pain in his leg was draining all his energy and he gave up. Almost hanging limply from his clenched fist. A woman looked at them as Fitchett began dragging the weakened body across the pavement towards the cafe, but he returned her look of concern with a glare and she hurried on. 'Come on Detective Sergeant,' he growled, 'you've come this far, let's see what you're really made of, shall we?'

A voice hissed at them and they both looked round. 'Terry, come on, you've gotta get out!'

'Phil! Thank fuck for that!'

Fitchett relaxed his grip and waited until Williams was almost upon them before diving forward and butting the young DC full in the face. The ferocity of the blow sent his head flying backwards, but as he struggled to keep his balance, Fitchett followed up and smashed him in the side of the head with his elbow. The sickening thud made Porter wince, but even before Williams had struck the ground, Fitchett had hit him again, this time a kick full in the stomach, the involuntary wail showing just how much damage it had done. When the body was still, Fitchett looked up and glanced around. Pedestrians were running away from him, their furtive glances failing to disguise their fear or hide their disgust. They had been reading about the English hooligans in the papers all week – and now here they were, fighting on the streets in front of them.

But Fitchett didn't notice them; he never did. Like pedestrians everywhere, from Camden to Copenhagen, they were just scenery. He wasn't interested in them. He turned to walk back to Porter, but a sixth sense developed in a thousand street brawls made him look round as another man came towards him, stopped and held up his hands in mock surrender. Fitchett lifted up his arm and pointed to him, the gesture as threatening as any weapon ever was. 'I don't know who you are but just turn round and fuck off, or you'll get the same.'

He stood for a second, his eyes boring through the man in front of him, daring him to come forward. And then, when he was sure that the message had got through, he took a step backwards and, without taking his eyes off the man in front of him, grabbed Porter and began dragging him backwards. 'Come on you, you're coming with me.' And then they vanished through the doors and into the noise and neon of the bar.

Fabio ran forward and leant down beside Williams. He was just starting to come round and, after shaking his head, sat up with a groan and put his hand to his face. 'Fucking hell, what hit me?'

'We must get you out of here,' urged Fabio. 'Can you move?'

Williams struggled to his feet and they began walking towards the car. Jarvis met them halfway and, without a word, dived under his DC's left arm and lifted him up to speed their progress. When they were safely back inside the Fiat, Jarvis turned angrily to Fabio, but before he could start, the Italian began.

'You shouldn't have done that Paul, it was stupid!' he shouted. 'You could have put my whole operation at risk.'

Jarvis glared at him. 'What do you mean, your operation?'

The Italian looked at him and raised an eyebrow. 'This is Rome, Paul, you have no power here.'

Jarvis almost exploded with rage. 'Listen, one of my officers is inside that bar over there and he's in great danger. I don't give a fuck what you say, we're going to get him out right now.'

Fabio looked towards the back of the car. 'What, you and a policeman who has just been badly beaten? And how do you plan to do that Paul? Like your SAS?'

Jarvis lowered his eyes for a second and took a deep breath to calm himself down. He was right of course, and this ranting was getting them nowhere. It certainly wasn't helping Porter. 'Look Fabio,' he said, using his name for the first time, something that did not escape the notice of either Williams or the Italian. 'He is my man and I am responsible for him. If we don't get him out soon, who knows what will happen?'

Fabio looked at him for a moment and nodded. 'OK. But this area is very dangerous for us now.' He turned and started the car. 'I have called for help, but we must wait – and we have to get the car away from here.'

Jarvis looked up as two police cars sped past and disappeared into the traffic in front of them, their blue lights and howling sirens sending an ominous sense of foreboding through the half-lit streets.

Fabio pulled the car away from the kerb and headed after them. 'I think the next few hours are going to be very bad.'

Jarvis turned and watched as the bar receded into the distance behind him. 'Yeah, but bad for who?'

Chapter 18
Tuesday, 26 October
20.45

Porter felt the door slam shut behind him and he realised that Fitchett had just removed his final hope of escape. Now, whatever happened, he was alone, his fate in his own hands. He finally summoned up the strength to pull away from Fitchett's grip and stumbled over to a table and sat down. He could tell by the pain and the swelling that his leg was getting worse, and after looking at it for a moment he let out a curse and lit himself a cigarette. The hot nicotine helped calm his nerves a little and so he looked up and, for the first time, studied the scene surrounding him. It was all dark brown wood, brass fittings and amber lighting. Classically Italian, and normally quite beautiful, but now plain ugly. Polluted by the forty or so Englishmen demanding drink from the small number of apron-clad waiters who scuttled around them. Shouting and screaming, the noise was oppressive.

'That's why everyone hates the English,' he thought. 'We're all so fucking ugly, we destroy anything beautiful just by being near it.' He glanced towards the door, but Fitchett was still there, glaring at him and making sure he didn't sneak out.

'You all right Terry?' He turned to find Hawkeye standing over him, a bottle of beer in each hand and a freshly lit cigarette hanging grimly from his bottom lip. He held out a drink and Porter took it with a curt nod.

For a second, he considered telling him he was a policeman and that this whole plan had been uncovered, but quickly put the idea aside. He still harboured hopes that eventually he would get out of this in one piece, so why commit suicide now? 'Yeah, as long as I don't have to stand up, I'll be fucking marvellous.'

Hawkeye gave him a grin and then looked up at Fitchett. 'What's up with him? He looks like he's got the right arsehole.'

Porter shrugged his shoulders. 'Fuck knows, PMT probably. Pre-match tension.' They both laughed and Porter started to relax a little more.

'Back in a minute,' shouted Hawkeye above the din and Porter watched as he vanished into the melee before returning to his cigarette and his bad knee. Then he glanced across at Fitchett and remembered what he'd done to Phil Williams outside. Poor bastard; he hoped he was all right. Fitchett would pay for that as well. He suddenly realised that if Williams had been outside, then Jarvis and the others would be as well. And if they'd tried to get him out once, then they would certainly try again. He took a long drink and relaxed a little more. Yeah, it would only be a matter of time now.

The gaunt features of Hawkeye fought their way back through the crowd and stopped beside him. 'Where's Billy? You seen 'im Terry?'

'No. Now you mention it, I ain't seen him since we got here.'

Hawkeye shrugged his shoulders and scanned the crowd. 'Maybe he's slipped out. I know he booked this place special, but I think we were supposed to be meeting some spics here or something.'

'And they haven't turned up?'

Hawkeye shook his head and continued looking around the room. 'No, apart from the waiters, the place was empty when we got here.' A look of relief suddenly crossed his face and he shouted out. 'There he is! Oi, Billy you cunt! Get over here.'

Evans came walking over, a nervous smile on his face. 'All right lads? Just been outside. The old sirens are working overtime.'

Hawkeye's eyebrows flew up. 'What? Is it kicking off then?'

'Think so. They're only over the back somewhere,' he said, gesturing towards the back of the bar.

Hawkeye smiled and took a mouthful of beer. 'Fucking top.'

Jarvis stood beside the car and looked around. They'd travelled about four hundred yards and Fabio had pulled over and parked. The traffic was mad and the noise manic, the drivers hammering their car horns and creeping forward to steal that extra inch, get home that extra millisecond early.

'How do you live with this?' he asked Fabio.

'It is always the same. We are used to it.'

Jarvis shook his head and bent down to look at Williams in the back seat. 'You OK?'

The young DC nodded. 'I'll live.'

The sound of a siren broke out above the general chaos and Jarvis instinctively turned towards it. It was close.

'It is getting tense, yes?'

He looked at the Italian and nodded. He could feel it. The electricity of aggression and fear that filled the air and set the nerves on fire. Airborne adrenalin he called it, and it was like an old friend. He'd felt it at almost every game he'd ever been at. From Stamford Bridge to the San Siro. 'We should get back,' he said, without looking round. 'I don't like the look of this at all.'

'Paul, your phone ...'

He turned round and then reached into his pocket and opened his phone with a shake of his head. He hadn't heard a thing. 'Hello.'

'Guv, it's Steve Parry. Listen, we're with the Italians in a street called the Via Veneto or something and it's all kicked off.'

Jarvis listened intently. Behind Parry's voice, he could hear the all too familiar noise of breaking glass and shouting.

'The Italians have gone in and made some arrests, but the fans around here are really wound up. Some guys from Sky have told me there's been some trouble at the station as well. It's gonna be a long night.'

'Just keep me informed Steve, all right?'

'Sure. Where are you?'

Jarvis looked around. 'Judging by the sirens, not far from you.'

'OK, gotta go.'

Jarvis closed the phone and looked at Fabio. He was speaking on the radio again and so he leant into the car. 'It's going off all over Phil. I've got to get back down there and get Terry out. You'd better stay here.'

Williams struggled out of the car and stood up. 'No, I'm all right, honest. Just a sore head.'

Fabio came round the car. 'The situation is bad. There are now large numbers of local fans coming into the area and one English person has already been stabbed. I think we must get to Bar San Marco quickly.'

They began walking down the road towards the bar, all the time straining to hear any noise above the traffic. Once or twice, they heard the scream of sirens in the next street and at one point Jarvis stopped and looked towards the skyline. He could have sworn he had heard the low rumble of thunder. Or had it been a roar?

Jarvis bit his lip and hastened his pace. He knew that, once trouble started, it inevitably got worse until the police really came down heavy on the hard-core. Usually, the problem was finding where that hard-core were, but this time Jarvis knew exactly. They were inside Bar San Marco. Forty of the worst hooligans England had to offer. They might not have been involved in any trouble yet, but he knew that wherever in the world they were, England fans were instinctively drawn towards each other. It was an inevitable peculiarity, but at the centre were always the Category Cs. The serious players. Like the queen ant throwing out orders from the nest while the soldiers ran around and did all the dirty work. He smiled at the analogy and then thought about Porter and hurried on.

Hawkeye had returned with more drink. 'I don't know about you, but I'm fucking starving.'

Porter sighed heavily: food was the last thing on his mind. He was more concerned with the pressing matter of survival. The door flew open and he looked up as three men came hurrying in. They looked harassed, or was it frightened? – he couldn't make out which – and began talking excitedly to anyone who would listen. Hawkeye moved over towards them, and then quickly returned.

'Fuck me,' he said excitedly. 'It's all kicked off in the next street. The fucking locals are revolting.'

News of the trouble spread through the bar like a whirlwind and, almost immediately, the level of noise rose and the atmosphere changed. It was no longer jovial: now it was aggressive, xenophobic. As if sensing the change, the waiters vanished, leaving the place in the control of the owner, who remained resolutely behind the bar like the captain of some sinking ship.

Porter looked around anxiously. Surely this was the last thing Billy Evans wanted tonight? After all, trouble here would just draw attention to them and that would have a knock-on effect. The police would be all over them before the game tomorrow. More men came into the bar, but this time, as the door swung open, he noticed that there were others milling around outside. He stood up and looked through the windows. There were about thirty lads out there. Talking excitedly among themselves and winding themselves up for later on. But their body language gave away their unease. Their heads were constantly moving. Watching the street for the first sign of trouble. Their expressions an odd mixture of bravado and fear.

'Bollocks,' thought Porter, before turning his head and searching for Fitchett. He was still by the door, talking urgently to one of the men who had just come in. *'No Surrender, No Surrender, No Surrender to the IRA'* ... cunts? He nervously lit a cigarette and looked around. Everyone was laughing except him, getting off on the buzz of violence. This was what they lived for – or was it lived off? The feeling that someone was looking at him made him turn towards the bar, and he caught sight of Evans sitting on a table. He was talking to the two Leeds fans from the car park, and every so often one of them glanced in his direction.

The realisation struck him like a thunderbolt. 'The bastard's setting me up!' That was it. 'Now or never,' he thought, and limped casually towards the door. Fitchett saw him and turned to block his path. The slight shake of his head and the dull look in his eyes said it all. He was going nowhere.

Suddenly, a hand spun him round and he felt a blast of hot, beer-laden breath on his face. 'Where the fuck are you going, nigger?'

'Bollocks!' Jarvis stopped and looked at the group milling around outside Bar San Marco. 'That's all we bloody need.' There were about thirty now, and the doors had been wedged open so God knew how many were inside. The sound of singing broke out again, more verbal adrenalin to build up the courage. The three of them ran through the still slow-moving traffic and across the road, distance the best protection they had for the moment. 'Where the fuck are your men?' he shouted at Fabio.

The Italian grabbed his radio and began shouting into it. 'They are coming, but there is more trouble at the station. They will be some time yet.'

A police car raced by on the wrong side of the road, its blue lights flashing across the front of the bar like lightning. Jarvis pulled out his phone and dialled Parry's number. 'This is going to kick off any minute,' he said nervously to himself. 'Steve! What's happening? ... Oh shit ... No we haven't. He's still in there. Just let me know if they come this way; we're in the ...' He looked toward Fabio.

'Via Saldra.'

'... The Via Saldra ... Oh, it's fucking marvellous. I've got a bar full of Cat Cs and street full of Cat Bs. Couldn't be better.'

He slammed his phone closed and looked at Williams. 'They've just sent the riot police in at the station. Some locals came off a train and steamed straight in to the English. Neal's gone down there. Steve's over the back somewhere, keeping an eye on a group of lads who are playing up.'

Williams let out a whistle and rubbed his head. 'That means it can only get worse,' he said.

The sound of singing made Jarvis look to his left as a group of men came into view. The one at the front was carrying a large Cross of St George above his head like some kind of medieval standard bearer, and they were soon among the others standing outside the bar. 'I think it just did.'

Terry Porter stood face to face with the man from the car park. Everything he despised was there right in front of him and he desperately wanted to strike out, to remove that smirk of hatred and bigotry for ever, but knew that if he moved, he was dead.

'I asked you a question, nigger. Where d'you think you're going?'

For a split second, nothing happened – and suddenly, all Porter could hear was silence. Not just any silence, but that special quiet you hear when something bad is about to happen. Like a car crash or a fight. When everything slows down and it's out of your control.

He stood there, waiting, and then a hand was on his shoulder, wrenching him backwards, ending the moment and releasing the noise. Hawkeye again, shouting and screaming. 'You fucking arseholes! You want some, do ya! Come on then, come on!'

The two men stepped back, angry grins still fixed to their faces. 'Well well. I never had you down as a fuckin' nigger-lover, Hawk.'

The bar was still in a state of happy chaos, but now people were turning to face the stand-off. Hawkeye stood there seething, his eyes almost out on stalks. He grabbed a bottle and expertly smashed the base off on the side of a table. 'That's fucking well it!' he said, his voice no longer manic, but calm and confident. 'I've had enough of you two cunts to last me for ever.' He moved forward, but Fitchett suddenly appeared and dragged him off through the crowd.

'No Hawk! They ain't worth it.'

The two Leeds fans followed, bobbing angrily on their toes and shouting. Urging Fitchett to let him loose. More shouting and the sound of breaking glass. Porter looked over at them and then turned quickly towards the door. With Fitchett gone, he could get out. Escape this madness he had found himself in.

He picked up a bottle and began walking, but felt something on his arm and reached across to touch it. It felt damp and he pulled his hand away and looked at it. Blood. His blood. He turned and looked into the grinning faces of the two Chelsea fans he and Fitchett had argued with at the service station earlier.

One of them held a Stanley blade in his hand. The damp edge glittering under the amber lamps. 'Oops, sorry about that. I'm gettin' really careless with this. I shouldn't even have it really, but y'know how it is.'

Porter looked at him, trying to work out what was going on. He could see he'd been slashed, but his brain wouldn't accept the information. There was no pain.

The hand shot forward and ran across his face, but this time he heard the sound of tearing. Was that skin?

'Oh, sorry. There I go again. I can't help myself.'

Porter went to speak, but the second man moved forward and grabbed him. 'Where's your mate? The mouthy cunt?'

Porter shook him off and moved backwards, clutching his face. He bumped into someone, who turned and shoved him angrily.

'For fuck's sake mate, watch ... Oh Jesus! He's been stuck!'

Fabio looked around and pointed down the road as three sinister-looking vehicles with blacked-out windows came into view. 'Here are the Carabinieri. Now we can clear the bar and find out who is in there.'

Jarvis looked at them. 'Thank fuck for that.'

He watched as they stopped and about thirty men in dark uniforms spilled out, their blue helmets and long black clubs clearly visible even in the darkness of the October evening.

'Wait here.' Fabio ran over and had a brief conversation with one of them before hurrying back across the road. 'I have told them about Terry; they will get him out.'

Jarvis nodded. He'd believe that when he saw it. Over the years, he'd seen enough incidents like this to know that nothing was that simple.

'We will also find out who is in there from Irriducibili,' Fabio went on, 'and end this.'

Jarvis looked around and gave Williams a wry grin. 'How will they do this?' he shouted above the noise.

Fabio turned and pointed. 'They will stop the traffic first, and then close the bar and move the people on. If they see anyone who we know, then they will be arrested.'

'What, from Lazio?'

Fabio nodded. '*Si*. *Or* maybe from Roma. Who knows?'

'And what happens if there is trouble?'

Fabio returned his eyes to the bar across the street. 'Then we will deal with it.'

Porter stood in the middle of the bar, swaying gently. He wasn't in any pain; he just felt completely shattered. But he wasn't going down. No way. It might be taking every ounce of concentration he could muster to stay upright, but he wasn't going to give them the satisfaction of seeing him on the floor. At least his knee had stopped hurting now, which was something. Around him, people were running about and shouting, but he couldn't make out what they were saying. What was it? Something about the police? Maybe they were on to him. He blinked: everything was blurry and out of focus. Was that Fitchett, fighting in the corner with the Chelsea? And where was Billy? He hadn't seen him for a while. Since ... Since when? Five minutes? Ten? Or was it longer? He felt himself being lifted up and sat down against a wall. Someone was kneeling in front of him, talking. Was it Hawkeye? He couldn't make out their faces, or hear what they were saying. And now they'd gone. Well that's nice. He leant back against the hard wood panel. What was all that noise? It sounded like a train. He wasn't on a train, he was in a bar. In Rome. And what was that smell? Like pepper. It was making his nose sting. He'd smelt it before, but where? Christ, he was tired. He'd be glad to get home and into bed tonight. Just have a quick five minutes now, though. No one'll notice.

Terry Porter closed his eyes. And the lights went out.

Chapter 19
Tuesday, 26 October
22.00

Jarvis looked on helplessly as the Italian police made yet another charge at the front of the bar. 'This is fucking ridiculous,' he shouted. 'We have to get in there.' He ran out into the road, but Fabio ran after him and pulled him back.

'The Carabinieri will not know who you are,' he shouted. 'You must be patient.'

'Patient!' yelled Jarvis above the chaos. 'That's a fucking joke. This is a bloody shambles.' He watched as the black sticks rained down on the bodies trying to force their way back through the door of the bar to escape the assault.

'A shambles,' he muttered under his breath, 'right from the start.' Rather than take their time, about ten policemen had simply walked up to the front of the bar and tried to move on the crowd gathering outside. The plan then being to go inside and pull out Terry Porter. But to the fans, this was the place to be. Their corner of little England in a foreign land – and they weren't moving. The situation had deteriorated rapidly and Jarvis had watched while first a hail of abuse, then a hail of glass had rained down on the Italians.

And within two minutes, there it was. Every tabloid editor's dream, England on the rampage. The police had pulled back and then gone in again. This time with the sticks, but the lads outside the bar were veterans. They'd been through all this before. Not just tonight in the backstreets of Rome, but all over Europe. For decades. They had stood firm and more glass was thrown, forcing back the police once again. The third time, the Italians had used gas. Firing it through the windows of the bar in an effort to drive out those inside, but the canisters had been thrown out. And then some of the boys inside had followed. The real headcases. With scarves around their mouths keeping out smoke and the prying eyes of the media. And now it was chaos. And Porter was still inside.

He turned to make his way back to the pavement, but the sight of a TV crew caught his eye and he ran over. 'Are you English?' he shouted.

'Yes, ITN.'

He pulled out his badge and held it up for them. 'Detective Inspector Jarvis, National Football Intelligence Unit. Can you film everything that happens here? I may need it as evidence when we get home.'

The cameraman nodded and returned to his filming.

'What's your name?'

The man holding the microphone turned to look at him. 'Brian Mason. We work out of Grays Inn Road in London. Just ask for me when you get home.'

Jarvis patted him on the back and ran back towards Williams. From inside the bar, a low rumble began and quickly spread to outside, where it grew into a roar. Jarvis had heard that same noise everywhere he'd ever been with the England fans. An ever-present soundtrack to their mayhem.

'They're pulling back, Guv,' shouted Williams, pointing across the street as more men came pouring out of the bar to reclaim the pavement. The blue helmets withdrew, and were followed by a hail of glass as the England fans regrouped. A few of them, given the chance, ran off down the road to escape the carnage, but finding both ends of the road blocked, turned back. Safety in numbers. But most stood firm and fought, embracing the golden rule: 'England run from no one.'

Another roar, and this time some of the England lads ran at the police. Chasing them down the road, but pulling back before they got too far.

'Shit!' exclaimed Williams as more police vans arrived to swell the number of blue helmets. 'It must be about four to one now.'

Jarvis put his hands behind his head, more as a gesture of frustration than fatigue. 'Don't feel sorry for the bastards,' he barked. 'They're getting exactly what they deserve. You just keep your eyes out for anyone we know.'

Williams returned his attention to the front of the bar as Jarvis scanned the street. He was trying to work out what he should do next, but finally resigned himself to the fact that he couldn't do anything but wait. The police began moving down towards the bar again, but this time their tactics had changed. Half of them came across the road and lined up in front of Jarvis, while the others hung back. After a few long minutes, a small snatch squad ran forward and grabbed three or four of the England fans. Dragging them away and into the back of the waiting vans.

Jarvis watched as they repeated the action twice more. It was effective, but ultimately flawed. They were just taking out the people on the periphery – and Jarvis knew better than most that many of them were simply there because, ironically, it was the only place where they felt safe. Even he accepted the fact that, when England were in town, police forces were indiscriminate in their treatment. Anything could happen to anyone. You just had to be English and be there.

He shouted over to Fabio, 'We'll be here all fucking night at this rate,' but the Italian simply held his hand up. He wasn't even listening. The snatch squad moved forward again but this time three men ran from the crowd, a large wooden table held in front of them like a huge shield. They charged at the police, ramming into them and sending them rolling back along the road.

Another roar went up – and this time a large group came pouring out of the bar and sent a hail of missiles across the road towards them. Jarvis and the others jumped as chunks of broken glass flew round their feet and shattered against the wall behind them. He waited until the bombardment had stopped and looked across the road towards the bar. This time the crew had stayed outside and were hurling abuse and gesturing frantically, geeing themselves up for the next attack.

A song broke out and quickly spread right through them and back into the confines of the bar. Angry voices singing '*No Surrender*' and then '*God Save the Queen*' at the tops of their voices. Arms punching the air. It was an incredible sight, broken glass and bravado. Every so often, a lone figure would break out from the crew and strut around in front of the ranks, screaming obscenities and throwing missiles before sinking back into the group, and anonymity. Jarvis looked over at the hordes of camera crews and journalists. They were loving every second of this. It was perfect press. The breakfast-table villains were right in front of them, to be captured for posterity. They'd never live down the shame of it when they got back home, but for now they were invincible, enjoying their fifteen minutes of fame.

Jarvis screwed up his eyes and peered across the road as, from inside the bar, a red light began to glow. A flare came flying out towards them, bouncing along the road and skipping over the chunks of glass and rubbish that were strewn across the tarmac. One of the blue helmets walked over and calmly picked it up, hurling it back. It came to rest against the wall, under one of the broken windows, the bright red mist pouring out of it making the whole scene even more surreal than it had been before, like a kind of Dante's *Inferno*.

Another roar, and the police went in again, batons flailing around and the steady thud, thud of hard plastic on skin and bone. It made him wince, but it worked. The crew drew back again; some got through the door, but others were forced up against the wall of the bar with no escape.

Jarvis watched as more of them were dragged away. Some were clearly hurt, blood pouring from head wounds, yet all were still prey to lone swipes from angry policemen. He shook his head. This was taking too long. More vans arrived at the end of the road but suddenly, as quickly as it had begun, it was all over. The euphoria had simply evaporated, replaced by a grudging acceptance among the England fans that the line had been reached, the point made. The police poured into the bar and emptied it in seconds, shoving bodies out through the door and frog-marching them to the waiting transport, their faces unashamed and arrogant, heads held high. He'd seen it a hundred times. England run from no one.

Jarvis walked across the road, searching frantically for the black face of Terry Porter. A few policemen angrily tapped their boots with their long batons as he passed, unsure if he was friend or foe, but he ignored them and carried on. His head turned from side to side in rhythm with the steady crunching of glass under his feet, looking at the faces being dragged away. Nothing. A man in a bloodied England shirt caught his eye and he stopped to look at him. He was sitting on a kerb, holding the corner of his flag to his head, his face blank and exhausted. Battle fatigue.

An Italian walked up and brought his stick down heavily across the man's shoulders. He yelled out in pain and jumped up. 'You fucking spic bastard,' he screamed. Another thwack, this time across the arm. More expletives. A second policeman appeared and grabbed the England shirt, pulling him round and shoving him backwards up the road in the direction of the crowd of bodies waiting for transport.

The shirt stumbled and fell. Another whack, on the legs, and he was up and moving. No swearing, just speed. Jarvis watched him go and shook his head. 'Animals,' he said to himself, unclear if he was talking about the fans or the police.

A shout caught his attention and Jarvis looked up to see Fabio in the doorway of the bar, gesturing furiously at him. He broke into a trot, stumbling through the debris and into the half-lit bar. It had been blitzed, every stick of furniture destroyed and strewn across the floor.

'Paul!' He turned round to where Fabio was standing. Behind him, a group of medics were working furiously on a man in the corner. 'Oh no!'.

He ran over and knelt down but they pushed him away. 'How bad is he?'

Fabio put his hand on his shoulder, and he stood up. 'He's lost a lot of blood, but they think he will be OK. He was stabbed. Here and here.'

Jarvis stared as the Italian pointed to his arm and his face. Shit, not his face.

'They will get him to hospital, but it must be quick.'

'Guv!'

Jarvis spun round to see Phil Williams in the far corner of the bar. Behind him, more medics were working. 'It's Fitchett!'

Jarvis threaded his way through the debris and looked down. 'He's taken a right battering and has been stabbed in the chest.'

'Will he make it?'

Williams shrugged. 'I don't know. They can't tell me much; their English ain't great.'

Jarvis let out a long sigh. 'It's a fuck sight better than my Italian.'

Fabio called them over. 'They are taking Porter to hospital now. Will you go with him?'

Jarvis thought for a moment and then nodded. 'Yeah, of course. Did anyone get away before you arrested them?'

Fabio shook his head. 'I do not think so. There is a back door, but it is locked. I think the owner went that way. We are taking the prisoners to a place near Fiumicino, the airport. They will be held there tonight until the magistrate can deal with them in the morning.'

Jarvis nodded. 'We must find Evans, and another man who was with him. I think his name is Hawkins. They will know what happened in here.' He ran his hand up the side of his head. It was hard to believe that so much damage had been done in so short a time. 'Fuck it. As long as you've got them in custody, they can stew till the morning.' He went to leave, but turned back. 'By the way, were your Italians in here?'

Fabio shook his head. 'Not that we could find. They may have got out with the owner but...'

'Well it looks like you won't have your riot now,' said Phil Williams.

Jarvis sighed and watched as two stretchers were carried past him. 'Yeah, but look what we've got instead.'

Fabio's radio burst into life. 'There is more trouble at the station. I must go.'

Jarvis nodded quickly. 'Phil, you go with Fabio and meet up with Steve. Let him know what's happened here. I'll be at the hospital. I need to make sure Terry's all right. And then I need to work out what the fuck I'm going to tell the DCI.'

Chapter 20
Wednesday, 27 October
08.45

Jarvis awoke with a start and sat up as a nurse in a crisp white uniform strode past and gave him a grin. Ordinarily, such a thing would have been the stuff of fantasies, but not this time. He felt like shit. God only knew what he looked like. He stood up, yawned and looked around. He was in the middle of a long white corridor. At one end were a set of swing doors and, at the other, some nurses were gathered around a desk talking. In front of him, a brown door carried the universal symbol of a male toilet, while behind, a large set of windows were filled with a set of white Venetian blinds. He suddenly remembered where he was and, more importantly, why. He walked along the corridor to the nurses' station and nervously stood beside it for a second. He had spent much of yesterday in a car with an Italian – but only now, when faced with a small group of females, did his total lack of language skills become a source of major embarrassment. 'Does anyone speak English?' he asked awkwardly.

A middle-aged woman turned to face him. 'Yes, I do. You are the policeman yes?'

Jarvis nodded and she smiled. 'Come with me, I will take you to your friend.' She put her hand on his arm and began to lead him back down the corridor. 'He is not good. He lost much blood, but he will get better.'

Jarvis closed his eyes, let out a sigh and stopped the nurse. 'Can you get me something to wash with please?'

She stopped and her grin became even broader. 'Si.' She led him past the large windows and into a bathroom. 'There is everything in here,' she said, indicating a large cupboard. 'I will be in the room across the hall with your friend.'

Ten minutes later, teeth brushed and freshly shaven, Jarvis walked into the room and looked at Terry Porter. He was a sight. A large white plaster covered the wound on his cheek and a bandage was wrapped around his arm. From his left wrist, a plastic pipe led up to a drip and he was connected to a heart monitor, but the regular beep it was emitting provided an instant source of comfort. The nurse looked up and smiled again. 'I will get a doctor to speak with you,' she said and left the room. Jarvis walked over and sat down, but within seconds the door opened and a young man walked in. His English perfect, with little accent, he introduced himself and studied the chart on the end of the bed. 'Your officer will be OK, but we will need to keep him for a few days. He lost a great deal of blood, a few more minutes and ...' The expression on his face showed Jarvis just how close it had been.

'Will his face be scarred?'

The doctor shook his head. 'Not a great deal. The wound was like an incision from a scalpel, it should heal perfectly.'

Jarvis sighed and half-smiled. 'How is the other man?' he asked without looking away from Porter.

'He is much worse. His ribs are broken and he has a fractured skull, but we are worried about the wound to his chest. I think it may have damaged his heart.'

Jarvis shook his head slightly and looked at the doctor. 'What a stupid waste.'

The doctor nodded. 'I think there will be more trouble today. The match is not for twelve hours yet and already they have deported many Englishmen.'

Jarvis raised an eyebrow. 'Deported?'

'Yes, it was on the radio just now. The Carabinieri have sent over one hundred people back to England. An aircraft left Rome earlier this morning.'

Jarvis dived into his pocket and pulled out his phone, but the doctor moved forward and held his arm. 'No, not in here. The machines ...'

Jarvis apologised and moved towards the door.

'Use the telephone at the nurses' desk. It will be easier.'

Jarvis stopped and turned round. He had to ask. 'Where did you learn to speak such good English?'

The doctor laughed. 'I studied medicine in London and came back to the Policlinico Umberto I last year. But while I was there I watched Vialli and Zola at Chelsea, so I know all about the hooligans – and this,' he said, gesturing towards the bed.

Jarvis smiled. 'Thanks doctor. Thanks a lot.'

Steve Parry was waiting in the Mondeo outside the hospital by the time Jarvis got outside. He dived in and slammed the door. 'Has anyone found out what the fuck is going on yet?'

Steve Parry shook his head and pulled away from the kerb. 'Neal and Phil are at the holding centre now, but it's a right cock-up.'

'What time did the plane leave?'

'Six o'clock. The Italians held it 'til then because they wanted it on the breakfast news.'

Jarvis looked at his watch: 9.10. 'So that's just over three hours ago. Where was it heading?'

'Heathrow; flight time's about two and a half hours. Bit less maybe. I rang Al Harris and he was getting on to Customs to make sure they stopped and checked everyone going through, but it'll be difficult.'

'Why?'

'Because hardly any of them will have passports, will they? If the Italians have sent any of our lot home, all their gear will still be in the cars.'

Jarvis grabbed his phone and dialled, but the battery was dead and he grabbed the one from the dashboard. 'Do we know if any of them were sent home?' he asked as he dialled.

'Not yet. According to the locals, there were a hundred and thirty-seven people put on the plane last night. They've also sent some of them to the local prison and there are about twenty still being held at the airport. Mostly just drunk and ...'

'Al! What's happening ... Right, so they're still being held at Customs ... Good. Look, have we got anyone looking for Evans? ... Then get in a car and get your arse down there. If he was on that plane, I want him held, is that clear? Good. If you need help, take the DCI ... Right, let me know what happens.' He turned the phone off. 'You got a lead in here?'

'Yeah, in the glove box. What's happening?'

'They're holding them at Heathrow for now, but apparently the place is in chaos,' he said as he plugged the lead in to charge his phone. 'Al reckons that another four to five thousand fans are on their way here and a load of them are flying through Heathrow. The poxy press are all over them.'

'How's Terry?'

Jarvis looked round, surprised at the question. It seemed totally out of place. 'He'll be fine. I don't think he'll be doing me any favours for a while, though.'

'What did the DCI say when you told him?'

Jarvis let out a low laugh. 'Thrilled to bits, he was. An officer in hospital and a very expensive operation fucked up. And that was before all this. He'll be having a bloody seizure.'

'Not down to us though, is it?'

'D'you think that really matters?' said Jarvis.

'Still, at least they've managed to keep the press at bay. The last thing we need is this coming out.'

'What did they tell them then?'

'They said his name was Edward Sampson or something. That'll keep them off the scent for a while.'

Jarvis looked out of the window as Parry headed out of the city towards the airport. 'Listen, once you've dropped me off, take Neal and get back to the car park. I don't give a shit what Fabio says, I want you to get into that Merc and see what you can find, OK?' Parry nodded. 'There's got to be something in that motor that we can pin on the bastard. 'Cause if there ain't, he's gonna get away with this.' He sat in silence for a moment and suddenly realised he was starving.

Jarvis threw open the door to find Fabio walking down the corridor towards him. 'Paul, I am so sorry. I do not know what has happened.'

Jarvis stopped and put his hands on his hips. 'You told me that this was your operation and now you say you don't know what happened. How can that be Fabio? Tell me.'

The Italian took his arm and walked him through a door and into a large room full of tables and the warm smell of coffee. Some men in uniform were eating and gave them an indifferent stare before returning to their food. The two men walked over to a servery and took some food and coffee before sitting down at a table.

'Paul, as I say, I do not know how this happened. When I left you, we had to deal with more trouble at the station and it was almost two o'clock before things were quiet. Then, I went back to my office, and home.' He took a mouthful of coffee and sighed gratefully. 'This morning, I had a call that this was going to happen – but by then it was too late ...'

Jarvis looked at him in astonishment. 'Hang on, are you telling me that the decision was taken without you knowing?'

The Italian nodded eagerly. 'Yes, by someone from the government. It was political. After all, why should we Italians pay for this? They are your hooligans, you deal with them. Come on Paul, you know that is what happens.'

Jarvis bit into a roll and chewed. 'But how can they do that without you? This was your operation.'

Fabio took a bite from a bread roll and shook his head. 'The prisoners were in the control of the Carabinieri, not me.'

'But you're from the Carabinieri.'

Fabio shook his head again. 'No Paul. I am from La Polizia, the state police. The Carabinieri are the military police. There are also Vigili-Urbani, who are the municipal police and we have another force who look after financial matters such as tax fraud. It is not usually a problem, but in a situation like this, with so much happening ... Well, you know. Things become confused.'

Jarvis shook his head in bewilderment. What a way to run a fucking country, he thought. 'Look, were any of the men detained last night deported this morning or not?'

Fabio nodded. 'Yes. From what I have been told, almost all of them. There are a few being held in Regina Celi, which is the prison here in Rome, but the others have gone, yes.'

Jarvis scratched the back of his head. 'Do we know if any of our lot are in prison?'

'No, I will take you there now and we will find out. But I must warn you Paul, it will be difficult to do anything today. After last night, we are expecting a great deal of trouble today and every policeman in the city is on alert for the game.'

'What, from all four police forces?' asked Jarvis sarcastically.

Fabio laughed. 'Come on, I will take you to the prison. By the way, are you going to the game tonight?'

Jarvis looked at him and bit his lip. The realisation hit him that, whatever happened now, for him and his men, this operation was all but over. He might well have missed Billy Evans, but at least if they had been planning anything, be it a drugs run or a riot, that had almost certainly been averted. That was something, he supposed. He looked up at Fabio and smiled. 'Well, it'd be stupid to have come all this way and not go, wouldn't it?'

Al Harris watched as the first of the men deported from Italy emerged from the arrivals lounge at Heathrow Airport. A thousand flashes illuminated the scene as the usual media scrum began, eager journalists desperate for their story. Some of the men came out with their heads covered, others with theirs held high, screaming about police brutality and pleading their innocence. Harris watched for a while, and then walked back into the customs hall and picked up the phone. After a moment, a voice answered and he took a deep breath. 'Guv, it's Al. From what I've seen, most of the lads you photographed at the hotel in London were on the plane, so I can only assume the lads who were with them were on it as well.'

'Was Evans on it?'

'No Guv, and neither was Hawkins.'

Jarvis and Fabio walked into the small room and smiled. 'Hello Graham, how are you?'

Hawkins looked up, surprised to hear an English voice in an Italian interview room. 'Who the fuck are you?'

Jarvis held out a packet of cigarettes and a lighter. Hawkins took them both. 'I'm DI Jarvis of the NFIU.'

Hawkeye shrugged and smoked silently.

'Tell me what happened last night.'

Another shrug. 'We were having a quiet drink and the wops came in, battered us all and nicked a few. That's it really.'

'Why did they nick you and not deport you with the others?'

'How the fuck do I know? Ask them.'

Jarvis sniffed and sat down. 'They say you threw a bottle and then attacked a policeman.'

Hawkins laughed. 'Bollocks.'

'That's what they're saying,' said Jarvis. 'Of course you know what that means, don't you?'

'No, but I suppose you'll tell me if I wait long enough.'

'You're going inside an Italian nick for a while.'

Another laugh. This time louder. 'Am I fuck. You're Old Bill so you know the score. They'll give it a few days and then kick me out. Get themselves a bit more press about how the English caused them so much trouble. It's all about propaganda – and if you don't know that, then you're in the wrong job, mate.'

Jarvis looked at him and smiled. He was probably right. 'How did you get here Graham?'

'Train.'

'Who with?'

'A few lads. Don't know all their names.'

'You're lying.'

Hawkeye looked at him, his face a picture of feigned surprise and indignation. 'That's not very nice, Inspector. Calling me a liar. I pay your wages you know, I deserve a bit of respect.'

Fabio let out a low snigger from the corner, but Jarvis went on. 'Cut the crap Hawkins, we know you drove down, we know why and we know who with.'

'Well if you know so much, why ask me all these bloody questions?'

'Where's Billy Evans?'

'Who?'

'Billy Evans. The man you drove down with.'

Hawkeye looked at the ceiling and slowly shook his head. 'No ... don't know who you mean.'

Jarvis stood up and leant on the table. 'Don't waste my fucking time, Hawkins.'

'Why not? According to you, I've got plenty.'

'Just tell me where he is.'

'Why? What's this bloke Evans supposed to have done then?'

Jarvis let out a huge sigh. 'Are you going to tell me where he is, or not?'

'No. In fact I don't think I'm gonna say anything else until I've seen a brief.' Hawkeye looked over towards Fabio. 'I take it you have a legal system here?'

Jarvis realised he was wasting his time and walked towards the door but stopped as Hawkins called him back. 'Inspector ...'

'Yes?'

'Thanks for the ciggies.'

'So ... where to now Paul?'

Jarvis scratched his head and reached into his pocket for his phone. He switched it on and looked at Fabio. The shrug of his shoulders said it all. 'Well, if he's not here and he's not back in London, then somehow, he must have got away last night. All we can hope is that we can spot him tonight or when he goes back to pick up his car.'

'Assuming he goes to the game, can we find out where he will be sitting?'

Jarvis let out a stifled yawn. 'Only if we can get hold of one of the tickets. They should all be in the same block. Did Hawkins have his in his effects?'

Fabio shook his head.

'Then it must still be in the Mercedes. Hopefully Steve Parry has managed to get into it. If not, we'll get the keys to the Lexus from Terry Porter and do it that way.' His phone let out a bleep to alert him that he had a message and he keyed in the number. It was Parry, asking him to call urgently. He dialled again and waited for a moment before the call was answered.

'Steve, it's Paul Jarvis. Listen, Evans hasn't been deported and he wasn't in the nick. At some point today he's going to have to get back to the Mercedes to get his stuff so hold back and keep an eye on it OK?'

'But Guv, didn't you get my message?' he replied, the anxiety in the voice clear to hear.

'Yeah, just now, that's why I'm calling.'

'No Guv, the Mercedes has gone.'

'What?'

'I said the Mercedes isn't here.'

Jarvis looked at Fabio. 'But how ... Didn't the locals see anything?'

'I think they did, but they don't speak very good English. Anyway, that's only half the problem.'

'Why? What d'you mean?'

'Well Guv, from what I can make out, and I might be wrong because this place is rammed out with England fans ...'

'For fuck's sake Steve, spit it out!' Jarvis said urgently.

'Sorry Guv, but from what I can make out, the Mercedes isn't the only car that's gone. They all have.'

Jarvis stood in the car park and glared at Fabio. They had arrived at the service station about twenty minutes ago and, after a frantic search, he had grudgingly accepted that what Parry had told him was true. 'How the fucking hell can your officers have missed twenty cars driving out of here when they had the registration numbers and the make of car? Tell me please? Because this operation has been fucked up from the moment you took it over'

Fabio moved forward angrily. 'No. *Your* operation was to follow a man who you suspected was planning to import drugs to England. *You* were wrong. *My* operation was to act on information you gave me and prevent a riot at the game tonight. I have done that.'

Jarvis let out an angry sigh. 'Your men were supposed to monitor this car park.'

'Yes, and they did. They were told to watch the car park and report when the coach came back, but of course, it did not come back.'

'But how did they miss all the cars leaving?'

Fabio let out a loud, ironic laugh. 'Look around you, this place is full of cars. Do you know how many passed through here last night? Hundreds, and many of them were English. There were also a number of fights here to deal with and ...'

Jarvis sighed and held up his hands. 'All right. I get the message.' He looked at his watch: 12.35.

'Guv?' Jarvis looked around to find Steve Parry standing next to him, an expression of bewilderment on his face. 'Aren't we missing the obvious here?'

'What?'

'Well how did he do it?'

'Do what?'

'How did he shift twenty cars if he was on his own?'

Jarvis looked around at the car park. It was full of Englishmen resting before they made the final leg of their journey to Rome. 'Fuck knows,' he replied. 'Maybe he just paid some lads to take them into the city and then drive them home tomorrow. I don't know.' He rubbed the back of his head and shrugged his shoulders. 'But, more importantly, where's the bastard gone now?'

Part Five

Chapter 21
Friday, 29 October
10.30

DCI Allen stood facing out of his office window. Jarvis could feel the glare even though he was sitting behind him, and it was making him feel very uncomfortable. Something not helped by the fact that he was totally shattered. After all, he and the others had only flown back late last night, having spent Wednesday evening and most of yesterday driving around Rome trying to spot Evans and the Mercedes – without success.

'So after all this time and effort, all we've ended up with is one officer in hospital, our informant on a life support machine, and, even if we could find our main target, nothing we can really charge him with.'

Jarvis looked down at his shoes. 'No Guv. But I'm hoping Terry Porter will come up with something when he gets home.'

'What about conspiracy?'

'To what Guv? I doubt we would get anyone to testify against him. Without that, it would never even get to court.'

'Has Evans turned up yet?'

'No, we tried to spot him at the game, but it was a waste of time. He could have been anywhere. I've got Customs keeping an eye out for him now. Chances are he'll come back through Dover or the tunnel. They'll notify us when they pick him up, and we'll see what he's got to say.'

Allen stood still for a moment and then turned to face his DI. 'So, all in all, this operation has been a complete waste of time then. You've got no evidence of anything and, if you were honest, you haven't even got a bloody crime to investigate. The assaults are down to the Italians.'

Jarvis's silence said it all and Allen moved over to his desk and sat down. 'How is DS Porter?'

'I spoke to him just now, he's fine, Guv. He'll be home in a couple of days. The Italians have interviewed him about the assault and he says he can remember who stabbed him, but there isn't much they can do now and we can't do anything. It'll just come down to his word against theirs.'

'And Fitchett?'

'Not so good,' said Jarvis with a shake of his head. 'He's still unconscious. He took a savage beating.'

'Have his family been informed?'

'Yeah, they've flown out to be near him.'

'How much do they know?'

Jarvis shrugged. 'Very little. They don't know he was working for us, if that's what you mean.'

Allen nodded grimly. 'Let's keep it that way. We've wasted enough time on this, I want it wrapped up today and everything handed to Special Branch. Write up your report and get it on my desk by this afternoon.'

Jarvis paced angrily up and down the incident room. He didn't take bollockings easily, and having to sit there while Allen ripped him apart had been a very uncomfortable experience. 'Right,' he said, spinning round to face the men in the room. 'Now that we've all recovered from our little break, we need to go over exactly what happened. If there's anything we missed or can pin on Evans, anything at all, I want to know.' He looked at the three men sitting in front of him: Harris, Parry, and White. With the exception of Al Harris, they all looked shattered, but that was too bad. At least Williams would get a rest: he was still in Rome, sorting out a way to get the unmarked police cars transported home.

Jarvis clapped his hands together to focus their attention. 'And for good measure,' he added, 'the DCI has just told me that this operation is being wrapped up this afternoon.'

'What about Terry and Fitchett?' asked Parry.

'Down to the Italians. We'll help them if they need it, but there's nothing for us to investigate. It was out of our jurisdiction. So ...' He looked around the room, waiting for a response.

'Well,' began Harris, 'I've interviewed a few of the lads who were deported, but they're all saying the same. That a mate lent them a car and they drove down. Apart from that, all they're doing is moaning about losing their stuff.'

'OK, then let's focus on the cars. Evans had twenty motors in Rome and now he's got no drivers, so how's he going to get them home? Transporter maybe?'

'He could just get some other lads to drive them back. Bung 'em a few quid,' suggested Neal White.

'OK, well let's make sure that they get stopped and checked out when they come back. Has that list been sent to Customs?'

'Yes Guv,' said Neal White. 'But they're not that confident of picking them all up. Twenty cars is a fraction of what comes across the Channel every day, especially if it's in dribs and drabs.'

Jarvis nodded. 'OK, get on to the ferry companies and Eurostar. If Evans books a ticket, I want to know.'

'Already done it,' said Harris.

'Good. Steve, you get to Evans's garage and see if you can find anything out. Take Neal with you.' He looked around the room. 'Have we missed anything? Anything at all?'

Parry and White shook their heads.

'Al?' Harris was staring into space, running something over in his head. 'What is it Al?'

Harris snapped out of his daydream and stood up. 'OK, bear with me a minute. Let me run something past you.' He walked over to the board and turned to face the others. 'We've assumed two things right from the start. That Evans was either staging a riot or importing drugs, right?'

Jarvis nodded slowly, unsure of where he was leading.

'But we've got no real evidence to support either of those, have we?' He looked around excitedly. 'The only proof of any so-called riot came from Fitchett, but no one found any Italians in the bar, did they? And your mate Fabio came up with nothing to link Evans with any political group, did he?'

Jarvis shook his head. 'Get to the point Al.'

'OK, OK. What if there never was any riot? It was all a front. The same with the drugs. That came from you, Guv. But it was just a hunch, you had no evidence to support it, did you?'

'No,' Jarvis conceded, 'but what are you getting at?'

Harris looked at him, a broad smile on his face. 'It's the cars.'

'Well, what about them?' interrupted Steve Parry.

Harris turned to him. 'It's the fucking cars. Look ...' He turned to the board, grabbed a marker pen and began drawing as he spoke, as if to illustrate his case. 'He took twenty cars to Italy, with twenty drivers. All the drivers got deported, leaving twenty cars and no drivers, yes?'

Jarvis moved closer and watched the saga unfolding on the board. 'Go on,' he said.

'We're waiting for the cars to come back – but they're not coming back. They never were! That was the whole point.' He stopped and looked around the room. 'We've just sat back and watched while he's smuggled twenty stolen motors out of the country, right under our noses.'

Jarvis looked at the board and smiled. 'It's a good theory Al, but it's wrong. All the cars were registered to Evans. What could he possibly have to gain by exporting his own cars? It makes no sense.'

'Insurance scam,' said Neal White.

Jarvis brushed the comment aside. 'What, report twenty of your own cars stolen on the same day? No insurance company would pay out without a major investigation.'

Harris looked at him and grinned. 'It's much more subtle than that.'

Jarvis looked at him and smiled. 'Well, come on then, Detective Sergeant. We're all ears.'

'OK, listen,' he said, the smile growing ever broader on his face. 'The only proof we have that they were his cars came from the DVLA in Swansea, right?'

'Well, ain't that proof enough?' asked White.

'No. I worked with the stolen vehicle squad for a while and they told me how easy it is to fool them. All you do is steal your car, right? Once you have that, then you find a second car identical to the first, and find out who the owner is.' He looked around excitedly. 'It's not hard, a bit of chat, ask the neighbours, that kind of thing. Once you have a name, you get a forged log book made up and send off the change of ownership slip to the DVLA. They send you a new log book, you make up some plates, stick them on the stolen car – and hey presto. As far as anyone is concerned, that's now your car.'

Steve Parry shook his head. 'It can't be that simple, what about the chassis numbers?'

Harris laughed. 'When you bought your last car, did you check the numbers matched the documents? Of course you didn't, no one does.'

Jarvis shook his head. 'No Al, you're wrong. If he was ringing cars, he'd never use his own name – because if anything happened, we'd trace them straight back to him.'

Harris shook his head. 'But that's the beauty of it. Look, he was sending out twenty lads right? He knew and trusted them all, that's why he asked them to go. But it doesn't take Einstein to guess that at least one of them would have been spotted by us at some point and we'd have run a check on the motor he was in. This way, it doesn't come back as stolen, it seems perfectly legit. And if anyone asks why our man is driving someone else's car, all he has to do is give them a letter of authority from Evans which, I bet a pound to a pinch of shit, he'd given all of them.'

'And in any case,' added Steve Parry thoughtfully, 'it was only a one-way journey.'

'Exactly, even less chance of getting picked up.'

'But why take them abroad, why not just sell them on here?'

Harris turned to Neal White. 'Because here it wouldn't work. He'd have to give them false identities and all that bollocks. That means hassle and time. Both of which would eat into his profits. This way, he uses his head, bungs some lads a few hundred quid to do his dirty work and, within two days, hands over twenty luxury motors, takes off the false plates and collects a small fortune.'

Neal White stood up and stared at the jumbled mess on the board. 'But where would they have been taken on to? The rest of Europe drives on the right.'

Harris looked at him and smirked. 'Ah, the innocence of youth. If you bothered to look it up, you'd find that there are plenty of countries who drive on the left like we do: Japan, South Africa, Pakistan, Malta, Cyprus, Australia, there are loads. Cars like these, they're worth a fortune abroad and were probably stolen to order. They could be anywhere by now, even the Middle East.' He reached over and patted the young DC on the head. 'Have you any idea what the estimated value of stolen and exported cars from Britain actually is, young Neal?'

White pushed his hand away and laughed. 'No, but with your age and experience Sarge, you'll be able to tell me.'

'You cheeky git. It's actually in the region of thirty million a year. Not to be sniffed at.'

He turned to Jarvis and shrugged his shoulders. 'Well? What d'you reckon, Guv?'

Jarvis sat down and rested his chin in his hands. He had to admit, the basic idea made sense. 'I like the idea Al,' he said. 'But there's a fatal flaw in your plan.'

Harris gave him a blank look and shrugged his shoulders. 'What?'

'Well, once he's ripped off the identity of twenty cars, their owners are effectively running around in cars which aren't registered with the DVLA right?'

Harris nodded and the others turned round to face their boss. The joy of seeing someone else's theory destroyed was something never to be missed.

'So what happens when they sell them on or have to tax them? It'll all come out and the path will lead straight back to Evans, won't it?'

Harris stared at him for a while and then grinned. 'I never said it was perfect, did I?'

The room exploded into laughter – and when it subsided, Jarvis held up his hand. 'I like the idea though, Al. And if he was using a false name and address, it would probably work.'

He tapped the side of his nose with his pen and then dropped it onto the desk. 'OK, if he turns up with the cars we've been wasting our time, but until he does, we've got nothing else to think about so we may as well give this some thought. Al, get on to the stolen car boys. Tell them what we've got and see if they can come up with anything that makes more sense.' Jarvis got up and began pacing around the room. 'And while you're at it, find out if they've got anything on our boy. You'd better give them the list of the motors as well, and see if any cars similar to the ones he took to Italy have been stolen over the past six months or so.'

He put his hand on Parry's shoulder as he walked past. 'Let's do some digging here. Steve, get on to the DVLA and find out when these cars were registered to Evans. And while I remember, get on to ITN. I asked them to film the trouble at the bar for me. The guy you need to speak to is called ... Shit. I can't remember, it's Brian something. Anyway, I want that film. Neal, you go to Romford and have a root around Evans's garage on your own. See if anyone knows anything.' He stopped pacing and surveyed the office. 'Of course, if this does pan out in some way, it means that all the lads who were deported were set up.'

Harris gave him a broad wink. 'Forty Cat Cs in a bar in Rome, and someone starts trouble. There's no way the riot police could get in without a fight. Especially if they've been fired up by someone.'

Parry gave a low sigh. 'If you think about it, getting deported, or at least a spell in prison, was almost inevitable.'

Jarvis began walking around the room again. 'Evans could have started the trouble himself and then slipped out the back door with the owner before it all turned really nasty.'

'In that mess, no one would have noticed either,' added Parry.

Jarvis stopped and turned to Harris. 'If you're right Al,' he said wearily, 'poor Terry never had a fucking chance.'

The room fell silent and Jarvis walked over towards the door. 'OK, let's get going on this and see if Al's right. I'd better have a word with the DCI and see if he'll give us some more time. Maybe we're getting somewhere at last.'

Neal White sat and stared across the road at the front of W. Evans Executive Motors Ltd. It was exactly how he had imagined it would be. A typical second-hand car site, all whitewashed walls and bright bunting. To the front, a large forecourt held a very desirable mix of about thirty Mercedes, BMW and Jaguar saloons plus a few 4 x 4 s. To the rear, a large glass-fronted showroom held even more cars. He could see at least one Porsche, two BMW convertibles and another Jaguar, this one an XK8. With a wry smile, he climbed out of his car and walked across the road to the forecourt. Close up, the place looked impressive, the cars immaculate. He looked over towards the showroom and, seeing two men sitting at a desk inside, headed towards it.

'Morning.'

They both looked round and smiled at him as he came through the door. Archetypal second-hand car salesmen. Dark suits and bright ties. 'Morning sir, can we help you?'

He reached into his pocket and pulled out his warrant card. 'Yes, I'd like to see Mr W. Evans please.'

One of the men got up, the smile fixed to his face. 'I'm sorry sir, Mr Evans is on holiday. We're expecting him back on Monday. Can I help you with anything?'

'I don't know. We'll see, shall we?' He turned away and looked at the XK8. 'Isn't that beautiful?'

The salesman was beside him in a second. 'It certainly is. Ninety-six model, sapphire blue with a cream leather and walnut interior. Air conditioning, special eighteen-inch alloys and a full service history. A snip for that price as well.'

Neal White looked at the windscreen and laughed. 'Thirty-two thousand! Do you know how many years it would take me to save that up?'

The salesman looked at him, his fixed smile not dropping for an instant. 'I can only imagine, officer,' he said.

'Do you mind if I wander around a little, get a feel for the place?'

The salesman opened his arms out wide. 'Of course not. Feel free. If there's anything you need, then just ask.'

White thanked him and turned to leave, but the man sitting at the table called him over. His face was a picture of smugness.

'We're a bit full at the moment, so we've had to put some cars round the back. There's a few trade-ins as well. They'll be more in your price range.'

'Thanks,' said the young DC, ignoring the sarcasm. 'But I'm not actually in the market for a car just now. I get one with the job.'

The man at the desk cocked his head to one side. 'Yeah, but those blue lights must be a killer with the birds.'

White let out a hearty laugh and walked over to the door. He pulled it open, but stopped and turned back. 'There is one thing you can do for me.'

'Please, just ask.'

'Could I see the log books to some of these vehicles?'

The salesman looked at him thoughtfully for a moment and then walked over and pulled the door open. 'I'd love to help officer, really I would,' he smarmed. 'But I'd have to speak to Mr Evans first. That is unless you've got a warrant?'

'Why would I need one?'

The salesman held out his arm, a subtle gesture but very effective. White nodded discreetly and walked through the door as the salesman added, 'I'm just the hired help here, officer. You wouldn't want to get me into trouble, would you?'

Neal White stopped and looked at him for a moment and smiled. 'Perish the thought.'

The door slammed shut behind him and he walked out across the forecourt. He was about to cross the road to his car when a thought struck him and he turned back. He could see the two men were sitting back at their desk. One was on the phone and the other was looking across the car park at him, but he wasn't interested in them. It had been staring him in the face and he'd almost missed it. He hurried across the road and jumped in his car, a smug smile of satisfaction on his face.

Jarvis snapped his phone shut and grinned across at Harris. 'Well Al,' he said cheerily, 'it looks like you may be on to something. Neal White reckons that Evans's forecourt is full to bursting.'

Harris looked across and furrowed his brow. 'So what?'

Jarvis shook his head and grimaced. 'Bloody hell, call yourself a copper? Last Sunday he took twenty cars to Italy: how can they have come from his garage?'

'Maybe he kept them somewhere else,' said Steve Parry, 'or his staff have simply replaced the stock.'

'Maybe, but maybe not.'

Jarvis rubbed his hands together excitedly. 'OK, I've got to see the DCI in five minutes so what've you got for me?'

Steve Parry picked up his notes and began flicking through them. 'I spoke to the DVLA: the twenty target cars were all registered to Evans over the past ten weeks. I also asked them how many others were registered in his name, and they told me that there are two. A BMW Cabrio and a Range Rover.' Jarvis moved around the office rubbing his hands. 'Probably his wife's car and his run-around.'

Jarvis nodded. 'OK, Al...'

Harris stood up. 'I spoke to the stolen car squad: they've got nothing concrete on our boy, but they know about him. His name's been linked to a few things in the past, but nothing worth investigation.' He briefly studied his notes and then continued. 'As regards stolen cars, I gave them the list of target motors and they burst out laughing. It seems most of them are on their top twenty most nicked motors register. But they'll have a look and get something to us in a couple of hours.' He looked across at Jarvis and gave him a grin. 'They liked the basic idea though. Asked me if I wanted to go and work for them.'

'What as?' laughed Steve Parry.

Jarvis watched them and smiled. It was good to have a bit of banter. It relieved the tension. He'd almost lost this whole operation – but now, maybe, he had a chance of getting it back. Regain a bit of credibility. He waited until the laughter had subsided and spoke up again. 'Right. Al, get back on to the DVLA and get a list of the previous owners of those twenty cars. When you have it, track them down and speak to them. I want to know everything there is to know about those cars.' He looked at his watch: it was almost three o'clock. 'I'd better go and see the DCI.'

Jarvis stood beside his DCI and stared at the London skyline. He'd briefed him on everything they had, and now he was waiting for a response. It wasn't long in coming.

'When are you expecting Evans to make an appearance?'

Jarvis shook his head. 'No idea Guv. If he's driving on his own, it could be three or four days. If he flies, he could be home already. We've alerted the airports as well now. They'll be keeping an eye out.'

'Good,' said Allen. 'But you say the men at his garage are expecting him on Monday?'

'Yes Guv.'

Allen sighed and looked away from the window. 'How much store do you put by this stolen car idea, Paul?'

Jarvis turned as his DCI sat down and motioned him to do the same. 'I don't know, to be honest. It sounds plausible, and some of it fits, but until we speak to Evans, we can't know anything for sure.'

Allen sighed and looked across the desk. 'OK Paul, I'll give you a week. If nothing has turned up by then, hand the lot over to the stolen car unit and let them deal with it.' Jarvis was about to argue, but decided against it and stood up to leave. If Evans turned up, or Terry Porter came up with something, that would be plenty of time.

A knock made him turn towards the door and he was surprised to find Al Harris standing there. He looked crestfallen, almost pale. 'Guv, we've just had a call from Italy. Gary Fitchett died from his injuries about an hour ago.'

Chapter 22
Saturday, 30 October
09.00

Jarvis and Harris stood in the arrivals lounge at Heathrow airport and surveyed the people pouring through into the concourse. 'There they are,' said Harris, and began walking over to where their two colleagues were standing, searching the crowd for a friendly face. Jarvis hung back for a second and then, with a sigh, set off after him. He wasn't looking forward to this at all.

'Hello Guv. How's things?'

Jarvis shook Phil Williams's hand, mulled over his response for a few seconds and smiled. 'A fucking nightmare actually, but forget that.'

He looked across at Terry Porter. He looked drained and the white plaster on his black face looked very odd. 'How are you doing Terry?'

Porter nodded slowly. 'I'll live. Still a bit tired though. Nothing a few weeks off won't cure.'

Jarvis let out a half-hearted laugh. 'I wanted you back at work this afternoon.'

'Well with all due respect Guv, you can fuck off.' He paused for a few seconds and then started laughing.

Jarvis relaxed a little. He picked up Porter's bag and they began walking slowly towards the car park. Porter was still limping badly and was using crutches to keep the weight off his knee.

'I'll need to speak to you for a while, Terry. We have to know what happened in that bar. I've seen your report, but we should go over it.'

Porter nodded. 'I heard about Gary. Bad business.'

Tell me about it,' said Jarvis. 'We've got Internal Investigations sniffing around now. There could be some shit flying around.'

'Why?'

'Come on Terry. An undercover copper ends up in hospital and an informant is murdered ... think about it. At the moment, we haven't even got anything to show for it.'

They walked in silence for a moment and then Jarvis stopped. 'Listen Terry, about what happened in Rome ...'

Porter put up his hand and interrupted him. 'Forget it Guv. It was my decision to go, not yours.'

Jarvis smiled thinly. 'Yeah, but I...'

'You didn't do anything. I knew the risks, I take the responsibility.'

Jarvis looked at him and nodded. 'Thanks. I needed that.'

They began walking again and Jarvis briefed Porter on the events of the past two days.

'So you think he was shafting us all, then?'

'Seems like it,' replied Jarvis glumly. 'To be honest, it's all we can come up with.'

A group of young women walked past them and Porter's hand came up to touch the plaster on his face. It was an involuntary action but it cut right through Jarvis like a knife. His eyes returned to the floor, guilt dragging them down.

'What are the Italians doing about Gary Fitchett?'

'I don't know,' said Jarvis lifting his eyes up from the polished floor. 'I take it they spoke to you?'

'Yeah, for some time, but I couldn't tell them anything. I thought I saw him fighting with some lads but, to be honest, I don't know. He did have a few run-ins during the trip, though. With some lads from Chelsea. I'll come back to the nick for a while and have a look at some pictures, see if I can pick them out.'

Jarvis smiled as they walked through the automatic doors to find Harris and Williams already sitting in the car. 'That'd be a help.'

He put Porter's bag in the boot and walked round to the far side of the car. The two men stood and looked at each other for a second before Porter spoke. 'I want the bastard who stabbed me as well. That's one face I'll have no trouble remembering.'

Harris turned to face the back as they climbed into the car. 'I've just had a call from Neal White, Guv. ITN have sent the film over. It'll be ready for when we get back.'

The five men sat through the film about three times before deciding enough was enough. It didn't make for pleasant viewing, and only a few of the individuals seen throwing bottles and missiles were identifiable. Only one of them was from the crew, and that was Hawkins. The other thing the film failed to do was shed any light on what had gone on inside the bar. Just a shot of two stretchers being carried out and a brief shot of the interior. 'Shit, I didn't even make the news then?' Terry Porter said.

Jarvis ejected the tape and handed it to Neal White. 'And a bloody good job as well. I don't want people knowing you're a copper.' He looked at White. 'Give that to the DCI on Monday. He'll want to look through it.' He ran his hand through his hair and looked up at the clock on the wall. It was lunchtime and he was hungry and thirsty. 'Come on,' he said, jumping up. 'Let's give ourselves a break for an hour. I'm buying.'

The others stood up but Terry Porter held up his hand. 'Not me Guv. I'm knackered. I need to get home.'

'I'll take you,' said Harris. 'You don't live far from me and I want to pop in and see the wife anyway. Just to remind her what I look like.'

Jarvis moved towards the door. 'OK. Listen, let's just call it quits for today. We can't do anything till Evans shows anyway.' The others got up and started to leave, but before White could depart, Jarvis called him over. 'Neal, have you got anything on this afternoon?'

'No, I was gonna get some kip.'

Jarvis grabbed him and led him out of the room and down the corridor. 'Come on. I fancy having a look at a few motors.'

'Well, well. It's my favourite policeman, and this time he's brought his chum. What can I do for you this time, officer? You saved up for the Jag yet?'

White smiled. 'Cut the crap. Has your boss turned up yet?'

The salesman shook his head. 'I told you, Monday morning. I'll tell him you called.'

Jarvis lit a cigarette and gestured towards the forecourt. 'How many cars do you shift a month?'

The salesman held up his hands. 'I can't tell you that, can I? You might pass it on to our competitors.'

'Or I may talk to the VAT man instead,' added Jarvis. 'And ask them to come down here and rip your books apart. Your boss would love that, wouldn't he?'

The smile flickered a little. 'Look, there's no need to get heavy, is there?'

'Then just tell me. It's just an idle question, to satisfy my curiosity.'

The salesman looked at White and then back at Jarvis. 'On a good month, we'll shift maybe twenty, twenty-five cars. Sometimes more, sometimes less.'

Jarvis raised his eyebrows. 'Not bad. What about last month? September? How many cars did you shift?'

The salesman looked agitated. He was on his own this morning and he didn't need this. 'I don't know, you'd have to ask the boss.'

'Guess,' said Jarvis, his tone becoming more aggressive by the second.

'It was a bad month. We only sold about fifteen motors; that's why the forecourt is so full. Why do you want to know?'

Jarvis jutted out his bottom lip and looked around. 'Just interested, that's all.'

The salesman jumped up and looked past them, nodding in the direction of the road outside. 'Look, here's the boss now. Ask him yourself.'

Jarvis and Williams spun round as a white BMW convertible turned onto the forecourt and pulled up outside the showroom. 'How the fucking hell ...?' muttered White.

'Never mind that,' hissed Jarvis, instinctively moving out of sight behind the Jaguar as the white car door swung open. 'Where's the Merc?'

Jarvis waited until the door of the showroom slammed shut and then he stood up to see Billy Evans walking past Neal White and over to the desk. He looked remarkably fit and well.

'Hello Billy.'

Evans almost jumped around. His face was a mixture of shock and anger. 'Fuck me! You nearly gave me a heart attack.' He patted his chest and leant against the desk, feigning a coronary. By the time he stood up, the smile was back, and so was the cockiness. 'Well, well. Inspector Jarvis. I ain't seen you for a while, have I? If I didn't know better I'd have a persecution complex. What's up now? You after a new car?'

Jarvis walked forward and shook his head. 'No Billy, not this time. You're nicked.'

Evans looked at him and laughed. 'What for this time? Unpaid parking? Having an offensive wife?'

Jarvis smiled. 'No Billy, I want to question you about conspiracy to commit offences abroad contrary to Section 5 of the 1998 Criminal Justice Act.'

'Bollocks.'

'Shut up and listen,' snapped White, as Jarvis continued.

'And your involvement in the murder of Gary Fitchett in Rome last Wednesday. You do not...'

Evans opened his eyes wide. 'Fitch is dead?'

Jarvis stopped talking. The shock in Evans's voice was real.

'Didn't you know?'

He shook his head. 'No, I heard he'd been in a ruck, but ...' He leant back against the desk and shook his head. 'Fuckin' hell.' He looked up at Jarvis and then turned round to the salesman. 'Call my missus, tell her what's happened and then call my brief. I'll be at...' He looked at Jarvis who handed him a card.

'Tell him his client will be here.' He turned back to Evans. 'You do not have to say anything. But it may harm your defence if you do not mention when questioned something which you later rely on in court. Anything you do say may be given in evidence.'

Evans nodded towards the forecourt. 'Come on then, let's get it over with. Your car or mine?'

Chapter 23
Saturday, 30 October
17.10

Jarvis took a deep breath, opened the door of the interview room and walked in. He nodded to Phil Williams, who simply said, 'Detective Inspector Jarvis has just entered the room.' Jarvis sat down and smiled. Across the table, Evans sat with his arms folded. His face wore a faint smile and he looked like he didn't have a care in the world.

'OK Billy, let's talk about the meeting in Great Portland Street, shall we?'

'Really Inspector, do we have to go over all this ground again? My client has explained all of this already. It was simply a meeting with a few acquaintances to finalise details of a trip to Italy for a football match. Nothing more than that. This story about a plan to stop the game is pure fabrication and you have no evidence to support it. My client freely admits that he lent each of his friends a vehicle to travel in, but he did not give anyone any money, he did not give them any tickets and he did not plan any riot.'

Jarvis looked at the solicitor sitting to Evans's left. He was a right smarmy bastard and, if anything, looked even more arrogant than Evans. Thirtyish and well dressed, he wasn't even wearing a suit. Just a black blazer, beige chinos and a pale-yellow open-necked polo shirt. If he didn't know better, he'd have sworn he had him on file somewhere. He looked the type and he certainly wouldn't have been the first brief he'd known who was partial to a ruck or two. 'But what your client says, Mr Higham, and what we know, are two entirely different things.'

'Then show us the proof, Inspector. If you have any.'

Jarvis looked down at his notes and flicked through them before looking up again. 'All in good time, Mr Higham. But let's move on, shall we? What happened at Bar San Marco, Billy?'

Evans ran his hand over his mouth and then shook his head. 'I don't know. I'd been there before, the last time England played, in ninety-seven, and we'd had a good time.'

'Who do you mean by "we"?' asked Jarvis.

'Me and most of the lads who went this time,' replied Evans. 'We go to nearly all the games and try and meet up somewhere. Anyway, this time, 'cause we were all going down together, I booked the place for a private party. So that me and the lads could go and have a drink in safety. I mean, no one else was supposed to get in.'

'Just you and your crew,' said Jarvis.

'My friends, Inspector Jarvis,' Evans corrected. 'My friends. But yes, just us. Next thing I know, some other lads turn up and kick it off. Well I tried to calm it down, but it started getting out of hand. So I got scared and baled out through the back door.'

Jarvis let out an ironic laugh. 'You got scared! That's a bloody laugh.'

'Now now Inspector ...' admonished Higham, leaning forward and wagging his finger. 'There's no need for that. I know that you suspect my client has been involved in hooliganism in the past – but if he had been, surely you would have been able to prove it by now? After all, you have waged a personal vendetta against him for three years.'

Jarvis glared at him and returned to his notes. 'So you never saw what happened to either Gary Fitchett or Terry Porter?'

'No. I was long gone.'

'Where to?'

'I just walked around for a bit. Keeping out the way. In the end, I jumped in a taxi and went back to my car.'

'Can you prove that?'

Evans shook his head and went to speak, but again, the brief leant forward. 'He doesn't really have to, Inspector.'

Jarvis nodded and reached down for a sheet of paper. 'I have here a statement from Terry Porter He says that you were present when he was attacked and that he believes that it was you who actually instigated the assault on him.'

'Bollocks,' said Evans. 'He's lying.'

'Why would he do that?' Jarvis asked.

'How do I know? But I'll swear on my mother's eyes that I must have left the bar by then, because I didn't see any assault.'

'Have you any other witnesses to back up this statement, Inspector?'

Jarvis smiled across the table at the solicitor. 'Not yet, Mr Higham. But we will have.'

'So at the moment, it comes down to my client's word against this ...' He looked down at his own notes and then smiled again, '... Terry Porter's.'

Jarvis looked down at the file for a few seconds and flicked through the papers. He wasn't reading anything, just thinking. He had nothing, and this bastard brief was making him look a right tosser. Even the fact that Porter was a copper wouldn't hold any sway in court. Unless he could come up with something, and soon, Evans was going to walk again.

He looked up from the file and smiled. 'OK Billy, let's talk about the cars for a while.'

'The cars?' said Evans, his face furrowed. 'What about them?'

'Well, can you tell me why you let these men drive your cars to Italy?'

Evans took a cigarette from the packet on the table and lit it. He blew the smoke directly across the table at Jarvis, who waved his hands across his face and let out an involuntary cough. 'Sorry,' said Evans. 'Why shouldn't I? They're my cars. If I want to let someone drive them, then why not? Is that a crime now?'

Jarvis smiled and shook his head. 'No, not at all. Not if they're legal.'

Evans let out a laugh. 'Legal, course they're legal. Taxed, insured, the lot.'

'That's not what I meant.'

Evans looked at him, a puzzled look on his face. 'What do you mean then?'

Jarvis glanced down at his notes and then looked up again, a broad smile on his face. 'I'll come back to that in a bit.' He pulled out a sheet of paper and ran his finger down it. 'Right, these cars ... Four Mercedes saloons, one Mercedes estate, seven BMWs, three Mitsubishi Shoguns, two Toyota Land-cruisers, two Range Rovers and a Lexus.' He looked up at Evans and smiled. 'Not a car older than M reg, most R or S: That's a lot of very expensive machinery Billy. How much would that lot be worth?'

Evans took a drag on his cigarette and smiled. 'Would that be trade or ticket?'

Jarvis looked at him and raised an eyebrow. 'How much ...?'

Evans looked up at the ceiling and pursed his lips. 'I'd say on a good day ... if I could sell the lot... I'd be looking at around about £430,000.'

Jarvis let out a low whistle. 'That's a lot of money Billy.'

Evans nodded. 'Well, I only deal with the best. You know that Inspector. Besides, I paid a lot less than that for them.'

Higham leant forward. 'What has this got to do with the matter in hand, Inspector? My client is a very successful motor trader and these vehicles are effectively business assets. Besides, having a garage full of stock is hardly a crime, is it?'

Jarvis smiled. 'I was just coming to that.' He took a deep breath and flicked through the contents of the folder. Now or never, nail the bastard. 'Of the forty men who travelled down in your vehicles, Fitchett is dead, Porter has just been flown home from hospital and Hawkins is in an Italian prison. And you're here of course,' he added as an afterthought.

'My client is aware of all that, Inspector;' said Higham impatiently.

Jarvis smiled, his eyes never leaving Evans's face. 'The others,' he went on, 'were all deported from Italy.' Evans stubbed out his cigarette and leant back in his chair. 'I know, terrible business all round.'

Jarvis leant forward slightly and focused on Evans's eyes. He was backing him into a corner and didn't want to miss the slightest flicker of a reaction. Now, go for it. 'You see, I have a problem now Billy.'

'What's that then, Inspector?'

'Well, we had a surveillance operation tailing your crew to Italy ...'

Higham held up his hand. 'My client has already explained that there was no "crew" as you call it. That is pure fabrication on your part.'

Jarvis ignored him and continued: 'On the evening of the attack on Porter and Fitchett, the twenty vehicles driven down were removed from the car park of the service area.'

Evans nodded. 'Yeah, that's right. But if you were following me, you'd have seen that.'

Jarvis ignored him and went on. 'I want you to tell me how that happened when all the drivers were either in hospital or custody.'

There was a slight hesitation and then Evans shook his head, as if puzzled by the naivety of the questions. 'Like I said, I went back to the car park and got there about midnight, something like that. Anyway, there'd been some trouble there during the evening and it all looked a bit dodgy. I didn't want to leave all my motors there so I managed to hook up with a couple of lads I'd met on previous trips and they spoke to their mates who offered to help me out. In the end, I had enough drivers and so we took the cars into Rome and stuck them in a car park.' He leant forward and lit another cigarette. 'It was simple.'

Jarvis looked thoughtful for a second and allowed his eyes to drop down to his notes. 'Don't lie to me Billy. That was impossible.'

'It's not. It's what happened.'

Jarvis lifted up his eyes and grinned. 'You couldn't have done it Billy, because you had no keys.'

Evans dragged on his cigarette and thought for a moment before leaning forward, the smile as broad as ever. 'I had spares with me.'

Jarvis laughed out loud and leant back in his seat. 'You took a spare set of keys for every car! Don't make me laugh.'

Another lungful of smoke and a long pause. 'Look Inspector, I'm not daft. Last time we went out there, as we walked into the ground, the police took all our change and all our keys. Only a few of us got them back; the rest had loads of hassle. I just planned ahead, that's all. In case someone didn't get their keys back or they got lost somewhere.' He took a final draw from his cigarette and stubbed it out. 'I mean, have you ever had to sort out a set of keys for a Mercedes, Inspector?' he said, his voice reeking of sarcasm.

Jarvis shook his head. 'I've never heard such a load of crap in all my life.'

Evans shrugged his shoulders and sat back.

'Well why don't you tell us what you think happened, Inspector,' said Higham. 'Or better still, tell us what you can prove. I suspect the latter version will be much shorter.'

Jarvis pursed his lips and took a deep breath. His temper was simmering nicely, but he wasn't sure if it was because of Evans's arrogance, his smart-arsed brief or his own failure to make any headway. He blinked heavily and then let out his breath slowly, regaining a bit of self-control. 'OK Billy. If all this is true, give me the names of some of these lads who helped you move the cars.'

Evans shook his head. 'I'd love to, but I only know them by their nicknames. I mean, when you're abroad with England you don't tell everyone your life history.'

'So you let people who you don't even know drive your cars?'

'I had no choice, did I?'

Jarvis let out a smirk. 'Don't bullshit me Billy.'

Evans held up his hands. 'Mr Jarvis, would I do that to you? I mean, what would be the point?'

'OK then. Where are the cars now?'

There was a pause and Evans leant forward and took another cigarette. His hands were solid as a rock. 'In France,' he said, as he lit up.

A horrible gnawing sensation began in Jarvis's stomach. 'What?'

'They're in France. Just outside Calais actually. In a warehouse.' He looked around the room. 'Well I'm hardly gonna leave four hundred and thirty grand's worth of motor in bloody Italy am I?' He leant back in his chair and inhaled a lungful of smoke. 'That's where I've been for the last few days. Getting them back.'

Jarvis fell back in his chair and looked at Williams. He was looking down, making notes, but his face was almost white.

'D'you want the address?'

Jarvis turned to face Evans again. His face was a picture of innocence.

Williams tore out a sheet of paper and, dropping his pen on top, slid it across the table. Evans picked up the pen and began writing. 'If you wait a few days, I'll be bringing them back over.' He paused and looked up, a wry smile on his lips. 'Now that they've been valeted.'

Jarvis looked down at his notes and shook his head. The bastard had an answer for everything.

'How did you get them from Rome to Calais so fast?' asked Williams.

'Oh that was the easy bit,' said Evans happily. 'I hung around the station after the game and just grabbed some lads waiting for trains. Bunged them a few quid and they were happy to do it.'

'And I don't suppose you know their names either; do you, Billy?'

Evans shrugged his shoulders. 'Sorry Mr Jarvis. I don't.'

'But why stop at Calais?' Williams went on. 'Why not bring them all the way over?'

Evans shrugged and held out his hands, palms uppermost. 'Easier for me. I mean, some of them lads were Scousers, for fuck's sake. Let 'em over here in my cars and they could end up anywhere. Besides, a mate offered me the space and my yard's rammed.' He looked at Jarvis and gestured to him with his hand. 'Well, you've seen it. Easier for me to leave 'em there, get 'em cleaned up and then bring 'em back and sell 'em. It's just easier. Besides ...' He paused while he looked at Higham. 'Bringing twenty cars over at the weekend would've cost me a fortune. It's cheaper in the week.'

'So if what you say is true,' said Williams, 'you'll have the personal effects of the others in the crew.'

Evans nodded and dropped his dog-end in the ashtray. 'Yeah, they're at my house. I brought 'em over with me in the Merc.' He looked around and grinned. 'Well, I wasn't coming across on the train, was I? I own a garage for fuck's sake.'

'So you have one of the cars at your house?' asked Jarvis, still unable to grasp the enormity of what Evans was telling him.

'Yeah. Had to see the wife first and get cleaned up, didn't I?'

'But you came back to the garage in a BMW.' Evans nodded. 'Yeah, the wife's. She's got the Range Rover today and the Mercedes stinks.' Jarvis stared at him, his face blank. 'I think we should have a break, Inspector,' said Higham. 'For refreshments.'

Jarvis shook his head and looked at his watch. It was almost nine. 'No Mr Higham. I am suspending this interview pending further enquiries.' He nodded to Williams, who terminated the interview for the tape and then switched it off.

'I take it my client is free to return home?' Jarvis stood up and walked over to the door. 'Your client, Mr Higham, is directly involved in a murder inquiry. He isn't going anywhere for a while.' Before the brief could answer, Jarvis walked out and closed the door behind him.

Chapter 24
Sunday, 31 October
09.30

'OK, unless we can come up with something concrete, this investigation is dead in the water.' Jarvis paced angrily around the room, his eyes concentrating on the floor rather than the two men in the room. 'Phil, chase up the French police, they must have been to this warehouse by now. Al, has anything come back from the stolen car boys yet?'

Harris sat up and held up a sheet of paper. 'Yeah. In the past three months, at least one car identical to each of the ones on this list has been stolen from somewhere in the southeast.'

Jarvis looked up from the floor. 'That's good.'

'But ...' Harris leapt back into the conversation. 'I also spoke to a few of the previous owners of the cars registered to Evans. They all say similar things. They either traded them in at Evans's garage or he bought them through trade ads in *Auto Trader*. Four were sold at auction, but they were all registered within a week of the sale, so chances are he bought it.'

Phil Williams put down the phone and looked up shaking his head. 'I just spoke to someone in Calais. They've got people there now. He'll call me as soon as they have something.'

Jarvis sat down on a desk and stared at the board. He'd sent Parry and White to Evans's house to search the Mercedes and check the chassis numbers matched the information from the DVLA, but wasn't hopeful that they would find anything. He sighed and rubbed his face.

'Of course, you know what he's done, don't you?' He looked up to see Terry Porter standing in the doorway, a broad grin on his face. 'Phil rang me last night and told me about the interview. I was lying in bed this morning and it all clicked.' Jarvis stood up and gestured for him to come in and sit down. 'It's so fucking obvious, when you think about it ...'

'Well, are you going to share it with us then or what?' asked Harris impatiently.

Porter sat down and slid his crutches under his chair.

Jarvis held up his hands in exasperation. 'Well...?'

'OK. Now hear me out before you say anything. We know Evans is a car dealer who specialises in executive motors. He's also a bit of a lad so, chances are, he isn't the most law-abiding citizen in Britain.'

Jarvis nodded. 'That's an understatement.'

'Right. He puts together, or is sent, a list of cars that are wanted in, say, the Middle East. Using his trade contacts, he then buys cars that fit that list. Either at auctions or he keeps back cars that are traded in and takes them over to France where they're out of the way. At the same time, he steals an identical car from somewhere and stashes it. With the people he must know, it wouldn't be that difficult.'

Jarvis looked at him and nodded slowly. 'Go on, Terry.'

'Well, once he's filled his list, both with stolen motors and legit ones, he simply sticks the real plates on the stolen car – and bingo. He can drive them to wherever, and unless he's really unlucky, no one will think anything of it.'

'So what you're saying,' chimed in Harris, 'is that once he gets to where he's going, he takes off the plates and, figuratively speaking, they go back on the real cars.'

'Exactly,' said Porter. 'He collects the money for the stolen motors from whoever his contact is and then sells the real cars through his garage.'

'And makes a fortune on both counts,' added Williams.

A smile spread across Jarvis's face. 'If you're right, he could have been pulling this scam for years.'

Porter nodded. 'But I doubt he's done anything this big before. It must have taken ages to plan.'

'You gotta admit,' said Harris, 'it's fucking clever. Even taking the real motors to France and then getting them valeted just in case.'

'Just in case of what?' asked Williams.

'In case he got caught. If the cars have been valeted, there'll be no forensic evidence, so there's no way we can prove that they aren't the cars driven down,' added Harris irritably.

'And you know what the best of it is?' asked Porter. The others looked at him quizzingly. 'You'll never be able to prove it. Those stolen motors will have vanished into thin air by now. They'll have been taken from the car park by his contacts and you'll never see 'em again.'

The room fell into silence, each man thinking of ways around what Porter had said but none finding any.

The phone broke the quiet and Williams picked it up and listened intently for a few minutes. 'That was the French police,' he said as he replaced the receiver. 'The warehouse Evans told us about contains nineteen English-registered cars. They match the list perfectly.'

'Nineteen ...?' queried Porter.

'He brought the Mercedes back,' said Harris. 'It's at his house, full of the crew's gear. I dare say your stuff will be down there somewhere.'

Porter laughed. 'Well, at least he's done the decent thing.'

The phone rang again and Harris took the call. He listened for a while and then lowered the receiver. 'It's Steve Parry, Guv. It's just like Evans said.'

Jarvis sighed. 'Do the chassis numbers match?'

The look on Harris's face said it all. 'Of course they do. Out of all of them that must have been the only car that was legit. Bollocks!'

'Shall I ask him to bring Terry's stuff back?'

'No, tell them to get the Mercedes back here. At least we can go through the bags and get confirmed details of the whole crew now. We're going to have to speak to them all in any case, to help the Italian investigation. By the way Phil, did you speak to Fabio yesterday and fill him in on all this?'

Williams nodded. 'Yes Guv. They've got nothing though. And I kinda got the impression that they may not be that bothered about investigating the murder. After all, whoever stabbed him was English and was in that bar. If no one's talking, there's nothing they can do, is there?'

Jarvis pursed his lips and nodded. He could see Fabio's point. No doubt the Italian taxpayers could as well. An English thug murdered by another English thug. The fact it took place in their city was almost irrelevant. Jarvis stood up and stretched his arms above his head. 'OK then. If what Terry says is right, how do we prove it?'

'Well I doubt any of the crew will say anything; besides, I doubt they know much,' said Williams.

'I didn't want to hear what we can't do,' said Jarvis testily. 'I want to hear what we can.'

'There is one way Guv.'

He turned to Terry Porter. 'Go on.'

'When you interview him, put this idea to him and see how he reacts. If he laughs it off, I'll come in and front him up.'

'What, tell him you were undercover?'

Porter nodded.

'Why?'

'It'd shock the shit out of him. He'd also work out that Fitchett was involved and was at the meeting in London. It might shake him.'

Jarvis shook his head. 'No Terry. I can't do that. You'd never be able to go undercover again.'

'What?' said Porter incredulously, 'and you think I will be? After this?'

Jarvis held up his hands. 'No, forget it. Besides, you're supposed to be on sick leave.' He sat there for a moment and looked at his watch. 'OK, it's a quarter to eleven. What time was Evans booked in yesterday?'

'Three thirty Guv,' said Harris. 'D'you want me to speak to the custody sergeant about getting another twelve hours' extension?'

Jarvis shrugged his shoulders. 'Give it a go, Al. But to be honest, we may not get it. All we've got so far is theories. And not a shred of firm evidence to back any of them up.' He looked at his watch again and stood up. 'I need to get hold of the DCI and run all this by him. Phil, get on to Evans's brief. Tell him I'll be interviewing him again at one thirty.' He looked at Porter, who was flicking through some of the interview statements taken from the deportees at Heathrow. He didn't like the idea, but it might well be the last card he had.

Jarvis sat and studied the faces of the two men sitting opposite him as Williams busied himself with the tape machine. Evans wore his usual smug grin of invincibility and Higham was just smarm personified. He would cheerfully have given either of them a good hiding. He drummed his fingers on the file in front of him and then flicked it open, shuffling through the papers to keep himself occupied. Allen hadn't been best pleased to be disturbed at home, but had listened intently while he filled him in on the events of the past two days. The suggestion that he bring Porter into the interview in an attempt to unsettle Evans had not gone down well. He'd eventually agreed, but only as a last resort. Jarvis snapped back to the present as Williams began the preliminaries for the benefit of the tape. This was his last chance. If he couldn't get Evans to open up or get him to make even the slightest mistake, then he'd have to let him go.

'May I remind you, Inspector,' began Higham, 'that my client has been in custody for over twenty-two hours.'

'I am aware of that Mr Higham. However, I have applied for a further twelve-hour extension to that. This is, after all, a murder investigation.'

'Of which my client has no knowledge,' Higham said brusquely.

'And no alibi,' added Jarvis. He looked at Evans, who simply shook his head.

'I didn't kill him, Mr Jarvis. You know that.'

'Then tell me who did, Billy.'

Evans held up his hands. 'If I could, I would. Fitch was a good mate of mine.'

Jarvis looked at him and raised an eyebrow. 'OK Billy, tell me about Terry Porter.'

'What about 'im?' asked Evans.

'Well, he says in his statement that there was a lot of friction because he was black.'

'Well I can't help that, can I? Not everyone is as racially tolerant as me. I mean, even the police force have their problems, ain't that right?'

Jarvis made a note on his pad. More to stop himself from laughing than anything else. He composed himself and went on. 'Porter says that on a number of occasions, you spoke to Fitchett about problems with the right-wing members of the crew.'

'Inspector, I must insist...'

Jarvis sighed. 'OK Mr Higham ... the party. And that on at least two occasions, once in the car park and once on the bus, he was attacked by the same two men. The second of those attacks, the one on the bus, was stopped by you.'

Evans shook his head. 'No, that's not true.'

'Well, why would he lie?'

Evans reached for a cigarette and lit up, sending clouds of smoke bellowing up towards the ceiling. 'I don't know. Ask him. Better still, ask some of the other lads, they'll tell you the same as me. Nothing happened.'

Jarvis stared across the table. 'Does the fact that Porter made a statement to us bother you, Billy?'

Evans looked at him and raised both eyebrows in mock surprise. 'Why should it? We all want the truth, don't we Mr Jarvis? Problem is, what he's said is wrong. That ain't helping anyone, is it?'

Jarvis flicked through his notes to give him time while he thought. Evans was unshakeable. Sooner or later, he was going to have to bring Terry Porter in. Not yet though.

A knock on the door interrupted them and Jarvis turned to see Steve Parry standing in the doorway. 'Can I have a word, Guv? Urgent.'

Jarvis got up and walked towards the door as Williams spoke for the tape, recording the fact that the senior officer was leaving the room.

Parry waited until the door was properly closed and started talking. 'We've been going through the stuff from the Mercedes. Terry's found the passports of the two lads who attacked him. Here's their names,' he said, handing Jarvis a piece of paper. 'Steven Daniels, known as Skinner for some reason, and Brian Hughes.'

'Do we know them?'

Parry nodded. 'Both are from Leeds and on the Cat C list. Hughes has done time for assault, not football-related though, and Daniels was detained in Dublin for a while before they kicked him out. They're well known as being card-carrying racists.'

'Nice lads then,' said Jarvis.

'Oh, the best.'

'Is that it?' asked Jarvis.

'No Guv. Get this. There was an envelope full of documents as well. All the log books, insurance stuff, all perfectly legit.'

'Yeah, go on,' said Jarvis sharply.

'Well in a couple of the bags, we also found some match tickets.'

'So?'

'Well they're all the same and they're all fake.'

'What d'you mean, the same?'

Parry held up two tickets. 'They're identical. Even down to the serial numbers. They're good copies, mind.'

Jarvis took them and grinned. 'Well that was careless. Let's see what he's got to say about that. How many were there altogether?'

'We found eight.'

'What, all the same?'

Parry gave him a broad wink.

'Nice one,' said Jarvis, and walked back into the room.

'DI Jarvis has just re-entered the room at 14.12,' said Williams for the benefit of the tape.

'Billy,' he said as he sat down and carefully hid the tickets under a sheet of paper. 'Do you know a Steven Daniels and a Brian Hughes?'

Evans furrowed his brow and slowly shook his head. 'No ... I don't think so.'

'Billy,' said Jarvis. 'Daniels was driving one of your cars four days ago. A green Mitsubishi Shogun.'

'Oh, you mean Skinner! Yeah, I know him. And Hughsie, of course. Sorry Mr Jarvis, you must think I'm a right prat.'

Jarvis raised an eyebrow in agreement and went on. 'Would you mind telling me where you know them from?'

Evans looked round at Higham who gave a discreet nod of his head. 'I've known Skinner for years. I first met him in ... Christ let me think ...' He looked at the ceiling and rubbed his chin dramatically. 'Sweden I think. Nineteen ...hmm. Yeah, nineteen ninety-two. European Championships.' He grinned again.

'And Daniels?'

'Can't remember. It was after that though. I meet a lot of people you know, I can't remember them all.'

Jarvis lifted up his eyes from his notes. 'Oh yes Billy. I know. So what if I told you that Terry Porter had identified these two men as being the ones who attacked him?'

Evans cocked his head to one side and scratched his ear. 'I'd say, good.'

'What?' Jarvis asked irritably.

'Well if they put him in hospital, they should be punished, shouldn't they? Stands to reason. But I wouldn't know much about it, because I wasn't there.' He settled back in his chair and reached for another smoke, lighting it off the stub of the old one.

Jarvis sighed wearily. That wasn't the response he was after at all.

'Inspector,' he glanced across as the solicitor spoke. 'Is there any chance that you are going to produce anything that remotely resembles evidence today? So far, all you have done is present the testimony of someone who, I assume, spent much of the past four days in an Italian hospital. Furthermore, as far as I can tell, you have no witnesses to back up a single word of what he says.'

Jarvis glared at Higham. The smug git was really starting to irritate him. Jarvis took the two tickets from under the sheet of paper. 'Do you recognise these, Billy?'

Evans leant over and looked at them. 'Tickets for the game in Rome. So?'

'We found them in your car.'

Higham shook his head. 'Really Inspector, my client and his friends were on their way to a football match. Is it really so extraordinary to expect them to have purchased tickets to get in?'

'Not at all,' said Jarvis calmly. 'But if those tickets are forged, as these are, then that is of interest.'

Evans leant forward and smiled. 'Well not to me it's not, because they're not mine and I've never seen them before. All right, they were in my car, but it was full of other people's gear. What d'you want me to do? Search it all for dodgy tickets?' He looked around at Higham. 'This is getting fucking ridiculous. Now I'm up for touting!'

Higham glared at Jarvis. 'I totally agree with my client. You're fishing, Inspector. You and I both know it. I insist you release Mr Evans immediately.'

Jarvis looked at him for a second, his face expressionless. Higham was right of course. He had nothing. Not a shred. There was only one thing left to do. 'OK Billy ...' he began, 'let me tell you what I think has been going on.'

Evans leant back in his chair. He looked calm but his eyes were blazing. Jarvis was pushing his luck now, and he knew it. 'I'm all ears, Inspector.'

Jarvis smiled and took a deep breath. 'You recruited a group of known hooligans and lent each of them a car to drive to Italy. You also gave them a match ticket and a sum of money.' Higham went to speak but Jarvis held up his hand and he stopped. 'However, those tickets were, as we have seen, forged. The reason for that is because you knew they wouldn't be used. I already have one statement that says you initiated the trouble in Bar San Marco. I believe you did that, certain in the knowledge that it would escalate and the riot police would become involved. Given the history of this fixture and the reputation of the people inside the bar, it was a pretty safe bet that most, if not all, would get detained or deported.'

Evans shook his head and smiled. 'Why would I do all that?'

Jarvis flashed him a glare and fished through his notes. The silence continued for a few seconds and then he looked up. There was no choice, he had to go for it. 'I believe that this whole trip was a front. You were not planning to attend this match at all. What you were actually doing was exporting stolen cars ...'

'Stolen cars!' Evans let out a loud ironic laugh. 'You've been out in the sun too much.'

Higham leant forward and put his hand on his shoulder. 'Just hear him out,' he murmured.

Jarvis nodded. 'The cars belonging to you which are currently stored in the warehouse near Calais are not, in fact, the same ones that were taken to Italy. Those were stolen vehicles wearing the number plates of your cars.' Jarvis coughed again and carried on. 'After removing the personal effects from the stolen cars, they were taken from the service station car park in Rome by persons unknown. You simply made your way back to Calais alone.' He stopped talking and looked up at Evans. The smile was still there, as smug as ever.

'It's a bloody good idea, Mr Jarvis. It might even work.'

Higham leant forward. 'Have you any evidence to back up one single word of this theory Inspector?'

Jarvis looked at him, a thin smile fixed to his lips. He'd given it a shot and it hadn't worked. Evans had just laughed the whole thing off. Now Jarvis had no choice. There was only one last chance to rattle the man sitting opposite him. 'I believe I can Mr Higham.' He scribbled on a piece of paper and handed it to Williams. He looked at it and with a low sigh, got up and left the room.

The three men sat, listening to the low hum of the cassette machine.

'I take it I'll be going home tonight?' said Evans.

Higham grunted. 'If I have my way you will. This is a bloody scandal.'

Jarvis looked at them and waited. He fixed his eyes on Evans, daring him to make eye contact, but he merely looked around the room and, after a minute or so, lit yet another cigarette. When the door finally opened, Jarvis leant forward and, without taking his eyes off Evans, said, 'DC Williams and Detective Sergeant Porter have just entered the room.'

Evans looked up at Terry Porter. For a second, he looked stunned, but if Jarvis was looking for even the slightest indication of fear or concern, neither was forthcoming. Evans started laughing. 'Well fuck me rigid! Now that's a turn-up for the books. I always wondered what an undercover copper looked like, and now I know.'

'Hello Billy,' said Porter, sounding slightly embarrassed.

'Well well. Terry. Shit man, you had me fooled.' He gestured towards the plaster. 'How's your face?'

'It'll mend.'

Higham leant forward and glared at Jarvis. 'Are you telling me that this is Terry Porter? The man whose statement you keep quoting from?'

Jarvis nodded. 'Yes I am.'

'And he's an undercover officer?'

'That's correct,' said Jarvis patiently.

Higham sat back in his chair. 'Well, Inspector Jarvis, I'm astonished. Despite having a man right in the middle of this, you still have no firm evidence to present against my client. In fact, I'll go further than that. You don't even have a charge to prefer against him, do you?'

Jarvis looked at him, surprised. 'Your client, Mr Higham, was involved in the murder of Gary Fitchett, was involved in conspiracy to commit offences outside the United Kingdom and was also involved in the theft of a number of motor vehicles – all of which have been exported out of the country.'

'And yet despite what I can only assume was a very expensive undercover operation, you are still unable to show us any evidence to support a word you say,' added Higham, caustically. 'Doesn't that tell you something, Inspector?'

The room fell into an awkward silence. Evans leant forward and dropped his cigarette stub in the ash tray.

'You must be fucking desperate, Mr Jarvis.'

'I think I would like a few moments with my client,' said Higham patiently.

'I think that would be a very good idea.' Jarvis nodded to Williams who suspended the interview and the three officers walked out, closing the door behind them.

'Shit,' barked Jarvis. 'That didn't go how I thought it would.'

Terry Porter looked at him. 'Guv, I have to say this. You've got nothing. You know that don't you? Even if it ever came to court, the conspiracy stuff will come down to my word against his. No one else is gonna say anything. And unless you can come up with something, the car theft idea is just that, an idea. We all know it's what happened, but we can't prove a word of it.'

Jarvis looked down at the floor and nodded. 'Yeah I know. I really thought he'd do something to drop himself in it.' He looked up at Porter. 'Sorry Terry, I shouldn't have done that to you. It just made you look a twat.'

'Oh thanks.'

Jarvis grunted, half laugh, half groan. 'You know what I mean. Go on, piss off home. I'll sort this mess out. It's all down to me.' He knocked on the door and walked back into the interview room.

Chapter 25
Wednesday, 17 November
11.20

Terry Porter sat and looked at the pile of paperwork on his desk. He wasn't supposed to have come back to work until Monday but boredom had taken over and, besides, he felt fine. Now, having been given all this work to do, he was having second thoughts. He looked at the others scurrying around the office and smiled. It was good to be back doing proper police work. He hadn't realised how much he'd missed the day-to-day office banter when he'd been undercover. He looked up to see Paul Jarvis standing and talking on the phone at the other end of the large open plan room. He looked agitated and, after looking over towards Porter's desk, hurried off in the direction of the DCI's office.

'Poor bastard,' Porter thought. Releasing Evans without charge must have been a real kick in the nuts. Especially now that the football unit's side of the operation had been all but wound up and was under an official investigation for the way it had been conducted. Hardly surprising, given that the key informant had been murdered. Jarvis would do well to escape with just a bollocking after that. Still, Porter had done his bit. He could hardly be blamed for anything. It wasn't down to him that the others in the crew had backed up everything Evans had said when they'd been interviewed. At least the stolen car squad had been impressed. Even if they weren't confident of ever proving anything. The phone rang and snapped him out of his daydream.

'DS Porter.'

'Hello. My name's Ian Shaw. From the *Express*. I'm just ringing to ask for your response to a story we'll be running in the paper tomorrow.'

'I'm sorry, you'll have to talk to the press office. We're not allowed to comment...'

'But Sergeant,' the voice insisted, 'this story is directly related to you.'

Porter felt a cold shiver run up his spine and he glanced down at the phone, his brow furrowed. 'What story?'

There was a pause and then the voice continued. 'Three weeks ago, on the night before the England versus Italy match, two England fans were attacked and stabbed during a major disturbance in a bar. The same disturbance in fact which resulted in over a hundred people being arrested and deported.'

Porter sat and stared into space as the mechanical voice droned on. The knot in his stomach was growing by the second.

'One of those men, his name was ... erm ... Gary Fitchett, died from his injuries. The second man recovered and was released from hospital on the Saturday morning after the match. The name we were given for that man at the time was Edward Samson. Have you any comment to make on that, Sergeant?'

Porter sat in silence.

'Right then ...' began the voice again. 'This morning, an Italian newspaper has run a story alleging that the second man was in fact an undercover police officer from the National Football Intelligence Unit. Obviously, this is a big story in its own right and we were planning to run it tomorrow anyway. However, I must tell you that, about two hours ago, we received information that alleges that you were that undercover officer. Would you like to comment on that?'

Porter leant forward and rested his forehead on his hand. This wasn't happening.

'Sergeant? Are you there?'

Porter looked at the phone. He wanted to put it down but simply said, 'Yes, and I have no comment.'

'OK,' the voice went on. 'But I think you should know that this information also alleges that Gary Fitchett received his wounds as a result of a fight with you ...'

Porter dropped the phone and stood up. He looked around and tried to work out what to do. He could hear the voice on the phone, calling out, but he didn't want to listen any more. 'Oh fuck!' he gasped, and headed as quickly as he could towards the DCI's office.

Jarvis stood awkwardly next to DCI Allen's desk and stared at the two men in dark suits sitting in front of him.

'I assure you Inspector Jarvis that this is no joke. According to the evidence we have, your DS is facing a charge of murder.'

'But you have to see this is all a set-up? It's so bloody obvious, it's ridiculous.'

A loud knock on the door made them all turn round as Porter came crashing into the office. He stopped and angrily looked around the room. 'Oh, so you obviously know then? Was anyone ever going to tell me?'

'Now hang on Sergeant ...' said Allen, holding up his hand to calm him down. 'We needed to get all the facts together before we spoke to you.'

Jarvis moved forward and gestured towards the two other men in the room. 'Terry, this is DCI Hayles and DS Jeffrey from Internal Investigations. They're here to try and sort out this mess.'

The taller of the men stood up. He was grey-haired but distinguished. His black suit was immaculate and he exuded authority and confidence. He held out his hand and smiled.

'Colin Hayles,' he said as Porter shook his hand. 'Terry, listen, I have to say this so that we get off on the right foot. Despite what you think, I'm not here to put you inside for something you didn't do. I'm here to prevent that. But to do my job, I'm going to need your help, OK?' Porter looked at him and nodded slowly. 'Good. Right, now first you tell me how you heard about this?'

Allen motioned for Porter to sit down and he collapsed in the chair vacated by Hayles. 'I just got a call from a journalist, the *Express* I think. There was a story in an Italian paper this morning. They're running it tomorrow but they've got more information.'

'What information?' pressed Hayles quietly.

'Erm ... they received something that says I killed Gary Fitchett. We had a fight and I stabbed him.'

Hayles nodded solemnly. 'And he named you?'

'Yes.'

Hayles stole a quick, and very anxious, look at Jarvis.

'Is that all he said, Terry?'

Porter shook his head. 'I don't know. I put the phone down and came here.'

Hayles rubbed his chin and walked around the room for a few seconds. 'OK Terry. Just to put you in the picture, let me tell you what we have already. Three days ago, an Italian newspaper received an anonymous letter which said that the second man injured in the stabbing incident in Rome was a British policeman working undercover. They contacted the Italian police and the NFIU for a comment but, obviously, no one gave them anything. Because of the murder inquiry, the police in Rome asked them not to run the story – but for some reason, and we don't know why yet, they ran it this morning.'

Porter looked at him. 'So when did you find out?'

Hayles gave him a rueful smile. 'We were contacted by the Italian police as soon as they received the tip-off.'

'And no one thought to tell me?'

'We hoped it wouldn't get this far,' chimed in Jarvis.

'What, you knew as well? Well that's great. Thanks Guv. Thanks a fucking lot.'

Hayles held up his hand. 'OK, let's keep this calm, shall we?' He looked around and then continued. 'Over the past two days, four men have walked into various police stations around the country and made statements alleging that they knew the name of the man who killed Gary Fitchett.'

'And they all named me, right?' hissed Porter, his voice full of irony.

Hayles nodded. 'Yes Terry. They all named you. Their versions are all slightly different, but in essence they all say the same thing. That Fitchett was taunting you with racist abuse and you attacked him with a knife.'

'That's crazy,' said Porter, looking around for support. 'In case no one noticed, I was stabbed as well.'

Hayles gave a slight shake of his head. 'They say that Fitchett also had a knife and fought back.'

'And of course none of these mythical knives have turned up?' said Porter sarcastically.

Hayles raised an eyebrow and carried on. 'A number of knives were found in the bar but the Italians failed to treat it as a legitimate crime scene. They were simply gathered up and put with everything else that was seized over those few days.'

'But why have these four come forward now?' asked Porter desperately.

'Two say that they were too frightened to come forward at first in case they were arrested; one says he hasn't been able to sleep with this on his conscience, and the fourth says that he's been on holiday and has only just heard about Fitchett dying.'

'And you believe that bollocks?'

Hayles gave a thin smile. 'It doesn't matter what I believe, Terry. The fact of the matter is that they've come forward with information relating to a crime. No matter what the circumstance, it has to be taken seriously.'

'What do we know about them?' asked Allen.

Jarvis looked up from the floor and then stood up. 'Well they weren't part of the crew we followed over,' he said wearily. 'But they were among those detained at the scene and deported.'

Porter shook his head and looked at the floor. 'I don't fucking believe this.'

Hayles looked at him and sighed as Jarvis sat down again. 'Look Terry, these four men are being interviewed again this morning – but as yet, none of them have mentioned the fact that you are a copper.' He glanced over at Allen and continued. 'However, if what you say is true and someone has told the papers your name ...' His voice tailed off. 'It can only be a matter of time before someone puts two and two together, right?'

Hayles nodded again. 'We should be able to keep your name out of the British papers though. For a while at least, but because the investigation will take place in Italy, that may not be possible.'

'What investigation?' asked Porter.

Hayles looked at him and sighed. 'Terry, at some point, unless we can come up with something to discredit these statements, the Italians will have to charge you. If not with murder, with manslaughter.'

Porter sat back in his chair and closed his eyes. This wasn't happening.

'But this can only have come from one person,' said Jarvis. 'It has to be Evans, it has to be.'

Hayles nodded his head in agreement. 'I totally agree. I have no doubt that he was the person who contacted both the Italian and British press and that these four witnesses are lying through their teeth on his behalf. But that is going to be very difficult to prove. If we question him, all he has to do is say that he told someone else about Terry and that whole line of enquiry is over.'

'Well whatever you say, we have to try,' said Porter standing up.

'No Terry.' said Hayles quickly. 'Not you. In light of what has happened, I have no option but to suspend you until further notice.'

'What!' shrieked Porter. 'I haven't done anything! This is a bloody set-up!'

'He has no choice Terry,' said Allen calmly. 'You know that.'

Porter looked around at the men in the room. Of the four of them, only Jarvis wouldn't make eye contact. He glared at him for a while and turned back to Hayles. 'Be honest sir, how bad is this?'

The tall DCI looked him full in the eye as he spoke. 'Bad Terry,' he said solemnly. 'It looks bad.'

Allen waited until Terry Porter had left the room before getting up and walking to the window. His office was silent except for the scribbling of DS Jeffrey, still making notes after the altercation with Terry Porter 'What's the next step, Colin?' he asked.

Hayles sniffed and sat down. 'As I see it, we're dependent on getting one of these statements withdrawn. But you know as well as I do, if these lads stick to their story, then there's nothing we can do.' He scratched the side of his nose and looked across at Jarvis. 'With the press involved, there's no way we can cover this up. The Italians will have to charge him.'

Jarvis shook his head angrily. 'But these four are well known ...'

'Don't be so bloody naive,' Hayles said angrily. 'That won't make any difference in court. These are four independent statements given at four separate stations in different parts of the country. The fact that these people have a history of hooligan activity is for the most part irrelevant.' He glared at Jarvis. 'I have to say this. Inspector, the way this operation has been handled has been very haphazard.'

Allen spun around angrily. 'Now hang on...'

'No, Peter ...' interrupted Hayles. 'Firstly, this operation should have been stopped and handed to Special Branch right from the outset. Secondly, the fact that Fitchett used Terry's real name was asking for trouble.'

'We had no choice,' said Jarvis. 'That's what he used to introduce him to Evans. After that, it was too late.'

Hayles paused for a while and took a deep breath. 'Finally, Terry Porter should never have been allowed to come into contact with Evans while he was being questioned. It goes against every rule in the book. And to be brutally frank, those rules were designed to prevent situations exactly like the one we are faced with now.'

Allen sighed and sat down. Hayles was right of course. They'd dropped Porter right in it.

'So what can we do now?' asked Jarvis sadly.

Hayles shook his head. 'My lads will go over the whole operation with a fine-tooth comb and see if we can discredit these witnesses. I'll also want to speak to the men that Porter thinks actually carried out the attack on Fitchett.'

'The Chelsea lads,' said Jarvis.

Hayles nodded. 'I'll only speak to Evans if I'm getting nowhere, but if he's as good as you say he is ...'

The shrug of his shoulders said it all, and Allen tapped his fingers on his desk in frustration. 'How bad is it, Colin?' he asked quietly.

Hayles sniffed and glanced out of the window. It was the first time he'd spoken to anyone without having eye contact. 'The Italians will want to question him, of course. But given this evidence, I have no doubt they will charge him with manslaughter. Possibly even murder.' He turned his gaze away from the window and stared mournfully at Allen and then at Jarvis. 'Because if I were in their position, that's exactly what I would do.'

Chapter 26
Tuesday, 8 February 2000
14.45

Terry Porter sat down and tried to take in what he had just heard. No, it couldn't be right. He wasn't guilty. He hadn't done anything. How could they have found him guilty? He looked across the courtroom at Hayles, but he simply stared back, his face showing no emotion but shouting volumes. Next to him sat Jarvis, avoiding eye contact altogether. The bastard had done for him, and he knew it. Terry closed his eyes and reflected on the past three days. Hoping he'd got it all wrong, that this was a dream. No, a nightmare. And he'd soon wake up and it would all be over. He'd be at home or in the office. Wading through dishes or paperwork. Either seemed equally attractive right now. He opened his eyes but it wasn't a dream at all. It was real. Very real.

He sighed and tried to work out where it had all gone wrong. The prosecution had wheeled in the four so-called witnesses, smartly dressed young men who had taken it in turns to lie through their teeth about him and what had happened. Telling the court that he and Gary had fought with knives in the bar and that he had struck the fatal blow. All lies. But they had believed it because they'd been arrogant and cocky and the defence hadn't rattled them at all. Then Jarvis had been called. Telling them all about the operation but admitting that the team hadn't been able to see him inside the bar. Admitting that yes, it was possible that he could have stabbed Fitchett, even though he couldn't believe ail officer on his team was capable of such a thing. And then the *piece de resistance*. They'd called Billy Evans to the stand. What a joke that had been.

Porter had listened while he told his side of the story. How he had planned the trip and how they had all travelled down together. But adding that Fitchett was a racist, and he and Porter had been arguing all the time. And how he had even had to pull them apart once, on the bus into Rome. The prosecution had then asked him to tell the court what had happened when he had got back to England. And he had told everyone how he had been arrested for conspiracy and how the police had thought he was the kingpin of the England crew, even though they had no evidence to back up either allegation. And then how they had been so desperate to charge him with something, they had even made up a story that he had tried to steal his own cars. Evans had made it sound so stupid even the Italian judge had laughed.

And then the clincher. They asked him if he knew who killed Gary Fitchett and he said he did. That it was Terry Porter. He had known all along. Someone had told him that there'd been a fight between Fitchett and Porter after he left the bar that night and that the two men had stabbed each other. But when he'd come back and been arrested, he hadn't said anything because he had believed he was already in serious trouble, so why make things worse for himself? And then, when they had brought in Porter and told him he was an undercover policeman, he had been convinced that they would try to pin it on someone else or cover it up altogether. They were capable of anything at the NFIU. Everyone who went to football in England believed that. After all, they had waged a vendetta against him for years and had already tried to charge him with a crime that hadn't even taken place. Terry Porter had listened while Evans had spouted one lie after another and no one had challenged him. They'd fallen for every word – and now he was going to an Italian prison. Convicted of manslaughter. A nightmare.

Billy Evans stood in the foyer of the courthouse and did up his Burberry jacket. It was freezing outside and the last thing he needed was a cold before his holiday next week. He looked up as a young woman walked over to him and smiled.

'Excuse me,' she said, her voice happy but with a hint of desperation. 'My name's Beverly Mills, from Sky News. I was just wondering if you had any comment to make about the case.'

Evans looked at her and smiled. 'Sorry luv,' he began. 'But it's going to appeal you know. I can't really say anything.'

Her smile faded a little and then returned. 'All I need is a general comment, nothing specific. For the news tonight.'

Evans smiled again and then looked over her shoulder as Jarvis came out of the court. His face was deathly white and, noticing Evans standing there, he veered over towards him.

'One day Evans,' he hissed angrily. 'One day I'll have you for this, you lying bastard.'

Evans looked at him and gently shook his head, his expression an odd mix of sorrow and pity. 'It's called justice, Inspector.'

Jarvis's face was suddenly scarlet with rage and he almost leapt forward but checked himself. Evans stared at him, one eyebrow raised and a faint smile on his lips. They both knew he had shafted the system, but there was no way Jarvis would ever get to prove it. Even if he survived the investigation, he was destined for other things. Well away from football.

'Have you met Beverly, Mr Jarvis?' he asked politely. 'She's from Sky News. We're just about to have a little chat.'

Jarvis took a deep breath and, without another word, turned on his heels and stormed through the doors and out into the cold. Evans watched him go and turned back to the young woman. A broad smile spread across his face like a naughty schoolboy. 'Bloody hell,' he said. 'He was a bit angry, wasn't he?'

The woman let out a short laugh. 'He has good reason to be. Word is that he's just been suspended and the NFIU are being disbanded.'

Evans gave the door a short, final glance. 'Is that right?' he said thoughtfully, turning back to face the eager young woman. 'OK, you want a statement, I'll give it to you. Are there any other reporters out there?'

The woman nodded. 'Plenty. This is a big story, Mr Evans.'

Evans smiled. 'Let's go then.'

He walked over towards the door but she grabbed him. 'Could you do it just for us first?' she pleaded.

He shook his head. 'No. What I've got to say won't take long and I'll only say it once.' He shook her off and burst through the doors into the cold.

At the bottom of the steps in front of the court, a large group of reporters were gathered, interviewing anyone who came out of the court-house, desperate to get a fresh angle on the story. They began calling out to him and he walked directly over to them, the young reporter trailing desperately in his wake. He stopped at the bottom of the steps and surveyed the scene. A dozen microphones were held out in front of him and the place was illuminated by a bank of bright lights. He closed his eyes and took a deep breath.

'I have a statement to make, if that's all right,' he said, looking around to make sure he had everyone's attention. 'In this court over the past few days, you have heard the truth about the British police force. How they coerce people into working for them, how they lie, cheat, try to fabricate evidence and how ... yes, how they try to cover up the actions of their own officers.'

He took a deep breath and carried on. 'You heard what went on in that courtroom. If it hadn't been for the courage shown by the people who gave evidence, this murder would have gone unsolved and the policeman responsible would have gone unpunished.' He paused for a second and looked around. 'The tragedy for Britain is that it took an Italian court to expose that crime.'

He stopped speaking and the place erupted with questions. 'Have you anything to say about the disbandment of the NFIU, Mr Evans?' shouted one of the reporters.

Evans held up his hand to quieten things down before he spoke. 'I'm sorry. I have nothing further to say, other than that I would just like to go home and get back to work.' He put his head down and thrust his way through the crowd. Within seconds, he was free of them and headed towards a row of yellow taxis parked by the side of the road. He climbed into the first one, gave the driver the name of his hotel and settled back into his seat as the car sped away from the kerb, past the throng of reporters and into the chaos of the Rome traffic. Within a few seconds, the car was anonymous, just one of thousands.

Billy let a broad smile drift across his face and pulled out his mobile phone. He keyed in the number and waited until a female voice came on the line. 'Hello love, it's Billy ... Yeah, it went exactly how I said it would. I'll be home in a few hours. We'll go out and celebrate tonight. I've had a right result.' He turned the phone off and settled back in his chair.

'Oh yes,' he said out loud to himself. 'A right fucking result.'

Also by Dougie Brimson

Rob Cooper, self-confessed football fanatic and editor of the United FC fanzine, *Wings Of A Sparrow*, returns from watching his team succumb to yet another defeat to discover that not only has he inherited an estate worth in excess of six million pounds, but that it has been left to him by an uncle he never knew he had.

However, even as Rob is struggling to come to terms with these two bombshells, he is hit with another. For the estate contains ownership of an almost bankrupt professional football club. And the terms of the will are such that Rob will only receive his inheritance if he takes over the running of the club and manages to keep them going for the coming season. The problem is, the club concerned are the local and very bitter rivals of the club Rob and his family have passionately supported all their lives.

But after wrestling with his conscience, and driven by his wife's desire for instant wealth, he accepts the challenge with a promise to the United faithful that he will do whatever he can to ensure that whilst his new club might survive, its supporters are about to experience the most depressing season in their history.

And so, in the full glare of the media spotlight, he sets out to do what most football fans could only ever dream about; humiliate their local rivals.

The trouble is, it just doesn't work out like that...

The Official Novelisation of the Movie
By Dougie Brimson

Sequel to the best-selling thriller, The Crew.
Soon to be a major motion picture starring Leo Gregory

GANG LEADER Billy Evans has ruled his turf in London for more years than he can care to remember. So long in fact, that even he realizes that things have become a little too easy.

So when an old adversary reappears on the scene, Bill sees a golden opportunity to not only reassert his authority, but to have some much needed fun.

Yet all is not as it appears. For this new enemy is far more powerful than any Billy has ever had to deal with before and he's about to discover that he's finally pushed his luck too far.

But this time it isn't the law that he has to worry about, it's something far more dangerous.

Published by Caffeine Nights Publishing Spring 2014

The Films of Danny Dyer

Danny Dyer is Britain's most popular young film star. Idolised by Harold Pinter and with his films having taken nearly $50 million at the UK box office, Dyer is the most bankable star in British independent films with one in ten of the country's population owning one of his films on DVD. With iconic performances in such cult classics as The Business, The Football Factory, Dead Man Running, Outlaw and now Vendetta, Dyer is one of the most recognisable Englishmen in the world. For the first time, and with its' subject's full co-operation, this book chronicles his film career in depth, combining production background with critical analysis to paint a fascinating picture of the contemporary British film industry and its brightest star. Packed with anecdotes from co-stars and colleagues, as well as contributions from the man himself, The Films of Danny Dyer is the ultimate companion to the work of Britain's grittiest star.

Published by Caffeine Nights Publishing 18th Nov 2013